Fatal Business

Pine County book 9

Dean L. Hovey

Print ISBNs
Amazon Print 978-0-2286-2214-7
LSI Print 978-0-2286-2215-4
B&N Print 978-0-2286-2216-1

BWL Publish

Books we love to u
Authors around the woru.
http://bwlpublishing.ca

Dedication

To Jerry Telker and Lori Berg

"There is no hunting like the hunting of man."
                                              -Ernest Hemmingway

Gone are the days when an author locked himself into a dark room with his Remington typewriter and a bottle of Scotch to pound out a manuscript without the aid of anyone but the voices in his head. I owe much to my legion of subject matter experts, beta readers, proofreaders, an editor, a cover designer, and my publisher who all collaborate with me to make these books a reality. Julie puts up with my hours on the computer and my distant stare as the characters reveal themselves and the plot to me. Deanna Wilson has evolved from my horse and cop consultant into the expanded role of early proofreader, commenting on the plot and characters, often reading a few out of context pages at a time. Fran Brozo, Mike Westfall, Clem MacIlravie, and Brian Johnson offer plot critique and are my muses when I've written myself into a corner. Anne Flagge and Natalie Lund proofread and correct my too numerous typos and grammatical errors. Jude Pittman, of BWL Publishing, has been marvelously supportive in getting my books into the hands of my readers. Most of all, thanks to you, the readers who provide me with feedback, plot ideas, and the energy to write.

Chapter 1

The sky turned gray as afternoon became early evening. The chickadees and squirrels rummaging through the dry leaves had retreated to safety as the orange and pink sunset faded behind gray clouds, leaving the forest in murky darkness. Roger Bartlett checked his watch. Although it was legal to hunt half an hour past sunset, the waning light was going to make his return walk to deer camp difficult if he stayed in his deer stand any longer. Scanning the forest one last time for the flick of a deer's tail, he declared an end to the day's hunt and slung his rifle over his shoulder.

Halfway down the crude ladder, someone called out to him. "Hey, Roger! You're packing it in early?"

With his feet on the ground, Roger looked for the person who'd called his name. A hunter's orange coat approached from the direction of his deer camp; the coat's color enhanced by the twilight. "Yeah, is that you Gary?" Not getting a response he added, "There's not enough light to see antlers."

Unable to discern the other hunter's face, Roger walked toward him in the quickly fading light. Bending down to slip under a leaning tree, he was struck by a blow that stunned him. The rifle was wrenched from his shoulder as he struggled to his feet. "What the hell?"

The ominous click of the gun's safety being pushed into the "fire" setting froze him. He stood slowly, putting his hands in the air.

A chilling chuckle rattled Roger further. "No need to put your hands up. Just make a run for it...you know, just so you have a sporting chance at escape."

"I don't understand."

The rifle butt hit Roger in the jaw, sending him sprawling in the leaves. "What part of *run* don't you understand?"

After struggling to his feet, Roger staggered away, slowly gaining momentum as his feet found a rhythm. Branches whipped his face as he stumbled on rocks and branches hidden under the leaves. Weaving between trees in the darkening forest, he ran, his breath rasping in the cold evening air. Focused on his feet, he saw the barbed wire fence just in time to put his hands up.

The rusty wires strained against the row of posts, making a screeching sound that seemed deafening in the quiet forest. He bent down to crawl between the strands when he heard footsteps approaching from behind. Panicking, Roger threw himself through the fence, the barbs ripping his coat and tugging at his gloves. A blow to his shoulder spun him around and threw him to the ground. The gunshot echoed off the trees, then quickly faded. Trying to understand what had happened, Roger attempted to push himself up, but his left arm wouldn't support him. Rough hands pushed him to the ground before groping into his front pocket.

"You won't need this. I heard the devil won't take cash." A moment later, the pressure on his back was released.

On his knees, Roger grabbed a nearby tree with his right hand, pulling himself to his feet. Behind him, the sound of the rifle ejecting the spent shell and chambering a fresh cartridge sent a chill down his spine. Staggering ahead, he plunged into the deepening forest.

"That's right! Run!"

Chapter 2

"911, what's your emergency?"

"Um, I'm not sure this is an emergency, but Roger didn't come in tonight."

Checking the clock, the dispatcher noted the time of the call, 21:11. "Please give me your name and location."

"I'm Justin Parker. We're at our hunting shack, east of Beroun, just north of County Road 14."

"Who is Roger and when did you expect him?"

"Roger's my father-in-law and everyone came back to the hunting shack shortly after sunset. We expected him to be here like four hours ago."

"Have you looked for him?"

"Yeah, three of us went out to his stand with flashlights, but he wasn't there. Gary's been honking the pickup horn every five or ten minutes so he could find us if he got turned around. We've called his cellphone, but he might've turned it off in his stand."

"Where's Roger's hunting stand?"

"We're hunting the western edge of the Chengwatana State Forest, east of Beroun."

"Does Roger have any health problems?"

"Um, he takes some pills, but I don't know what they're for."

"I'll dispatch a deputy to your location."

"I'm driving a blue Chevy pickup. I'll meet him on the county road."

Chapter 3

Sergeant Charlene (C.J.) Jensen started her morning shift with a briefing at the Pine County Sheriff's Department. Sheriff John Sepanen sat with one hip on a desk across from C.J. and Pam Ryan, just coming on duty. Sandy Maki, who was coming off the night shift, had mud up to the knees of his uniform pants. Each of them had a cup of coffee and they listened intently to Sandy as he recapped his shift.

"We spent the night searching the west edge of the Chengwatana State Forest for Roger Bartlett, who didn't return to his hunting party's cabin last night. We found his hunting stand. There wasn't any sign of a problem there. His hunting party owns eighty acres abutting the state forest and the three other hunters in his party had walked most of their property without finding him before I arrived."

Sepanen nodded. "What happened after you met the hunting party?"

"I called Frank Mercer, the conservation officer. He brought in a four-wheeler about ten o'clock and checked the west edge of the state forest while the hunting party and I rechecked their property. We quit about midnight, just after the snow started. Frank suggested there'd be a better chance of finding his footprints in the snow this morning."

The sheriff nodded. "I called in the reserve deputies. They'll be at the Beroun fire hall at eight. The Department of Natural Resources (DNR) is sending four forestry people and Frank Mercer to the meeting. I'd like you two, Pam and C.J., to join them. Wear orange coats or vests because it's still deer season and there are hunters in the woods."

C.J. waited for the sheriff to leave, then took his place, sitting on the corner of Pam's desk. "I heard that you've decided to go back to your maiden name, Ryan?"

"I talked to Floyd and the sheriff. They both agreed that there is some risk of unwanted phone calls or contact if I use my married name professionally. Besides, everyone around here, and in the neighboring departments, knows me as Pam Ryan. Changing to Conrad would confuse people for a while."

"I think that's wise," C.J. agreed. "You don't need creeps and perverts tracking you down by your married name. Using your maiden name provides another layer of insulation between your work and personal lives."

* * *

The meeting at the Beroun fire hall was brief. The DNR would focus their search in the state forest. C.J. and Pam volunteered to patrol the roads west of the forest. The fire department and sheriff's reserves were going to walk the swampy woods around the hunting stand and surrounding forest.

C.J. drove a single-lane dirt road west of the lost hunter's deer stand. The road was now snow-covered and muddy. Several sets of deer tracks crossed the road but there was no sign of human activity. Chickadees flitted between the trees, and downy snowflakes swirled, creating a Christmas card image.

The road crested a small hill, revealing Cedar Lake, only recently iced over and now snow-covered. There was a small cabin on the north shore and C.J. decided to check it out, even though it was miles from the search area. Parking near the cabin, she walked to the small porch overlooking the lake. Footprints made after the snow started, but now dusted with fresh flakes falling to the ground, approached from the lake and crossed the porch.

Studying the tracks before walking onto the porch, C.J. announced her location to the dispatcher. She reached for the doorknob, hesitating when she realized it was coated with frozen blood. An involuntary chill ran over her body. She looked around, rechecking her surroundings. She'd been surprised by an attacker in a similar remote location. Her mind flashed back to the events that resulted in a physical confrontation and a gunshot wound to her leg.

Her knock on the door went unanswered. A question about entering without invitation ran through her mind. *Exigent circumstances* was the term for entering a building without a warrant in a situation where someone's life might be at risk. She pulled her pistol, switched on her flashlight, and turned the doorknob with her gloved hand. The knob didn't turn, but the door swung open with a push. The door jamb was splintered, apparently when someone broke in. "Sheriff's Department!"

The unlit interior was as cold as the surrounding woods. Worn furniture was neatly arranged, facing a stone fireplace. A kitchen area was to her right, with a table and four chairs, a stove, refrigerator and cabinets. The area was neat, probably just as the owners had left it in the fall. A short hallway led to two open doors. Snowy footprints led into the living room, then ended. A blood trail continued through the door on the left.

With her heart pounding and her breath making billows of steam in the cold air, C.J. followed the blood, scanning the flashlight beam ahead and leading with her pistol. She hesitated, staring at the frozen blood drops on the floor. Her mind raced back to her childhood, deer hunting with her father, trailing a wounded deer through the woods east of Cloquet. Her father had explained that he'd messed up. A good shot would've killed the deer quickly and it would've run no more than twenty or thirty yards. They'd followed a trail of blood drops for hours before finding the wounded deer that her father dispatched with a single shot. Whoever had left this blood trail was injured but might be alive.

She stepped into the doorway of a small bedroom. An orange-clad person lay on the floor in a puddle of blood. "Hello! Are you okay?"

When the person didn't move, C.J. realized there was no steam rising from the person's breath. She holstered her gun and moved ahead, avoiding the blood on the floor as she neared the body. The left shoulder of the orange coat was blood soaked. The stocking cap on the man's head sat askew over unseeing eyes. Checking the man's neck for a pulse, she knew he was dead. The pooled blood was frozen, and his skin temperature was as cold as the room.

"Dispatch, I need backup and an ambulance at Cedar Lake." She paused her call to the sheriff's department non-emergency phone number, then added, "No sirens. Please notify the sheriff."

After disconnecting from the dispatcher, she chose the medical examiner's number from her phone's memory. It was answered on the second ring, "Good morning, Sunshine. I didn't expect to hear from you this morning."

"I'm afraid this is a professional call," C.J. said to her friend, Eddie, the ME's assistant. "I have a hunter who died of a gunshot wound."

"Hang on," he said. "Where are you?"

Considering her remote location and the difficulty she'd have giving directions to the cabin, she said, "I'm east of Beroun, in a cabin on the north shore of Cedar Lake." She continued her description of the route, ending with, "By the time you get here from Duluth, dozens of vehicle tracks in this morning's snow will lead you to the cabin."

"Tony's in his office making calls," Eddie said, referring to Tony Oresek, the St. Louis County Medical Examiner. "We'll be on the road in ten minutes."

"Thanks."

"Say, there's a new brew pub in the East End. I was told they have a great IPA. When do you have an evening free?"

The mental transition from requesting the coroner to the topic of dinner took C.J. a moment. "Um, I'm on day-shift right now. I could meet you there any evening, as long as I have time to walk Bailey before we meet…and get home at a decent hour."

"My social calendar is…empty. How about tonight at 5:30?"

"My social calendar is in the same sorry state. I'll call if I'm running late."

C.J. ended the call. Thinking about the upcoming evening with her male friend, who wasn't a boyfriend, made her smile. The happy aura evaporated when she realized she was standing on the porch of a cabin with a dead body inside. For Eddie, dealing with dead bodies was a fact of his life, so he was very casual about the topic. For C.J., any death was shocking.

* * *

While she waited for backup, the ambulance, and ME, C.J. backtracked the hunter's footsteps from the cabin. She followed the indistinct trail through the snowy yard, carefully stepping around the footprints made by the orange-clad man in the cabin. The hunter's footprints kept to the shoreline for over a hundred yards before approaching the cabin. A gust of wind blew the fluffy snow off some of the hunter's footprints, exposing blood droplets between them.

An occasional shot rang out in the distance as hunters fired at deer. One shot, very close, startled C.J. and she squatted down, trying to minimize her profile in case a hunter's bullet flew her direction. While waiting for more shots, C.J. mulled what she knew.

"*If this is the missing hunter, he's over a mile from his deer stand. There isn't a rifle inside the cabin, so he'd dropped it somewhere. The snow started around midnight, so the trail was made after that. New snow had fallen in his tracks, so the hunter had arrived at the cabin in the very early hours of the morning. His body was cold and the blood frozen, so he's probably been dead for hours.*"

Flashing red and blue lights approaching from the road caught C.J.'s attention. She walked back to the cabin and met Pam Ryan, the Pine County Sheriff's Department investigator, as she stepped out of her unmarked cruiser. "I think I've found our missing hunter." C.J. nodded toward the cabin. Snapping on rubber gloves, she led Pam up the steps and into the small bedroom. C.J. was surprised when the overhead light came on when Pam flipped the switch. "I guess the owners left the power on."

Pam surveyed the scene. "Have you checked his pockets?"

"I decided to wait until you photographed the scene."

Pam got busy taking pictures, so when the ambulance arrived C.J. ushered the crew around the footprints and blood, and into the small bedroom. Taking in the scene, the male/female ambulance crew stood silently in the door. The body was on the floor, near the foot of the bed. The rest of the room, including the bed, dresser, wardrobe, and nightstand, were undisturbed.

C.J. let them collect their thoughts, then said, "Can you declare him dead?"

The middle-aged woman who led the crew nodded, then pulled on rubber gloves and uncoiled a stethoscope from her pocket. Skirting the blood on the floor, she unzipped the man's coat and pressed the stethoscope against his chest. She touched the man's gloved fingers and gently lifted his arm.

Standing, she turned to C.J. "Rigor mortis has already started. He's been dead at least three hours, maybe more."

Pam pulled on a pair of purple nitrile gloves and knelt next to the body. Unzipping an outer chest pocket, she removed a slip of paper. "The deer hunting license was issued to Roger Bartlett, with an address in Askov."

"That's our missing hunter," C. J. said.

She slipped the license into an evidence bag, then patted the man's pockets. "He's got his phone and wallet. There's no cash, but his driver's license and a debit card are here. Slipping off the man's left glove, she slid up his sleeve. "He's

17

wearing his wedding ring and a wristwatch. He wasn't shot in a robbery."

C.J. considered that information while looking at the body. "The bullet's exit wound is on the front of his shoulder. He was walking or running away when he was shot." She paused, then added, "He's missing his hunting rifle, but all his other valuables are here. That makes me think he was shot accidentally. We should check the rifles of his hunting party to see if any of them have been fired. They're probably the people who were closest to his hunting spot."

"That's an interesting theory." Pam nodded. "I wonder if Sandy and his hunting buddies looked for his rifle under his tree stand. If he was shot there, he might've dropped his rifle and it might be lying on the ground right below it."

C.J. hesitated. "It may have been an accidental shooting, but we can't dismiss the possibility he was targeted. If that's the case, his gun might be somewhere along his backtrail, and he may have been running from his attacker."

"You were looking at his footprints in the snow when I pulled into the yard. Was he running when he approached the cabin?"

"His footprints were close together, like he was walking very slowly. If he was bleeding out, he could've been running out of steam." She looked out the window at the swirling snow. "If you guys have this under control, I'm going to follow his backtrail as far as I can before it fills in anymore."

Pam stood and pulled off the purple gloves. "I'll come with you. Give me two minutes to put the camera away and stow the evidence bags."

"I've got this," C.J. replied. "You can deal with the evidence and next-of-kin notification."

Before C.J. got out of the living room, Pam had her arm. "I'm coming with you."

"I've got this."

Pam stiffened, then led C.J. to the porch where they were out of the ambulance crew's earshot. "You've barely recovered from being shot. You are not wandering into the woods without backup. Agreed?"

C.J., who was ten years older than Pam, smiled. "Yes, Mom. I'll play nice."

"Listen to me, dammit. It's deer hunting season. There are hundreds of armed men out there. I wouldn't go anywhere in those woods without a partner. Being a local girl, you should know that."

"Fine. Hustle your butt before Bartlett's prints disappear under the snow. I'll notify the dispatcher."

* * *

19

The backtrail became less distinct as they moved farther from the lake. Brush whipped their faces and tugged at their uniforms as they walked through the woods. C.J. stopped and pointed at the brushy woods ahead. "We're going to lose this trail soon. When I kneel, I can look ahead and see slight indentations in the snow. Do you have many purple gloves in your pocket?"

"A few, but not hundreds. What do you need?"

"Tie a glove to a branch here. That'll give us a point where we're sure we had a trail. If we lose his prints, we can come back to this point and re-examine the snow to see if we can pick up the trail again."

Tying a thin rubber glove to a low branch, Pam asked. "Where did you learn that?"

"My dad taught me that when we were tracking a wounded deer. He tied his red bandana to a branch, then he'd drop a glove farther on and send me back for the bandana. We lost the trail a couple times, but we'd go back to the bandana. Then, we'd circle that spot until we found the trail again."

Pam looked back at their footprints and the faint trail they'd been following. "With this snow, I don't think there's any point in circling. We know the victim's footprints are covered."

Tipping her head back and looking at the sky, C.J. nodded, "You're probably right. Let's go back to the cabin."

When they started their return trek, Pam posed an idea. "I've got a pretty good fix on our location when we stopped tracking. I'll look at the county map when I get back to the bullpen and see if that lines up with Bartlett's property. He might've walked directly from his deer stand to that cabin."

"I wonder if he knew the cabin's owner?"

"He was walking in the dark without a flashlight or compass. He probably stumbled on the cabin by accident."

C.J. paused as a thought struck her. "He had a cellphone in his pocket. Why didn't he call his hunting buddies?"

"It was turned off."

"I'm sure he had it turned off in his deer stand. You wouldn't want it to ring just as a big buck was walking into range."

"But why wouldn't he turn it on to call for help after he'd been shot?"

Staring at the trail ahead of them, C.J. shook her head. "It could be that his battery was dead. Or he was paranoid about powering it up and having the glowing screen give away his location to the shooter."

"There's a third possibility: He might've been in shock. People don't reason well after a major trauma. Travis said soldiers do all kinds of stupid things after they'd been hit by gunfire or been tossed around inside a Humvee by an IED."

"I've always wondered about the soldiers who are awarded medals for heroism. No rational person would expose themselves to massive enemy fire."

Pam stopped. "Except to protect or save your friends. Wouldn't you do that for another deputy whose life was in danger?"

Blowing out a breath, C.J. considered Pam's words. "I'd like to think I would. It's hard to say how you'd react in the heat of the moment. I suppose you never know until you've been there."

"I've been there. No thought is involved. You act on total adrenaline overload." Pam looked in C.J.'s eyes. "We're brothers and sisters in this department and in law enforcement. We put our lives on the line, not only to protect each other, but to protect innocent civilians. It's who we are."

"I've never had to…"

"Bullshit. Last spring you followed a teenage girl into a dark shack. You were trying to protect her, and it nearly cost you your life." Pam paused. "And I'm sure you'd do the same for me."

C.J. started walking. "What I did wasn't heroic."

"That's what every hero says. They were doing their job. Or they were protecting their friends and comrades."

With the cabin in sight, C.J. changed the topic. "I called the medical examiner. Eddie said they'd be on the road in a few minutes, so they should arrive shortly."

"I'll release the ambulance crew and wait for the ME."

Blowing out a breath, C.J. said, "I'll notify Mrs. Bartlett."

"I'll check the victim's phone battery. That may give us more insight into what happened after the shot."

Chapter 4

C.J. drove to the Askov address on Roger Bartlett's driver's license. She located the house a few blocks off Highway 23, on the outskirts of Askov. Main Street had once been a bustling Danish community but when the construction of I-35 bypassed town, the storefronts changed and many of the jobs moved. The town still had a mom-and-pop feel, but it felt deserted. The streets, with their Danish names, seemed out of place in a county now populated by hundreds of ethnicities.

After waving to a woman walking into the small grocery store, C.J. turned onto Kirke Alle and passed a large Lutheran Church. Bartlett's 1920's two-story house had a short concrete driveway and a detached double garage. An older Buick and a muddy Ford pickup stood in the driveway. C.J. parked on the narrow street and walked up the sidewalk.

A young man wearing an orange flannel shirt with a camouflage pattern answered the door. His eyes looked tired, and he had at least two days beard growth. "We were wondering when a deputy would show up," he said, holding the door open in an invitation to enter.

Caroline Bartlett sat on the couch, surrounded by sodden tissues. The news of Roger's death had apparently been delivered. C.J. took a seat in an upholstered chair near the end of the couch.

"Mrs. Bartlett, I'm sorry to inform you that your husband is dead."

Having said the words, C.J. flashed back to the day a sergeant and chaplain arrived at her door to announce the death of her husband in a car accident. Tears welled in her eyes.

Caroline Bartlett nodded and held the box of tissues out to C.J. "Gary told me. Do you have any details?"

"He'd been shot, then walked to a cabin on Cedar Lake. I found his body there this morning."

Caroline's eyebrows went up. "You found him?"

"Yes. He'd broken into a cabin for shelter. I saw his footprints and followed them into the cabin."

"How did he get from his deer stand to Cedar Lake?"

"I followed his footprints, and it appears he walked there last night."

"But Cedar Lake is a mile from where he hunts."

After taking out a notepad and pen, C.J. asked. "Do you know anyone who owns a cabin on Cedar Lake?"

Caroline glanced at Gary. "I don't think so. I mean, we've seen the sign for Cedar Lake, but I don't know anyone who owns a cabin there." Gary shook his head.

'Has your husband had any disputes with anyone lately?"

Caroline's eyes went wide as the implication of C.J.'s words hit. "You don't think his shooting was accidental?"

"We have to consider all the possibilities. It's likely he was shot accidentally by another hunter, but I need to explore the scenario that someone shot him intentionally."

"Roger owns a tire retreading shop. There's nothing to dispute. He buys truck tires that have blown out. His guys put new tread on them, then they ship a truckload of them to a distributor who resells them. There are no unhappy customers, just a distributor who bids on a truckload of tires."

"Does he have any unhappy employees? Has he fired anyone lately? Does he get along with the people who own the buildings near his shop?"

Looking at Gary, Caroline shook her head. "I'm sorry, but I don't know anything about his business. I don't see how anything there would result in a deer hunting shooting. I mean, he was in the middle of nowhere. It's not like someone other than their hunting party would even know where his deer stand is located."

"Gary, are you one of the deer hunting party?"

"Yeah, Roger's my dad. There were six of us, five other than Dad. We're all relatives. Two are my uncles. The others are my cousin and my brother-in-law. We get together every year."

"Do you all get along?"

"Oh, hell yes. We stay in a shack on the land, playing cards and drinking half the night. There's lots of friendly kidding, but we all get along fine."

"There were no problems the night before the hunt?"

"We laughed until our bellies hurt. Hank missed a big buck, and we all gave him a hard time about blowing his big chance."

"Hank wasn't mad at Roger over the kidding?"

"Not at all. Dad was probably the most sympathetic of the hunting group. If Hank would've been mad at anyone, it would've been me. I cut the tail off his hunting shirt. The tradition is that if you miss a buck, you lose the tail off your shirt, and it gets pinned to the wall. When you get a buck, you have to sew it back on again. Hank wasn't pleased about the ritual, but my dad had no direct involvement in the hazing. He laughed along with the rest of us."

"Is Hank's deer stand near the place where Roger hunts?"

"I suppose they're a couple hundred yards apart."

"Did anyone shoot and miss a deer yesterday?"

Gary opened his mouth, then stopped. "Tom shot a doe. You don't think his shot..." After considering the question further, he shook his head. "No, Tom shot east, toward the state forest. Dad's stand is west of Tom."

"Did you hear any shooting from other hunting parties?"

"There's always shooting around us. Lots of people hunt the state forest."

"Did you hear any shots coming from your dad's area?"

"There may have been. I don't remember any, but shots echo in the trees and it's kind of hard to determine their direction."

C.J. closed her notebook. "So, there may have been shooting from Roger's direction?"

"There probably were shots from the west, but I couldn't say exactly where they originated."

C.J. looked at Caroline Bartlett, whose eyes were red from crying and said, "Thank you for seeing us. I'm sorry for your loss."

* * *

Alone in the cabin, Pam tried to turn on Bartlett's phone. After two attempts, she assumed it was dead and quit. She sat on a cold kitchen chair and contemplated the murder and what to do next. Only the victim's feet were visible through the open bedroom door, making the view less terrible than staring at the man's unseeing eyes and the pool of blood around his torso.

Pam tipped her head back and contemplated the ceiling. "Dang it, Floyd. Why did you dump this on me? I'm not ready for this." She pulled out her phone and dialed a number from her contacts list.

Floyd's familiar voice said, "Hi, Pam. How are you doing?"

"I'm staring at a dead guy's feet and cursing you for dumping this new role on me. I'm not ready to be an investigator."

"Mary's at the shop and I'm sitting here reading the newspaper and watching *The Dukes of Hazzard* reruns. A cup of coffee and a caramel roll would taste awfully good."

"I'm waiting for the medical examiner. I'll give you a call when they've got the body loaded."

Floyd waited a moment, then asked, "How bad is it?"

"A wounded hunter walked to a cabin and died on the floor."

"It sounds like an accidental shooting. Is there something that makes you think it's something else?"

"I don't know. Maybe. Maybe not. The victim walked at least a mile to get here after the shooting."

"Who's working it with you?"

"C.J. is notifying the victim's wife. She might have some insights after she's free."

"You two are a good team. You'll figure it out."

"I wish I was as confident as you are. I hear a truck outside, so the ME is probably here. I'll give you a call when we wrap up."

"If it takes long enough, you can buy me lunch instead of a roll."

"I'd buy you a steak dinner if you'd unretire and rescue me from this."

Floyd laughed. "It'd take a lot more than a steak dinner to pry me out of retirement. Call me when you're free."

* * *

Floyd sat in a booth reading a newspaper. A coffee cup pushed to the side, made Pam wonder how long he'd been waiting.

Peggy, the owner, spotted Pam come in and brought a cup and coffee pot to the booth. "Are you two just having coffee or would you like menus?"

Glancing at the white board near the door, Pam wrinkled her nose. "I'm trying to lose the weight I put on when I was pregnant, but a hash brown skillet sounds awfully good. I'll have the eggs over easy and the hash browns crispy."

"I'll have the same," Floyd said as he folded the newspaper. He watched Peggy go into the kitchen, then leaned close. "I've learned that a large portion of carbohydrates helps me think. Someone told me the carb rush stimulates your creative process."

"There are more grease calories in Peggy's skillet breakfasts than carbs."

Floyd leaned back. "You've got to be careful about grease. Sometimes the ideas slide right through your brain if there's too much cholesterol in your blood."

Pam laughed. "I didn't think it would be possible to laugh again after this morning, but somehow you got a chuckle out of me."

"Part of retirement is not taking life too seriously."

Wrapping her hands around the coffee cup, Pam asked, "How's Mary?"

"That depends on whether you're talking about her medical condition or her head."

"Start with her medical situation."

"She had a scan and there's no sign of cancer. She has to be rechecked in a year, but the oncologist says there's no reason to believe the cancer will be back."

"What's wrong with her head?"

Floyd shook his head. "She's nuts. Ever since the wedding she's working like she's possessed. I pointed out that the point of my retirement was so we could be together and do things. She's convinced the shop will go under if she's not there every hour it's open."

"What are you going to do about that?"

"She's trying to whip the books into shape so it'll sell. We're meeting with a realtor next week, but one of the women who work for her is interested in buying it."

"How is married life?"

With a sheepish grin, Floyd picked up his coffee cup. "It's a lot like living together, except Mary doesn't feel like she has to cater to my every need."

"Is that good or bad?"

"You know how that goes. There's good and bad to everything. Since I'm home most every day, Mary thinks I should fix supper." Floyd glanced around to make sure no one was listening. "That's backfiring because my cooking is so bad, she prefers eating out."

"You cooked for yourself before Mary came into your life."

Floyd grinned. "I wasn't trying to convince Mary I wasn't a chef back then."

Peggy delivered their breakfasts on platters, then set a squeeze bottle of ketchup on the table. "Besides coffee refills, what else can I get you?"

Surveying the mountain of food on the platter, Pam shook her head. "I don't need anything else."

Floyd unfolded a napkin and spread it on his lap. "Tell me about your murder."

"I'm not sure if it's a murder or an accidental death." Pam said as she squirted ketchup on her hash browns. "The guy died of a gunshot wound, but there's nothing to indicate it's anything but a tragic accident."

Floyd chewed on a strip of bacon as he spread grape jelly on a slice of buttered toast. "Considering there are a hundred thousand armed hunters wandering the state opening weekend, it's amazing there aren't more accidental shootings than there are."

"C.J. and I followed the dead man's footprints and blood trail a quarter mile. His trail came from the direction of his deer stand."

"Did you recover his rifle?"

"It wasn't in the cabin, and we didn't find it on his backtrail. Sandy said they looked around the deer stand. He didn't find Roger's rifle or a blood trail."

"Had he been robbed?"

"His wallet, watch, and wedding ring were all in his possession when C.J. found his body. He was in full rigor mortis, so he'd been dead for hours before he was found."

Floyd pushed his hash browns into a puddle of ketchup with the corner of his toast. "So, he was shot some time between when his hunting party last saw him and midnight."

Cocking her head, Pam frowned. "I'd assumed he'd been shot about sunset, then walked until he found the cabin."

"Is there any evidence to support that?"

"Well, his hunting party didn't miss him until it got dark."

"Let's assume he came back to the shack for lunch and returned to his deer stand shortly after that. He could've been shot any time after he left the shack."

Pam closed her eyes. "You're right, although he would've been bleeding for nearly twelve hours before he died."

"You said you found a blood trail. Was he dripping or gushing blood?"

"It was dripping."

"With the cold weather, he could've been bleeding a long time."

Pam sighed. "True."

"Was the cabin in the direction of his hunting camp?"

"The cabin was west of his stand, the exact opposite direction of his hunting shack."

Floyd ate in silence for several minutes. "I'm thinking out loud," he resumed, "so bear with me. If he'd been accidentally shot, why wouldn't he go toward his hunting camp? Was he disoriented? Or was he afraid to go toward the camp because…"

Pam nodded. "Because he knew the person who shot him, and he was trying to get away."

"There's another possibility," Floyd said, sliding his nearly empty plate away. "He accidentally shot himself. It seems like every year there's some poor soul who drops his gun out of his tree stand, the gun goes off, and he gets hit."

Shaking her head, Pam pushed her plate back and signaled for a coffee refill. "He was hit in the shoulder, and it appeared the bullet went straight through, like he'd been standing at the same level as the shooter."

C.J. walked into the restaurant, nodded to Pam, then slid into the booth next to Floyd. She hugged him and kissed his cheek. "Hey there, retiree. How's life?" She signaled for coffee.

"Retirement is better than working."

Snorting, C.J. shook her head. "You don't miss the rotating shifts, hours of boredom, and paperwork?"

"I miss this. Having coffee with you two really livens up my day."

C.J. cocked her head and raised her eyebrows. "Do you buy that, Pam? Do you really think having coffee with us is better than retirement?"

"Daisy and I were getting into *The Dukes of Hazzard* when Pam called."

In unison, Pam and C.J. asked, "Who's Daisy?"

"I finally named the pup that showed up on my doorstep."

"How big is Daisy now?" Pam asked. "Did she grow into those big feet?"

"She's gotten bigger, but I suspect there's some Corgi in her bloodline. She filled out but her legs aren't any longer."

Peggy delivered coffee to C.J. and topped off the other cups. "Anything for you, C.J.?"

"Since Eddie's been taking me out for two or three meals a week, I've been struggling to fit into my uniforms. I'll stick with coffee."

Pam leaned close. "Did you learn anything from talking to the victim's widow?"

Waiting while a customer paid his bill, C.J. shook her head, then sipped her coffee. When the customer left, C.J. checked to see if anyone else was listening. "Not really. Their son was at the house and had broken the news about the victim's death. The widow seemed suitably distraught and in shock."

"Isn't Roger Bartlett the guy who owned the tire recapping business in Askov?" Floyd asked.

C.J. nodded. "His wife mentioned that and something about his partner."

Floyd leaned back and stared at an antique hand mixer mounted on the wall. "I went to his shop to interview one of his employees a few years ago. It's dusty and stinks. Back then, he had a crew of paroled convicts working for him. It was a messy job that involved lots of heavy lifting, so he had a tough time finding employees. I think his business was one of the few places an ex-con could get a fairly good paying job."

"I remember a lot of ex-cons and people on work release from the county jail working as busboys and dishwashers around Cloquet," C.J. said. "Some of them were really smart people, but no one trusted them to run a cash register or handle money."

Floyd blew out a breath. "There was a CPA convicted of embezzling money from her employer. She got a job as a clerk for one of the local counties, then worked her way up to bookkeeper. Everyone said she was way too smart to be filing paperwork and sorting the mail, but the lure of the money, coupled with a gambling problem, was more than she could stand. She was back in prison within two years."

C.J. leaned her elbows on the table and stared at Pam. "Since you're the new investigator, and I'm supposed to be on the road, I guess you're the one who'll have to visit the dirty, stinky tire company."

"Give me a break," Pam protested. "I've got to..."

C.J. smiled at Floyd. "She's too green to be an investigator. She can't even come up with an excuse to avoid a miserable assignment."

Floyd put his hand on C.J.'s shoulder. "I'd love to hang around for the rest of this discussion, but the coffee is starting to back up on me. Please let me out of the booth."

Watching Floyd walk to the restrooms, C.J. slid into the booth. "How's Mary doing?"

"The doctor said she's clear and doesn't need to return for a year."

C.J. breathed a sigh of relief. "I was afraid to ask."

"You don't want to interview the tire company employees?" Pam asked.

"I'll come with you, but I really don't want to walk alone into a building filled with ex-cons. I'm barely able to sleep with the lights off after my incident at the hunting shack. I'm talking with the psychiatrist the sheriff suggested, and we're making progress. But my PTSD kicked in the other day when a guy stood too close to me in the grocery checkout line."

Pam picked up the bill from the edge of the table and slid out of the booth. "It's probably a good idea to have two people listening and asking questions anyway. You and I pick up different vibes and nuances from people."

Pam was setting a tip on the table when Floyd approached. "Thanks, this was fun."

Peggy leaned across the counter. "You should come back tomorrow, it's cinnamon roll day."

Inhaling deeply, Floyd closed his eyes. "I can almost taste that cinnamon roll. It's especially good because Pam is going to pay for it." He opened his eyes. "What time would you like to meet? Ten o'clock works for me."

Pam pointed a finger at C.J. "She's buying tomorrow."

"Hey, I'm the one trying to lose weight. Cinnamon rolls are *not* on my diet."

"I don't care which of you buy, it'll still taste sweeter."

Peggy laughed. "Floyd, you're taking advantage of these women."

"I am," Floyd said as he stepped out the door.

* * *

Askov, founded by Danes avoiding military conscription in the 1800s, still celebrated a rutabaga festival each summer. Pam drove past the Rutabaga festival sign, already painted with next year's dates. The Pine County Historical Society Museum was inside the old Askov school. With C.J. following, they passed old

39

store fronts. After passing a bar/restaurant on the north end of town, now in its second or third reincarnation since her arrival in Pine County, they turned and followed the road until they reached a big barn with an attached pole building. The smell of hot rubber and sulphur hung in the parking lot air as they exited their cars.

C.J. wrinkled her nose. "Can you imagine working in this smell all the time?"

"Maybe your sense of smell goes numb after a while," Pam said as they approached the entrance.

"I'll have to scrub myself raw before I meet Eddie for supper."

Pam stopped at the door. "I wonder how Bailey will feel about the smell?"

"She'll probably roll in my clothes."

The door opened into a small office where the smell was even more intense. Every surface seemed to be covered with fine black powder. A gray-haired man with heavily tattooed arms turned from his computer and acknowledged their uniforms. "How can I help...two of Pine County's finest?"

"We'd like to speak with Roger Bartlett's partner."

The man smiled, exposing a mouthful of crooked or missing teeth. "Joe Callahan's on his quarterly Las Vegas junket and Roger's not around. I guess you're stuck with me."

40

"You are?" Pam asked.

"Iggy."

"Iggy is an interesting nickname," C.J. said.

"It's short for Ignatius."

Another man, bare-chested with several days of beard walked in and tossed a stack of papers on the desk. His skin glistened with a sheen of sweat on top of the myriad tattoos on his torso and arms. He gave the deputies and the man behind the desk a disgusted look. "Or ignoramus." He pointed at the papers he'd just thrown on the desk. "This load is crap. Most of them have nails in them and they've all been recapped a half dozen times. It's taking the guys a half hour to grind and patch them. We're losing money on every tire we handle."

Iggy threw his hands up. "I'm having problems getting loads across the Canadian border. Joe told me to get some tires in here from wherever I could, or he'd fire my ass. This was all the buyer could find right now."

"Call him back and tell him he can pull the nails and patch them himself."

Pam realized that C.J. had stepped behind her. She'd turned so her back wasn't toward the entrance door and the fingers of her right hand were flexing near her holster. C.J.'s eyes were fixed on the corner. Following C.J.'s eyes, Pam saw the Rottweiler sitting in the corner. His ears

41

were back, and his eyes were moving between the two deputies.

"Is your dog aggressive?" Pam asked.

Iggy looked at the dog. "Zeus, sit."

The dog hesitated, then sat. His muscles remained taut, and his eyes never left Pam and C.J.

"Zeus is our security system. We don't have cameras or an alarm system. Anyone who's ever seen Zeus knows not to come around here when the shop is closed."

"Yeah," C.J. said. "I can see how that would be effective."

"Have you heard about Roger Bartlett?"

"It's a small town. Everyone knows Roger is missing."

"C.J. found Roger this morning. He's dead."

Iggy stroked his chin with his dirty index finger. "I suppose that means his kid will want to try and run the place."

"You say that like it's a bad idea," C.J. said.

"His kids are all college grads who think we need to modernize and automate. They don't understand that we're competing with a thousand Far East companies with workers who make ten bucks a day. That, and there's no way to automate. Each tire is inspected and handled individually. Like Weasel said, we've got a load of tires with nails and punctures. The guys pull each nail by hand, inspect the plies, patch the holes, then grind the surface. No machinery can do that."

Iggy stood up. "Would you like a tour?"

The offer sounded friendly, but there was an undercurrent of challenge being laid to the female deputies. "Sounds good," C.J. spoke up, covering Pam's hesitation and giving her partner a minute to adjust.

The hum and bumping noise coming from the other side of the wall became a roar and banging when Iggy opened the door between the office and work area. He took two pairs of scratched safety glasses from a case mounted on the wall. "Wear these all the time back here." He then handed them plastic wrapped packets of foam ear plugs. "Scrunch these up and stuff them in your ears."

Having used eye and ear protection on the shooting range, Pam and C.J. were accustomed to their use. With their safety gear on, Iggy led them to a workstation where a well-muscled man held a grinding wheel against a spinning truck tire. They watched in fascination as the machine ground off the tire tread.

"Why don't you leave the tread on for anchoring the new layer?" C.J. asked.

"The tread surface is too smooth for the new rubber to anchor," Iggy shouted. "When Charlie gets through grinding the tread off, we've got a nice rough surface for the primer."

43

Done with the grinding, Charlie shut down his machine, lowering the noise level significantly. Without looking up at the deputies, he stopped the spinning tire, pulled it off the hub, and threw it onto a pile stacked on a wooden pallet. He glared at them before retrieving another used tire from a different pallet. He mounted it on the hub and started spinning the tire for grinding.

As the howl of the spinning tire started, C.J. leaned to Iggy. "Charlie hardly looks big enough to be tossing those tires around by hand."

Iggy turned his back on the operation and led them to a slightly quieter spot. "Don't let Charlie hear you say that. He's only five-foot-three with his shoes on, but he's wiry with a bit of a Napoleon complex."

"He's got a chip on his shoulder?" C.J. asked.

"He's a scrapper. I think his nose has been broken more times than any hockey goalie I've ever known."

"Charlie doesn't say much," Pam shouted to Iggy as Charlie glared at them.

"He's a man of few words who doesn't have much time for cops," Iggy replied. He led them to another station where a man in gray coveralls was thumping a hammer on the surface of the tire. "Weasel checks the tires for ply separation, then repairs punctures."

Weasel didn't look at them either, instead focusing on the tire. After thumping, he ran his fingers around the inside of the tire. Halfway around, he stopped and picked up a large pair of pliers. He pulled a long screw from the inside of the tire, then dabbed a syrup-like black goo on the hole. Not as muscular as Chuck, Weasel slid the tire off his workbench and rolled it ahead of himself.

Following Weasel, they made a corner where a man had a bald tire on a slowly turning hub. He painted black goo on the surface of the bald tire. Sensing the visitors behind him, he turned. The hair on the nape of Pam's neck bristled as the balding blond man leered at her, his eyes slowly checking her out from her shoes to her hair. He got a lascivious grin when their eyes met. He stared at Pam for a moment, then repeated the process, looking at C.J.'s uniform.

"You fill out that bulletproof vest nicely," he said, grinning and staring into C.J.'s eyes.

Holding his stare, C.J. said, "Pam, have you noticed that the dirtiest old men have pricks proportional to their tiny brains?"

Iggy stepped between C.J. and the man, whose face was reddening. "Ole doesn't mean anything by stuff he says. He just likes to get a rise out of people. He was always getting under the prison guard's skin. Let's go to the next station."

A red-haired man with a sunburned look cut a strip of wide rubber from a roll, then applied it to a slowly turning tire. He stopped the tire when the first end of the new rubber came around, then he carefully trimmed the excess rubber from the overlap. Ignoring the touring deputies, he used a hoist to lift the tire to a round, hollow chamber. Once in the chamber, he sealed it. A loud hissing noise came from the machine, then the chamber opened, and the tire emerged with tire tread molded into the rubber wrap.

"Igor takes the molded tires to the curing chamber. They're heated under pressure overnight. In the morning he'll pull out the finished tires."

With the tire in the cure chamber alongside a dozen others, Igor looked at Pam and C.J. Igor's head was shaved, exposing a variety of tattoos, including two eyes on the back of his head that appeared to be watching behind him. Igor barely glanced at Pam, but when he saw C.J. he cocked his head, as if to say, "hi," then went back to the next tire.

Iggy led them out of the building onto a loading dock. A forklift was loading pallets of tires into the back of a semi trailer. "This is the end of the tour. We load the finished retreads into the trailer, and they go to a wholesaler who sells them to trucking companies."

Looking at a pile of randomly tossed tires behind the building, C.J. asked. "Are those incoming tires?"

"Those are the tires we can't recap. Most have cuts in the sidewalls or a ply delamination we can't repair."

"What happens to them?" Pam asked.

"A guy picks them up. I guess he chops them into chunks. He paints them the color of redwood, then bags them up and sells them as landscaping mulch. Some are used as fill to stabilize soft spots in the bogs."

"They're not mulch. They don't degrade," Pam said as they walked down a narrow passageway toward the office.

"That's above my pay grade," Iggy replied, as he put their safety glasses back into a dusty rack. "You can throw your earplugs in this wastebasket."

Pam stepped to a chair, then realized it was covered with the fine black rubber being ground off the tires and decided to stand. "Tell me about the employees, Iggy."

"Most have been with us a couple years. There's some turnover if guys get better jobs, but Roger pays well and, well, there aren't a lot of jobs for cons just getting out of prison."

"They're all on parole?" Pam asked.

"Yeah. It's their first job after getting released."

C.J. looked at a calendar from a tool company. It featured a scantily clad young woman holding a wrench. "Tell me about Igor."

"He's on parole like the rest of them."

"Why was he in prison?"

"All our guys are federal parolees. They violated a variety of federal laws. Roger doesn't like to hire guys who've been in the drug trade. They tend to go back to their old buddies and are then arrested for parole violations, either drug use or firearms possession. We mostly hire guys who committed white-collar crimes."

"White-collar crimes like money laundering, or...?" Pam asked.

"Charlie was in for embezzlement. Weasel fenced stolen art."

"And Igor..." C.J. asked.

Iggy blew out a breath. "Igor and his girlfriend were busted for human trafficking. They had a string of illegal alien girls."

Pam frowned. "That's a state crime."

"Yeah, well they were taking them to trade shows and conventions. I think the feds called it an interstate criminal operation."

C.J. took out a notebook. "What's Igor's last name?"

"Igor is just his nickname because he's got an accent that sounds Russian. Aleksandr Lianin is actually Romanian."

Pam watched as C.J. wrote down the name. "How did he get assigned to the Sandstone Prison? I thought federal judges put people in prisons near their homes and there aren't many Romanians around Pine County. Actually, I can't think of a single Romanian family."

"Igor has never explained it, but I suspect his life might've been in danger if he'd been imprisoned near his home. He might've testified against someone important to get a lighter sentence in a prison far from his business associates."

Closing her notebook, Pam considered shaking Iggy's hand, then looked at the fine black dust on everything and decided against it. "Thanks for the tour and information."

C.J. opened the outside door but stopped when Iggy spoke. "Just because these guys are white collar criminals doesn't make them pussycats."

"Are you saying the community isn't safe around them?"

Iggy checked the door to the work area, making sure no one was listening. "I don't think they're a physical threat, but I wouldn't co-sign a loan with any of them."

Feeling edgy, C.J. checked the parking lot as she closed the door behind them. "What does it say when a convict warns you about his co-workers?"

Pam stopped at the bottom step. "Remind me of the recidivism rate for convicts."

"In Minnesota, it's twenty-five percent. That's well below the national average of sixty-six percent."

"Yeah, I think half those guys will be behind bars again." Pam pulled a tissue from her pocket and blew her nose as they walked to their cars. "I feel like I inhaled a pound of ground rubber while we were in there."

C.J. leaned against the fender of her cruiser. "I thought it was interesting that they wanted us to wear ear plugs and safety glasses, but not masks."

"None of the workers wore masks."

C.J. stared at the door. "I saw packs of cigarettes at every workstation. I suppose a little rubber dust is insignificant if you inhale tar and carcinogens on your breaks."

"I hope Igor gets lung cancer and dies a slow painful death."

Chuckling, C.J. said, "And it wasn't even you he was ogling."

"I didn't need to be the object of his attention to be creeped out by his leer."

"I wonder if there are women who find that approach endearing?"

Pam dabbed at her nose with the tissue. "It apparently worked on someone. How else would he attract a stable of girls to pimp out?"

"I can't see him being the recruiter. He must've had a partner." C.J. paused. "What now, Madam Investigator?"

Pam shook her head. "I'm going to look up Aleksandr Lianin's file to see if he's ever been charged with murder."

"I'd check all the employees. Just because Roger supposedly hired white-collar criminals, doesn't mean they don't have other arrests on their records."

"I miss Floyd. He would've reminded me of things like that."

C.J. smiled. "Wow! I've been elevated to Floyd's level."

Pam shook her head. "Actually, I think I'll start calling you Rosco P. Coltrane."

C.J. tried to remember why Rosco's name was familiar, then made the connection. "Oh no. I'm not the inept sheriff from *The Dukes of Hazzard.*"

"Bailey is the twin of Rosco's slobbering basset hound."

"Fine, if I'm Rosco, then you're Enos, the equally inept deputy."

"I'd rather be Daisy Duke, in the cute shorts."

C.J. rolled her eyes. "Daisy was as dumb as a stump."

Laughing, Pam replied, "Like Enos was any smarter?"

C.J. put up her hand to end the banter. "Let's get back to reality. I'll look for Bartlett's backtrail and rifle while you check the criminal histories of the tire company employees."

Pam put up one finger, like she'd had a sudden thought. "Did you find it coincidental that Joe Callahan is in Las Vegas? I'll see if he has any arrests, too."

"It doesn't make any difference if Bartlett's shooting was accidental. On the other hand, if someone tried to make it look accidental…"

"I think you're right about the coincidental Las Vegas trip. It'd be interesting to know if that's an every deer hunting season event, or if he just happened to choose this time to be gone."

C.J. leaned on the top of her car. "It'd also be interesting to know if Bartlett and Callahan were equal partners, and what happens to the ownership now that Bartlett is dead."

"Sandy gave me the names of the hunting party. I'll take a look at them, too."

A shot rang out in the distance, followed by two more quick shots. C.J. turned in the direction of the distant shots. "It's warming up and the snow is melting. I'm going back to the cabin to see if I can follow Bartlett's backtrail. We need to recover his rifle."

"There are a lot of acres to search between Bartlett's deer stand and the cabin. If his trail disappears when the snow melts, your chances of finding his rifle are slim."

C.J.'s eyes lit up. "We know a deputy with a dog!"

"Do you think you can talk him into coming up here?"

C.J. opened her car door. "The worst he can do is say no."

Chapter 5

C.J. searched her call log for the number of the Chisago County K9 officer she'd contacted for assistance the previous spring. She selected Pat Radosovich's cell phone number and touched the call button. She was preparing to leave a message after the fifth ring when the call was answered.

"Here's the deal, C.J. If there's evidence in a flooded ditch, you'd better have hip boots because I'm not the one wading in this time."

Laughing, C.J. said, "There are no flooded ditches involved."

"Are you calling to tell me Floyd is buying coffee as thanks for the last time I helped?"

"Floyd retired, but I'm willing to buy you a cup of coffee. I might even have a couple Milk Bones in my car for Woody."

"Floyd finally retired?"

"He put his papers in last spring, after the last time you helped me."

"I suppose he was at that point in his life. I assume this isn't a social call. What can I do for you?"

"We found the body of a hunter last night. I want to follow his backtrail to find his rifle." C.J. paused. "Can you help me out?"

"I heard there was a hunting accident near Cloverdale. Is that the case you're on?"

"A hunter died of a gunshot wound. We're still trying to determine if it was an accident."

"C.J., you're talking to a cop, not the media."

"The wound was probably made by a deer rifle, so it could've been an errant shot or accident."

"The tone of your voice says you're not convinced that is the case."

"There are still questions to be answered and finding the victim's rifle may put some of them to rest."

"Give me a few minutes to call my sergeant."

"I'll be waiting."

* * *

Pam got a cup of coffee and sat down at her computer. She'd just entered Aleksandr Lianin's name into the National Criminal Information Check (NCIC) system when the sheriff walked in. "Have you decided the dead hunter was an accidental shooting?"

"I'm not ready to say that yet."

With the coffee pot gurgling, the sheriff sat in Pam's guest chair. "Is there evidence he was shot intentionally?"

Pam leaned back. "The victim was the co-owner of the tire recapping business. They employ parolees from the Sandstone Federal Prison, and I was just going to check the NCIC database to see why his employees were arrested."

"Most murders are prosecuted by the state and the convicts go to the Stillwater or Oak Park Heights prisons."

"The guy who toured us through the recapping shop said their employees were white-collar criminals. I'm going to verify that."

The coffee pot stopped gurgling, signaling the end of the cycle. The sheriff stood, then paused. "You learned a lot from Floyd. I'm pleased that you're digging into this case as diligently as Floyd would've."

"Thanks."

After retrieving his mug from the coffee maker, the sheriff stopped by the door. "This is the highest profile case we've got going. Keep me informed."

"I will," Pam said to the empty doorway.

Back at the computer, Pam finished typing in Lianin's name and waited. After a few moments, rather than Lianin's rap sheet, a note popped up with a name and phone number in the U.S. Marshal's Office. She wrote the name and phone number on a notepad, then punched the number into her desk phone.

"U.S. Marshal's Office, how may I direct your call?"

"I'd like to speak with Wayne Parker."

After a minute of instrumental music, a man's voice answered. "This is Deputy Marshal Parker, how can I help...the Pine County Sheriff's Department?"

"Deputy Parker, I'm Pam Ryan. I'm investigating a death and Aleksandr Lianin's name has come up during my inquiries. When I entered his name in NCIC, I received a message to call you."

"Ms. Ryan, let me call you back in a couple minutes."

Knowing Parker wanted to verify her identity, Pam said, "Call the Pine County Sheriff's Department non-emergency number and ask for Investigator Ryan." She gave him the phone number and hung up.

Within a minute, a button flashed on her phone and the dispatcher paged her to answer line one. "Deputy Marshal Parker?"

"I'm sorry for the subterfuge, Investigator Ryan, but it's way too easy for a reporter or criminal to call in representing themself as a law enforcement person seeking information. What's your interest in Aleksandr Lianin?"

"I'm investigating a suspicious death and I'm doing background checks on all the victim's employees. Mr. Lianin is one of the employees. I'd like to know why he was imprisoned in the Sandstone Federal Prison."

"Mr. Lianin's location is...sensitive information."

"I have no interest in revealing his location. I'm only trying to gather background on a group of people who may be suspects in a suspicious death investigation. I received anecdotal information that he was part of a human trafficking organization."

"That would be the information available in the FCIS database."

"Marshal Parker, I feel like we're playing twenty questions."

"I'm sorry if I seem evasive, but Mr. Lianin was offered certain guarantees in return for his cooperation in a Federal RICO case."

"You make it sound like he's in a witness protection program."

"I think you know I can't comment on that."

Pam wrote *witness protection?* on her notepad. "You can neither confirm nor deny."

Parker was silent. "This is an extremely sensitive situation. What can I say that will remove Mr. Lianin from consideration in your investigation?"

"Your assurance that he's not a hit man or murderer would be a big step."

"He pled guilty to a non-violent crime."

"We both know that's not the answer to my question. Prosecutors arrange plea bargains for lesser crimes all the time to get witnesses to testify against their co-conspirators." Pam wrote, *what would Floyd ask*? Then she was struck by an obvious question. "Is his name actually Aleksandr Lianin, or is that an alias provided by the government?"

"I'm afraid I have a meeting. Please remove Mr. Lianin from your suspect list and good luck with your investigation."

About to ask for Lianin's real name, Pam realized she was listening to a dial tone. She redialed the US Marshal's office and was informed that Wayne Parker was out of the office and unavailable. After hanging up, Pam searched the internet for the 215 area code. She leaned back and stared at the computer screen. Parker was in the US Marshals Philadelphia office.

The sheriff was reading when Pam knocked on his doorframe. "Do you have a second?" She closed the door behind her and sat in a guest chair. "I just had the strangest conversation with a US Marshal in Philadelphia and I'm not sure what to do next."

* * *

C.J. was driving through Sandstone when her cell phone rang. "Hi Pat, can you help me out?"

"I'm free after lunch. Since you're buying, where would you like to meet me?"

"Are you familiar with Nicoll's Café in downtown Pine City?"

"Not really, but I'm sure I can find it. I'll meet you there in forty-five minutes."

* * *

C.J was sitting in a back corner booth in Nicoll's Café when Pat Radosovich walked in. He looked through the crowded eating area and spotted a waitress gesturing towards C.J.'s location.

"You must be a regular," Pat said as he slid into the booth.

"It's the most convenient café when we're at the courthouse or sheriff's department offices. Don't be surprised if the sheriff and county prosecutor walk in."

Esther, a long-time Nicoll's waitress, brought a coffee pot to the table and flipped over Pat's mug. "The lunch special is a Rueben with fries or potato salad. C.J.'s having a California burger."

"The Rueben sounds good to me," Pat said.

Esther, matronly and outspoken, glanced at Pat's wedding ring. She topped off C.J.'s coffee and said, "Too bad he's married. He's cute."

Pat chuckled as Esther left. "Is our waitress the local matchmaker?"

"No, she just likes to needle me about being forty, widowed, and unmarried."

"Is your leg healed?"

The question caught C.J. off guard. The gunshot wound she'd suffered while wrestling with a suspect was still tender, both physically and mentally. She took a second to compose her answer. "It's healing. My chances of being hired as a swimsuit model are gone."

Radosovich saw C.J.'s attempted humor for what it was, a way of deflecting the question, and he moved to safer ground. "Tell me about your hunter."

Interrupted only by the delivery of their sandwiches, C.J. reviewed the events leading to the discovery of Bartlett's body in the cabin, her attempt to follow his backtrail, and her visit to the tire recapping shop with Pam Ryan.

"Pam's off restricted duty now?"

"Her son, Luke, is six months old and Pam's back, unrestricted and full time."

Between bites, Pat nodded toward C.J.'s sleeve. "You weren't a sergeant when we did the drug search last year."

"Floyd told the sheriff I should be promoted to his old position when he retired."

"Congratulations. How are the rest of the deputies taking that move?"

"A couple of them are mildly irritated, but overall, I've been accepted as a competent member of the department." C.J. paused. "The guys are taking it better than one of the county board members. The sheriff took one board member aside after he made a derisive remark about 'that woman deputy who couldn't hold her own in a fight with a teenager'. No one overheard the conversation, but I guess the sheriff set him straight. At any rate, no one has given me any flak since then."

After taking his last bite of the sandwich, Pat wiped his hands on a napkin. "Who's watching Bailey the farting dog now that Pam's out of the office?"

C.J. nearly choked on her last bite of hamburger. "Who told you about Bailey?"

Pat pushed his plate back and smiled. "The central Minnesota law enforcement community isn't that large."

"Sandy Maki had an undercover assignment over the summer. It must've been with you guys."

Signalling for a coffee refill, Pat nodded. "He and his wife were introduced to us so we wouldn't blow their cover if we saw them working. I guess Barb's tattoos and personality lent credibility to Sandy being part of the drug culture. Is it true she used to date a biker?"

"Pam told me Sandy met her when he was investigating a murder. I guess Barb's relationship with the biker was abusive and Sandy rescued her by arresting her boyfriend."

"That's just crazy. I've never heard of a cop dating a biker chick before."

C.J. nodded. "Yeah, they had to overcome a bit of culture clash, but they're making it work. Barb is very intelligent, but people miss that when they see the tattoos and her hard appearance."

"Like I said, she gave Sandy street credibility during his undercover stint. The drug task force was able to bring down a major supplier who'd always shied away from previous undercover stings. Barb sealed the deal." Pat paused. "You dodged the question about Bailey."

"I have her in doggie daycare three days a week. Now that she's outgrowing her puppy stage, I can leave her loose in my apartment without coming home to messes." C.J. signalled for their bill. "She's good most of the time."

"Most of the time?"

Pulling two twenty dollar bills out of a clip, C.J. handed them to the waitress. "Keep the change."

Esther patted Pat's shoulder. "Too bad you're married. C.J. would be quite a catch. Do you have an unmarried older brother?"

"All my siblings are sisters," he said as he slid out of the booth. "But there is one deputy who's a recent divorcee. I'll tell him about C.J. when I get back."

"Attaboy," Esther said as she gathered the dirty dishes. "C.J.'s not getting any younger. I wouldn't want her to stay single past her shelf life."

"I have a shelf life?" C.J. asked as she stood.

"You know how it is, honey. Men like their women skinny and young. You're good on the skinny side, but you should think about touching up the gray in your hair."

Snorting, Pat steered C.J. toward the door before she could respond.

"Gawd, you'd think Esther's been talking to my mother," C.J. said as they stepped onto the sidewalk.

"She's a hoot!"

"That's great for you. You're not the one who was told to 'touch up her hair.'"

"I'm parked down the street. Which direction are we going?"

"Drive north, over the river. You can follow me from the VFW parking lot."

* * *

The Cedar Lake cabin was a twenty-minute drive from Pine City. Radosovich let Woody, his K9 partner, out of the back door. Ignoring C.J., the dog rushed to a patch of tall grass and lifted his leg. After peeing, he ran to C.J. who knelt and rubbed his neck.

64

"Do you have a piece of the victim's clothing? Woody needs a scent to track."

"The victim died in the cabin. I assume Woody can get scent from the victim's blood."

Hooking the dog on a leash, Pat followed C.J. into the cabin. Woody moved quickly around the living room and kitchen, sniffing everything. When they led him to the bedroom, the dog froze and sniffed the air tentatively.

"I think he knows someone died here," C.J. said.

"Yeah. I can smell the blood, but Woody is picking up more than we smell." Pat led the dog to his car.

"What are you doing?"

Popping the lid to the car's trunk, Pat reached inside while the dog sat, wagging his tail. "I use an orange tracking harness," he said, taking a long leather lead and orange harness out. Woody immediately stood, anticipating the fitting of the harness around his chest.

"Good thought," C.J. replied. "I've got an orange vest to wear in the woods.

"Wear comfortable shoes or boots. We'll be running."

C.J. pulled on her vest. "Running?"

"If Woody's on a scent, I'll let him follow the trail and run along behind."

"I thought that's what the leather lead was for?"

"If we're following him through underbrush, I don't want to crawl under every deadfall and through every briar patch."

"We can't keep up with a dog," C.J. protested. "I've chased Bailey for blocks when she's found something interesting to sniff. Then I caught her."

"Woody will look back to see if we're following, but he's going to range back and forth following the scent cone."

"I thought he'd follow the footprints?"

"He's trained to follow scent. Footprints disappear on solid ground or in water. He follows the scent left by the person he's trailing. It's more reliable and harder to disguise."

Radosovich stripped off his heavy belt and replaced it with a nylon belt with only a holster. He switched his gun to the lightweight belt, then pulled on a brown backpack.

C.J. pulled on a pair of hunting boots and tied the laces. "What's in the backpack?"

"It's a hydration pack with a water bladder. If we all run a long way, we're going to need water. How far are we from the hunter's deer stand?"

"It's a couple miles on the map." C.J. stood, then cocked her head. "Do you think we're going to run all the way to the victim's deer stand?"

"Is that a problem? Woody and I run two miles at least three times a week."

Tipping back her head, C.J. groaned. "I run a mile once in a while, but Bailey stops at every fire hydrant and signpost."

With his smile spreading, Radosovich attached the lead to the dog. "Try your best to keep up."

"You do realize that I'm not an eighteen-year-old cross-country runner."

"Did you just admit that you're old?"

C.J. put her pistol into a clip-on holster and put her duty belt in the car, then closed the car's trunk and locked the doors. "I admitted that I'm past my prime running years and out of shape."

Back at the cabin's steps, Pat ordered the dog to sit. "Here's the deal. I'm going to watch the dog. He's going to give me signs he's on the trail or struggling to find scent. Your job is to watch our surroundings. Since it's hunting season, yell out if you see someone in orange. They should see the dog's orange harness, but I don't want some idiot taking 'sound shots' at the dog when he hears something that sounds like a deer."

"Pam and I found droplets of blood on the victim's trail until the tracks disappeared, so there should be a good scent trail. It's warmed up enough to melt the snow where the sun hits the ground. I assume Woody can follow the blood trail even if it's melted off the snow."

"Scent is hydrophilic. It loves wet conditions and lingers on grass and leaves. These conditions should be just about perfect." Radosovich unclipped the lead and said, "track."

Woody raced ahead in the wrong direction, then cut back until he crossed the blood trail. After taking a left turn, he ran ahead. C.J. loped along behind them, scanning the trees ahead of them for blaze orange.

Woody ran past the spot where C.J. had earlier lost the trail in the snow. Pausing briefly to sniff Pam and C.J.'s final footprints. With her hands on her knees, C.J. gulped air. "I'm sucking wind and we've hardly started." She looked at Pat, who was barely breathing heavily. "Can we slow Woody down until I catch my breath?"

Pat held up the lead and called the dog, who hesitated, but bounded back. "It's open ahead of us. I'll put Woody on the lead for a while. He won't be happy, but we'll only have to trot to keep up."

"Oh good, I'll only have to jog for a hundred yards." Standing up, C.J. waved them on. "Go, I'll be right behind you."

Pat held the dog back. "No, I won't put the dog at risk. You have to be with us to watch for hunters and other risks. We'll go at your pace, but no faster."

Drawing a deep breath, C.J. uttered, "I should've had Pam do this."

"Why? Does she run?"

"I don't know if she runs, but she is ten years younger than I am."

Walking ahead with the dog straining at the lead, Pat smiled. "I suppose she didn't need to color her hair to find a boyfriend."

"Stuff it, Radosovich."

"She had more shelf life."

"I have a boyfriend who thinks my shelf life is just fine." As soon as the words were out of her mouth C.J. knew she'd just admitted to a virtual stranger that Eddie, the medical examiner's assistant, was more to her than an occasional dinner partner. Her relationship with Eddie was complicated. She'd decided she wasn't ready for a *relationship*, but dinner with a male friend was comfortable. Eddie was gentlemanly and put no pressure on her to move their friendship past casual dinners. If anything, Eddie seemed even more reluctant to approach the issue of intimacy than she was.

"Your boyfriend must not be local, or Esther wouldn't be needling you."

C.J. shook her head. "I'm not talking anymore. I need to save my breath for...breathing."

They jogged across the open meadow, following the dog who was ranging farther to the sides as they approached a tree line.

"Why's he going so far off the trail?"

"The scent trail is less distinct here than it was closer to the cabin. I suppose the scent is older or your victim wasn't bleeding as much here."

With the dog into the trees, they found a set of human tracks going through the snow under a stand of balsam firs. Pat motioned to C.J. "Cut around the side of these pines. Make sure there isn't someone on the other side waiting for a deer to run out."

Sprinting ahead through the brush along the edge of the balsam thicket, C.J. stumbled and fell. Grabbing a branch to pull herself up, she tested her ankles to make sure they weren't sprained, then sprinted ahead, pushing the brush away from her face as she forged ahead.

"What the hell?" She heard a voice say from above her.

She looked overhead and saw an orange jacket. "Sheriff's department operation. There's a dog coming through."

The man, who was on a platform twelve feet above the ground, stood and slung the rifle over his shoulder. "I saw them in the balsams. I couldn't see you coming, but I knew no deer was going to make that much noise."

"Are there any other hunters in this area?"

"Naw. They're all napping until the evening stand."

Leaning against the tree, C.J. caught her breath. "Did you see someone run through here last night?"

"Something or someone came through last night after sunset. I was climbing down from my stand, and I heard commotion."

"What time?"

"There wasn't enough light to see a deer, so it must've been after 5:30."

"But did you *see* anyone?"

"Nope. I just heard something running through, making as much noise as you."

"Did you hear any shooting from the east last night?"

"You know, I did. I kind of thought maybe the noise I heard was a wounded deer."

"You didn't check?" C.J. asked, looking around for Woody and Pat.

"It wasn't my deer. So, no, I didn't check." The hunter looked away from C.J. "A dog just ran out of the balsams. Is that what you're looking for?"

"The handler will be right behind him."

Still looking at the evergreens, the hunter said, "Yup, there's the guy."

"You only heard one shot?"

"Just one. That's all it takes to bring down a deer if you're a careful hunter."

"Did you see any other hunters in the woods yesterday?"

"I didn't see anything except chickadees and a couple noisy squirrels."

"What's your name?"

"Herman Kessel. I live by Big Pine Lake." The hunter looked toward the dog again. "You've got a lot of questions. Does this have something to do with that lost hunter?"

"The sound you heard after sunset may have been him walking through here."

Wiping his nose with a red bandana, the hunter frowned. "Whatever went through wasn't walking, it was running."

"Running?"

"Just guessing based on the amount of noise I heard, I'd say definitely running. He was crashing through the balsams." Kessel nodded to his left. "Your partner is waving. I think he's looking for you."

C.J jogged in the direction Kessel was looking. She found Woody sitting at heel next to Radosovich.

"I thought you got lost."

Pausing to catch her breath, C.J. shook her head. "That hunter heard a shot shortly after sunset, then heard something run through after dark."

"There are a few footprints in the balsams, tamaracks, and moss. Whatever or whoever went through was running and stumbling. There's a spot where something fell to the ground and Woody was all over the scent there."

"Was there a puddle of blood?"

Radosovich shook his head. "There wasn't any visible blood, but the snow had melted in that spot."

C.J looked at the dog. "Well, I've caught my breath. I suppose we should move on. If the victim was running, we should be where he was shot in about fifteen minutes."

Anticipating the command, Woody's tail started wagging frantically.

Pat released the lead clasp. "Track."

Ranging from side to side, Woody ran through the underbrush, stopping occasionally to make sure Pat and C.J. weren't falling too far behind. Nearly twenty minutes later, the dog stopped and started barking.

"What does that mean?" C.J. asked.

"It usually means he's being held back and wants to run. Maybe he's stuck in some brush."

Woody was racing from side to side as they approached. When they neared, they could see he was stopped behind a four-strand barbed wire fence. Orange thread hung from barbs between the two uppermost strands.

"I think our hunter went through here," C.J. said.

"I wouldn't bet on that," her partner replied. "There's no time stamp on those fibers. They could've been left there any time."

C.J. took an evidence bag and a blue plastic glove from her back pocket. "The victim's jacket was torn. I can have the lab test these to see if they match."

After collecting the fibers, they walked down the fence line and found a loose spot in the bottom wire. Woody slid under the wire, followed by C.J. Radosovich passed his backpack to C.J., then he slid under the wire.

They paused and drank water from the backpack. "How far are we from the victim's deer stand?" Pat asked.

C.J. looked around. "This fence is probably the west edge of the hunting party's property. His stand isn't far from here."

Woody raced ahead as Radosovich slipped the backpack straps over his shoulders. "We should be close to where he was shot."

They found Woody circling a tree thirty yards from the fence. "Why is he circling?" C.J. asked.

"Look at his tail. He's found something."

A hunting rifle was leaning against the tree where the dog was circling. Snow had accumulated in the riflescope, and the rest of the gun was wet from melted snow.

"The rifle looks like it's been standing here since the snow started," C.J. said.

Radosovich bent over and sniffed the muzzle. "It's been fired recently."

C.J knelt, and the dog immediately went to her, nuzzling her face. She looked back, toward their trail, then the opposite direction. "The snow covered up a lot, but it looks like there are two sets of prints coming from the east, but only one set continuing on." She stood. "Can Woody find a spent cartridge?"

"Lacking any other scent, yes. But this area is covered with the victim's scent. You'd do better bringing a metal detector out and searching the area with it."

C.J. looked west at the barely visible fence line. "Do you think he was shot from here?"

"Here's a theory: his attacker took the gun away from the victim and chased him here. The fence slowed or stopped the victim, giving the shooter an easy target."

"Gettysburg."

Radosovich frowned. "What?"

"My parents took us to Gettysburg when we were kids. Longstreet charged the Union line, but his men had to climb over a split-rail fence a hundred yards from the Union position. The hesitation set them up as easy targets for the Union infantry and artillery. If there hadn't been a fence, Longstreet probably would've routed the Union infantry. Instead, they had to climb the fence while under fire. The pictures showed Confederate soldier's bodies stacked like cordwood on both sides of the fence."

"I must've slept through Civil War history," Radosovich said, clipping Woody to the lead.

C.J. stared at the fence. "I was at the Gettysburg battlefield and stood at the monument where the First Minnesota regiment ran forward to reinforce the broken Union line. Over 80 percent of the regiment was killed or wounded in that engagement, the most casualties of any Union or Confederate regiment, in any Civil War battle. It brings tears to my eyes just thinking about it."

Radosovich put on a pair of rubber gloves and unloaded the rifle while C.J. composed herself. "I assume there's a road near here that'll be an easier walk than going back the way we came."

"Yeah, there's a township road a couple hundred yards south of here."

Chapter 6

NCIC searches confirmed that the employees of the Askov Tire Company were white-collar convicts. The search for Joe Callahan showed that he'd been arrested in 1988 for smuggling cases of Cuban cigars from Canada, hidden in boxes labelled walleye fillets. He'd been fined $1,000 and forfeited the cigars. More interesting than his criminal record was his Canadian address, in Thunder Bay, Ontario.

After starting another cup of coffee, Pam pondered the new information while the coffee maker gurgled. Of all the employees at the tire company, Joe Callahan was the only one never convicted of a felony. With a fresh cup of coffee, she went back to the computer and typed in Roger Bartlett's name. The NCIC site pondered the request for a few seconds, then displayed, 'no records'.

While considering that information, Pam leaned back and held the mug in both hands. "Floyd, what should I do next?" she asked, staring at what had been Floyd's desk. The dispatcher's page broke her concentration.

"Deputy Ryan."

"Are you investigating my father's death?" the female voice asked.

The caller ID showed MBartlett. "Who are you?"

"I'm Michelle Bartlett. Roger Bartlett was my father. I assume you've arrested his slimy partner."

Setting her cup aside, Pam picked up a pen and pulled a notepad close. "What makes you suspect your father's partner?"

"He's a slimy douchebag who used my father."

"His being an unsavory character doesn't make him a murderer."

Michelle gasped in frustration. "You don't understand. The man is capable of anything. My skin crawls every time I see him."

"First of all, we're not sure your father's death was anything but a hunting accident. Secondly, Mr. Callahan was in Las Vegas at the time of your father's death."

"Just because the jerk didn't pull the trigger, doesn't mean that he's not responsible for Dad's death."

Tapping the pen on the notepad, Pam asked, "Is there something specific that makes you suspect your father's partner was involved in his death?"

"There is no specific event, just years of his shady dealings and…sliminess."

Pam suppressed a chuckle, wondering if sliminess was even in the dictionary. "Tell me about his shady dealings."

"There are millions of truck tires recapped in the US every year. Millions. But Callahan has them shipped in from Canada, along with all the recapping materials. It makes no sense. He told Dad he got better prices in Canada because of the exchange rate between Canadian and American dollars, but it just didn't add up."

"I'll look into this information. Thanks for the call."

"Um, Deputy Ryan, there's more."

"Go ahead."

"Callahan hit on me when I was a teenager. I was flattered, but I'm sure his attention was more than flirtation. He asked me to meet him for burgers and stuff, but I always chickened out at the last second. I think he might be a pedophile."

"Thanks. I'll check into that too." Pam hung up and leaned back and thought to herself, *"What in hell am I supposed to do with this information. Michelle is obviously overwrought about her father's death. How much of what she told me are emotions and how much is fact?"*

* * *

With Woody on a leash, C.J. and the dog handler walked down the gravel road that ran parallel to the track they'd followed through the woods. Woody walked quietly at his handler's side, occasionally looking up to make sure he wasn't getting ahead.

"I wish Bailey would behave like this," C.J. said. "She pulls me along when we walk and if I let her off the leash, I'm afraid I'd never see her again."

"Woody had months of intensive training before he was assigned to me, then we had weeks of training, learning to work together."

C.J. sighed. "I don't have the time to put in that much effort, and I'm not sure Bailey would ever behave as well as Woody. She'd catch the scent of a squirrel or bunny and she'd be off to the races."

"That's every dog's instinct. You have to train them to overcome their natural instincts."

C.J.'s cell phone rang, and she struggled to get it out of her pocket before the call rolled over to voicemail. "Hello."

Eddie's familiar voice made her smile. "Tony finished the PM on Roger Bartlett with no surprises. He died from blood loss."

"Could you tell how far away the shooter was when the shot was fired?"

"Far enough so there wasn't any burnt powder residue on the orange coat, so more than a few feet."

"What else can you tell me?"

"He had some antemortem bruising on his face."

"I suppose that could've been caused when he fell out of his tree stand after he was shot. Is there anything else?"

"Not a lot. He was hit by an expanding bullet, like a deer hunter would shoot. Bartlett was an average guy. He had a little atherosclerosis and a slightly enlarged liver."

"Atherosclerosis?"

Eddie laughed. "There was some plaque accumulation in his arteries, no more than most fifty-year-old guys, and he probably drank a fair amount of liquor causing a fatty and enlarged liver. Aside from that, he was healthy. I'll run a toxicology screen to see if there was anything unusual in his system, but as far as you're concerned, he bled to death from a gunshot wound."

"It appeared that the bullet passed through his shoulder, so there's nothing to link it to a particular gun."

"Tony recovered some lead fragments from the wound channel, so we might be able to compare them to another cartridge, but there's no bullet for comparison to link the deadly shot to a specific gun."

"We just recovered a gun. The dog found it on Bartlett's trail through the woods. It's been fired recently, and I have several unfired cartridges from the magazine."

"If you bring me one of the cartridges, I can compare the alloy in the lead core to the fragments found in the wound. That won't say those shells are the same box of shells, but it can say they're not if the alloys don't match." Eddie hesitated. "If you brought me a shell tonight, I could have results for you tomorrow...and I'm available for supper."

"You just want me to bring the bullet up tonight because it's my turn to buy."

Eddie hesitated, as if he was checking to see if anyone was listening. "I like your company, no matter who buys."

"I'll give you a call after I've cleaned up and walked Bailey."

"You don't need to clean up for me."

C.J. laughed. "I've been running after the tracking dog for an hour. Trust me, I don't even want to be trapped in a car with myself. I'd leave my socks on the ground if I wouldn't have to ticket myself for littering."

Pat laughed and leaned close to the phone. "This is Pat Radosovich, the K-9 officer. C.J. is so gamy the dog is straining at his leash to get farther away from her."

Eddie chuckled. "I'm convinced. Call me when you're leaving home."

C.J. ended the call and put the phone in her pocket.

"Is Eddie the boyfriend you mentioned?"

"I may have overstated the depth of our relationship. We're work colleagues and friends. We have dinner together when I'm in Duluth."

Pat smiled. "Friends make pretty good spouses."

"I'm… It's too soon since my husband's death. I need a friend more than I need a lover. Eddie understands that."

"You can't predict or control what your heart feels. You'll heal. Circumstances change."

"I don't want to forget my husband."

"He'll always be a part of who you are. That won't change. But you might find room for someone else someday."

"Is that Radosovich philosophy?"

"It's just observing people and life. We all grieve in different ways at different paces. Some people never get past the loss of a spouse. Others are able to hold the memory close, but still find love with another person. Look at Floyd and Mary. I never thought Floyd would get past the loss of Ginny, his first wife. He hasn't let go of her memory, but he's found someone who understands that and is helping fill the void Ginny's death left."

"Floyd said he took Mary to Ginny's grave and explained to Ginny that they were getting married. He told Pam and me that he wasn't struck by lightning, so he thinks Ginny felt it was okay for him to move on."

"If something happened to me, I hope my wife would find someone to make her happy." He paused, then added, "But I hope she waits until my side of the bed cools off before she invites someone to use my pillow."

C.J. was relieved to see the Cedar Lake cabin's driveway ahead of them. "It looks like we got back to our cars before dark. I was beginning to wonder if we'd taken the wrong road."

Pat bumped shoulders with C.J. "I get it. You've had enough of my philosophy about an uncomfortable topic."

"It's not that…"

"Don't bullshit me. My wife tells me all the time that I don't know when to stop chewing a bone. You're free. Next topic. How about those Vikings! It looks like they're good enough to make the playoffs."

C.J. laughed. "What have you been smoking, Radosovich? They lost half their defense to injuries, and they have two receivers who can't catch passes that hit them in the hands. They'll be lucky to win half their games."

"I'm serious. Things are starting to gel for them. Just wait."

They stopped next to Pat's bumper and C.J. bent down and ruffled Woody's ears. "You're such a good dog." Then she stood and put her hand out to Radosovich. "Thanks for the help…and philosophy."

"You can pay me back."

"How?"

"The sheriff's planning a prostitution sting and we need a woman none of the local Johns will recognize."

C.J broke into laughter. "You are kidding! What John wants a forty-year-old hooker?"

"You're cute and you seem to have all your own teeth."

C.J. gave a dismissive wave. "Talk to the sheriff about using Pam Ryan if you need someone. She doesn't have gray in her hair."

Pat pulled a towel out of his trunk and started drying the dog. "Think about it. You owe me now."

"If your Chisago County Johns are so desperate that they'll accept me as a hooker, you'd better start buying them glasses."

C.J. opened her trunk, set the rifle on a blanket, then swapped her boots for shoes. Pat waited until she was in her car. Then, he turned around and drove down the driveway with C.J. close behind.

Eddie was sitting at the morgue reception desk when C.J. walked in. She handed him a cartridge in a plastic evidence bag. "Here's one of the shells from the gun we recovered."

Eddie signed the custody tag, then locked it in a file cabinet. "I'll take a look at it tomorrow. What are you hungry for?"

"Since I'm paying, I think you get to choose."

Eddie stood and pulled a jacket off a peg by the door. "I think an enchilada and beer would taste really good. Let's go to the Mexican place next to the brewery."

"I'll limit myself to one margarita. I have to drive home and walk Bailey again."

With a sly grin spreading across his face, Eddie said, "As long as you're buying, maybe I'll try the lobster enchiladas. I've heard they're great."

"I know that's a lie. No one makes lobster enchiladas."

"I guess we'll see."

Their table overlooked Lake Superior, C.J. and Eddie made small talk. C.J. filled Eddie in on her trek through the woods, and Eddie talked vaguely about some of the interesting cases they'd had since their last dinner. They'd driven separately to the restaurant and walked through the parking ramp, stopping at C.J.'s car.

"Thanks for driving up," Eddie said. "I always enjoy our dinners."

"Yeah, well, I had to bring the cartridge up for you to test anyway."

Jamming his hands in his pockets to ward off the cool Lake Superior breeze, Eddie stared at his shoes. "Our dinners are the highlight of my weeks. They're a nice break from the cop shows on TV."

"Since Floyd retired, you're the only person I can confide in. All the rest of my colleagues are too close, and anything said seems to get leaked around the department."

Eddie laughed. "I don't have that problem. I can talk to Tony during the post-mortems. He's so focused on the autopsy he doesn't remember what I've said."

Fingering her car keys, C.J. stared at the lake. "I'm really glad we've connected. You don't mind me talking about cop stuff and…most men are more interested in being invited up for a drink after dinner."

"It's a different world than the one I left for Nam," Eddie said, staring at his shoes. "I was into booze and one-night stands. I was so naïve and stupid. Now, I'm happy to get out of the house for dinner and have an interesting conversation."

"Bailey's going to be irritated that I'm home so late. I'd better go." C.J. hesitated, then impulsively leaned forward and kissed Eddie's cheek. "Good night," she said, quickly unlocking her car and getting in.

Eddie stepped back and watched her drive out of the parking garage. "Well, that was strange," he said to himself.

Chapter 7

Pam spent a mundane evening at home with Luke and Travis, ignoring the day's activities. She went to bed, but her mind refused to shut down. She tossed and turned, replaying the day. Then she considered her next steps in the investigation.

Travis turned on the lamp at midnight. "Are you going to sleep, or are you just going to toss and turn all night?"

She moved to the kitchen table and made notes of the things that came to mind. At 1:12 AM she set the pen aside, finally out of ideas and questions.

The alarm clock jarred her awake at 6:30. When she reached to turn it off, she realized that Travis was already in the shower. Groggy from lack of sleep, she made a pot of coffee and laid out clothes.

"Luke's not awake?" Travis asked as he walked damp from the bathroom.

"I'm not functional yet. Could you deal with him this morning?"

Travis pulled on boxers, shaking his head. "You slept like a baby when Floyd was around, and you were helping him with the investigations."

"I had no idea how consuming investigations were when he was deciding what needed to be done, and I was just executing his plans. I'm going nuts."

"Don't overthink it or you'll go into analysis paralysis."

"What?"

"Young lieutenants would get caught in their first firefight and there'd be so much information coming chaotically to them that they couldn't decide how to process it all, and what to do. We called it analysis paralysis. I pulled one fresh West Pointer aside and slammed him against a Humvee to get him out of the line of fire. Then I stuck my nose in his face and said, "Make a decision because guys are getting killed while you're trying to replay classroom war game scenarios in your head."

"What did he do?"

Travis smiled. "He did something very smart. He said, 'Sergeant, take over while I call in air support.'"

"That was smart?"

"The sergeant was seasoned, with more than a dozen firefights behind him. He knew exactly what to do and did it quickly and efficiently."

"And the lieutenant?"

"He learned how to be a leader from an experienced combat veteran." Travis buttoned his shirt as Luke started making noises from the nursery. "You've been training with a seasoned veteran for years. It's time for you to step up and lead."

"It's stressful."

Travis grinned as he walked out of the bedroom. "That's why they pay you the big bucks."

"What big bucks?"

* * *

Pam hung up her jacket, set her notes on the desk, and started a cup of coffee. With her hands braced on the counter like she was supporting it, she stared at the coffee dribbling into the cup.

C.J.'s voice startled her. "I think the counter will stay put without you holding it down.

Self consciously, Pam stood. "I wasn't worried about the counter. I was thinking about the case."

"What conclusions have you come to?"

"I only have questions, no conclusions."

"The gun we recovered from the woods yesterday matches the son's description of Roger Bartlett's deer rifle. I brought a cartridge to the medical examiner so the bullet fragments they recovered from the body can be compared to the shells in the gun's magazine."

Lifting her mug out of the Keurig, Pam nodded. "Did you check the gun for fingerprints?"

C.J. carried her empty mug to the coffee maker and popped a pod into the top. "There weren't any prints on the gun."

"That's odd. I'd think Bartlett's prints would be all over it."

"I thought the same thing," C.J. replied. "Then I thought, '*He was wearing gloves when he handled the gun*'."

"I'd expect him to leave prints on the gun when he oiled and loaded it."

The coffee dribbled into C.J.'s mug as she nodded. "I went through the same thought process. So, I checked the cartridges in the magazine, and they're covered with prints. I think someone wiped the gun after they shot Bartlett."

"That points us away from an accidental shooting."

C.J. pulled her mug out of the Keurig and discarded the used pod. "That, and Bartlett running the opposite direction from his deer camp after the shot. Those pieces don't add up to a hunting accident."

Pam held up a sheaf of papers. "Take a look at these."

C.J. accepted the papers and sat down. "These are the criminal records of all the Askov Tire employees?"

"Every one of them is a federal parolee."

After leafing through the pages, C.J. asked, "Where's Igor's sheet?"

"He was in Sandstone to get him away from his cronies after he testified against them. I spoke with a US Marshal who declined to provide much information, but made it clear I wasn't supposed to poke around in his past."

"He must've done something really bad. I mean, the feds set up mob murderers with new identities and relocate them to remote towns. They don't go to prison."

"All I know is what the marshal told me. Maybe his lawyer wasn't as shrewd as the mobsters' lawyers."

C.J. leaned back and sipped her coffee. "Or Igor did something so heinous the judge wouldn't accept his plea bargain unless it included prison time."

Pam shivered. "Just thinking about him makes my skin crawl."

The sheriff walked into the bullpen and started a cup of coffee. "What makes your skin crawl?"

"One of the guys who works for Bartlett's tire company ogled me."

The sheriff drew a breath and blew it out. "Sadly, that's not illegal."

After finishing the last of her coffee, C.J. set the cup aside and stood. "On the other hand, if he's driving a car with a cracked taillight or loud muffler, I can make him squirm a bit."

The sheriff pulled his cup out of the coffee maker and wrinkled his nose. "I hate to be vindictive, but I understand where you're coming from. Is there some other reason to be suspicious of him?"

Pam nodded. "He's a federal parolee who was moved to Sandstone for his own safety and placed in the prisoner's witness protection program after he testified against his co-conspirators in a human trafficking prosecution. I think we need to keep an eye on him and be diligent if there's any hint he's into the same thing here."

"How would we do that before there's a missing teen? Do you have any suspicion that he's doing something illegal now?"

Deep in thought, Pam closed her eyes. She shook her head. "I miss Floyd. He'd have some thought about monitoring Igor."

The sheriff smiled. "You know, all Floyd ever did was ask questions that brought you to the solution. I just threw out two questions to you. Figure out the answers." Then he departed for his office.

Pam looked at C.J. "Floyd always warned me not to discuss cases when the sheriff was around. He likes to send us off chasing his wild ideas."

C.J. picked up the NCIC printouts and leafed through them again. "You know, any of these crimes could be committed over the internet. We should check their addresses and see if they have cable/internet connections. If we have any suspicions that these guys have reverted to their old crimes, we could get a search warrant to look at their internet activities."

"No judge is going to issue a warrant because Igor ogled me."

C.J. waved the sheaf of paper at Pam. "These guys are all on parole. The bar for checking their activities is lower than for a private citizen. Find their addresses, then talk to their parole officers. Maybe you wouldn't even need a search warrant to get their internet activity."

Pam started an internet search for the parolee's addresses as C.J. put on her jacket. "Where'd you go for dinner with Eddie last night?"

C.J. froze. "How did you know I ate out with Eddie?"

"Pat Radosovich called earlier to see if we'd found any fingerprints on the rifle you recovered."

Letting out a sigh, C.J. shook her head. "We ate at the Mexican place next to the brewery. It was good."

Without looking up, Pam nodded. "We like the food there, although I prefer the British pub. They have a lot of comfort food on their menu."

"British food is hardly comfort food for a Scandinavian like you."

Still concentrating on the computer screen, Pam shook her head. "Grandpa Ryan was Irish, so part of our family heritage is eating boiled dinner and his favorite vegetable was peas. There's that, and British cooks don't over-season their food. Nothing my mother ever cooked burned my mouth, so that's what's comfort food for me. I never ate pizza, spaghetti, chili, or tacos at home. They were all treats when we went out or after I left for college."

"You've lived such a sheltered life."

Pam looked up from the computer. "All the employees list the same address. It's a fire number east of Askov. I wonder if they're living in an old farmhouse."

C.J. walked to Pam's side so she could see the computer screen. "Who's their parole officer?"

Pam went back to the NCIC and typed in a name. "Kurt Olson appears to be the parole officer for all of them. It looks like he's in Sandstone." She picked up the phone and dialed the listing for Olson.

"You don't actually expect to catch him?" C.J. asked.

"I'll leave him a message." The call rolled over to voicemail and beeped. "This is Pam Ryan from the Pine County Sheriff's Department. A couple of your parolees have come onto our radar in a suspicious death investigation. Please call my cell phone."

After listening to the message, C.J. waved. "I'm out of here. You've got my number if anything interesting comes up."

"Hang on," Pam said, picking up her cellphone. "I'm texting you the address listed on the parolees' files. Drive by when you get a chance."

"Let's be clear; I'll drive by, but I'm not knocking on the front door."

"Are you afraid Igor will answer?"

With a dismissive wave, C.J. left. As she walked away she said, "I don't really want to run into any of them in a dark alley."

A nervous shiver ran over Pam's body as she thought about the prospect of being one-on-one with Igor. *Not in a dark alley, or even in the well-lit grocery store.*

Barely out of the courthouse parking lot, C.J.'s radar chirped as a pickup raced down the county road on the east side of the courthouse. The radar flashed 80 mph. The speed limit was 55. She turned on her flashing lights and accelerated to catch up with the pickup that had quickly put nearly a mile between them. Announcing her location to the dispatcher, she glanced at her speedometer which was quickly approaching triple digits.

An oncoming car pulled over to the shoulder as she approached Beroun, the next town north of the courthouse. Slowly catching up, she saw the pickup's turn signal. Assuming the driver had seen her flashing lights, she eased off the accelerator. To her surprise, rather than pulling to the shoulder of the road, the pickup turned into the driveway of the county recycling center.

She announced her location to the dispatcher and followed the pickup onto the gravel driveway. By the time she turned, the pickup was out of sight, leaving a dust plume in the direction of some dumpsters. A minute later she was parked behind a young man dressed in a camouflage coat and dirty jeans. He was hurling black garbage bags into one of the bins marked GLASS ONLY. She stepped out of her car just as he tossed the last bag into the bin. Seeing the flashing lights in his peripheral vision, he froze, about to say something, but apparently unable to come up with a plausible excuse for speeding.

"Um, I was just...um...throwing some recycling in the bin."

"Your bags didn't sound like breaking glass when you tossed them in."

The man looked around as if he was going to run. "Our...um...garbage man...um...didn't take all our...um...bags."

"So, you just dumped a pickup load of garbage into the recycling bin."

"Hey!" a female voice yelled from somewhere behind C.J. "You can't dump your recycling until I check your driver's license."

The young man glanced at the heavyset woman waddling toward them.

"Sonofabitch," he uttered. Then he glanced at his pickup, as if weighing the option of driving away.

"Don't do it," C.J. warned. "I'm going to ticket you for speeding. Fleeing an officer after a stop means you go to jail."

"Shit."

The woman was out of breath by the time she crossed the thirty yards from her little hut to C.J.'s car. "What did you dump? That didn't sound like glass recycling."

"It was just garbage."

The woman put her hands on her hips. "That ain't no garbage bin. If you've got garbage, you have to take it over to the compactor and it'll cost you two bucks a bag."

The guy looked at her with disgust. "Well, I'm not digging it back out."

Raising her eyebrows, C.J. said, "That's exactly what you're going to do. Then you're going to pay two bucks a bag, and you're going to carry it over to the compactor."

"But there's like eight bags!"

C.J. looked at the woman. "Sounds like he owes the county sixteen bucks."

"It sure as hell does! Now toss them bags out of the recycling bin and haul them over to the compactor."

C.J and the woman stepped back and watched the guy climb over the top of the six-foot high bin. He landed with a crash on broken glass. The woman stuck her hand out. "I'm Wanda."

"Nice to meet you. I'm C.J."

"I heard 'bout you. You're that new woman cop from Cloquet."

C.J. smiled. "I am."

"I'm glad you showed up. These kids think they can just dump their crap anywhere. Truth be told, I have to look in all the bins at the end of the day and sort out anything that went into the wrong bin. It's bad enough digging shopping bags out of the aluminum cans, but it's a real pain in the butt digging anything out of this glass recycling bin."

Black garbage bags flew over the top of the bin, some hitting the side of the pickup. Most landed on the ground. After the ninth bag, the guy climbed out of the bin.

"It appears there were nine bags. You owe the county eighteen bucks," C.J. said.

"Listen, I don't have eighteen bucks. That's why we don't have garbage pickup."

C.J. looked inside the pickup. "You've got a carton of cigarettes and they cost about nine bucks a pack."

"I've got to prioritize. I need gas for my truck, and I've got to pay the rent."

Wanda nodded toward the truck. "I might forgo the dumping fee for a couple packs of Marlboros."

The guy closed his eyes. "What a rip off. I'll just dump the bags at the gas station next time."

"What did you say?" C.J. asked.

"What?"

"Did you just say you'd dump your garbage at the gas station next time?"

"I might have said that. Why?"

"Because that's a hundred dollar littering fine."

"Aw shit. What am I supposed to do with it?"

C.J. pushed one of the bags with the toe of her shoe. "I suppose you could pay for garbage pickup like most everyone else. Or you could bring it here and pay the dumping fee." She stepped behind the truck and took a picture with her cellphone.

"Hey, what are you doing?"

"After I write your speeding ticket, I'm taking this picture of your truck to the gas stations and restaurants around town to see how many of them have video of you dumping in their garbage bins."

"Hey, it's not just me doing it."

C.J. put on a surprised expression. "Really? Who else is doing it?"

The man stopped, considering what he'd just said.

"Do you take turns making dumping runs with your roommates?"

"I'm done talking," he said, turning toward the pickup. C.J. followed close behind, unsure of his plans, but ready to react. He pulled the carton of cigarettes off the dash and handed two packages to Wanda. "Here. I'll go dump my stuff and get out of here."

Wanda took the cigarettes and was about to return to her hut when C.J. stopped her. "You're going to reimburse the county for the value of the cigarettes, right?"

Wanda gave C.J. an *are you serious* look. "Sure. Whatever." Then she stomped away.

C.J. checked the guy's license number on the computer, watching him until he'd dumped all his bags. He was about to get into the pickup when she stopped him. "Willard Jones, I need to see your driver's license and proof of insurance."

"I gave that fat woman the cigarettes. She said we're good."

"License and insurance, please."

The guy pulled out a worn leather wallet and handed C.J. his driver's license. I go by Will. My dad was Willard."

"I need to see your proof of insurance too."

Will blew out a breath. "I just changed companies and the new insurance card hasn't come in the mail, yet."

"I'll write the ticket for speeding and no insurance. You can bring the insurance card to the judge when he hears your case and he'll dismiss that charge and you'll only have to pay the speeding fine."

"Listen, I can't afford a speeding ticket."

"Then you shouldn't have been driving thirty miles an hour over the speed limit."

"Come on. I'm late for work."

C.J took out her citation book and started writing Will's driver's license information on a ticket. "I guess you'll have to work a couple hours of overtime to pay for the ticket."

Will looked around nervously. "Listen, if I could help you with another crime, would you consider not writing that ticket?"

C.J. stopped writing. "What crime?"

"Will you skip the ticket if I tell you?"

C.J. stopped writing out the speeding citation. "It depends on what you've got to offer. If you tell me about kids littering the playground, you're getting the ticket. If you tell me about someone who buried his wife in the backyard, I'm listening."

"I was at karaoke night in Henriette, and I overheard this old guy complaining to the bartender about getting ripped off. Some woman came to his door selling knee braces. She said her company would give him fifty bucks, cash, if he ordered a brace from her. He told her he didn't need a brace but was intrigued by the offer of cash. She said all she needed was his Medicare number because her company had their own doctor to write the order for the brace."

With a dismissive wave, C.J. lifted her pen to complete the ticket. "That's Medicare fraud. I'm not interested."

"Wait! It's all local. The woman claimed she was working for a start-up brace company." Will tipped his head back and closed his eyes. "He said the woman was from the...aw shit, I can't remember. Wait! It was Finlayson. She said she worked for the Finlayson Brace company."

"And this guy felt he was ripped off?"

"Yeah. He said he got some paperwork from Medicare saying they'd paid for a brace, but he never saw the woman again and never got the money or a brace."

"Do you know the guy who was ripped off?"

"Naw. He's one of the barflies who hang around Henriette. He's there every karaoke night, so I assume the bartender knows who he is."

After putting her pen in her pocket, she folded her citation book. "I've got a half-written ticket here. I'm going to follow you out of the recycling center. If you're driving the speed limit all the way to Rock Creek, I'll rip it up. If you're going one-mile-an-hour over the speed limit, I'll pull you over and finish writing the ticket."

"What if my speedometer is off?"

"In that case, you'd better be going under the speed limit."

Jones blew out a breath and shook his head. "Fine."

As she followed Jones, who was driving 53 mph in the 55 mph zone, C.J. thought about his comments. If someone was running a door-to-door Medicare scam, they wouldn't hit only one person. *"How many senior citizens had given up the Medicare numbers and how many fraudulent bills had been submitted on their behalf?"* C.J. asked herself.

She stopped following Jones in Pine City and ordered coffee in Nicoll's Café. Using her smartphone, she did an online search for the Finlayson Brace company. She got dozens of hits, all for brace and brake companies in Finland. Her only hit in Finlayson was for a repair shop that advertised brake repairs.

Changing the search parameters, she searched for brace manufacturers in Minnesota. There were dozens, mostly small companies who built custom orthopedic braces. They were often associated with physical therapists or orthopedic surgeons. Most of them were located in the major metropolitan areas, the closest being in Duluth.

Pam slid into the booth across from C.J. and signaled for coffee. "Are you playing solitaire or Tetris?"

C.J. handed her phone to Pam. "I'm looking for the Finlayson Brace company."

Scrolling through the listings, Pam shook her head. "I don't see anything in Finlayson. What makes you think there's a brace company there?"

After the waitress poured Pam's coffee and topped off the other cup, C.J. explained her conversation with Will Jones.

"Huh. I suppose it was someone who cruised through, hit a few dozen senior citizens, then moved on."

Cradling her coffee cup, C.J. shook her head. "This feels local. Why would someone from outside the area choose Finlayson for the location of a fake company?"

"I suppose she pulled up a map and found a town people would recognize as local. That way they'd feel like they were supporting a local business."

"Supporting a local business and ripping off Medicare."

"Did you drive through Askov and look at the parolee's house?"

"I got sidetracked by the speeder and his garbage." C.J. snapped her fingers. "If you're bored, you could check with the local gas stations and businesses who have an outside Dumpster. Will Jones said he and his roommates have been dumping their garbage at the gas stations rather than paying a rubbish company for pick up."

"I don't think I've ever been that bored. And, unless the gas stations are complaining about it, I'm too busy to poke that bear."

"How's the Bartlett investigation going?"

"Bartlett's daughter called again asking if we've arrested her father's partner."

Checking her watch, C.J. realized it was nearly noon. "Did you come here for lunch?"

"That was my plan," Pam replied, signaling the waitress for menus.

They ordered lunch, talked about the lack of progress on the murder investigation, Pam's son Luke, and C.J.'s dog.

Pam chuckled after mentioning C.J.'s dog. "Is Bailey still a fart machine or have you changed her diet?"

"It doesn't matter what I feed her; she turns the room blue at least twice a night. She farts, then looks at me like it's my fault, then she walks away."

"Bring her over some night. I'd like to take some pictures of Bailey and Luke. They were so cute together."

"Name the night. I'd be happy to skip whatever's on television."

"We've got nothing going on in the evenings since Luke was born. Come over tonight and you can eat supper with us. Travis was throwing meat, carrots, and potatoes into a crockpot. I don't know what it's called, but it'll be tasty and filling."

"You'd better call Travis to make sure he hasn't made other plans."

Pam raised her hand. "Trust me, we have no other plans for tonight. You and Bailey come over any time after six."

"That sounds like fun. I'll change, take Bailey for a short walk, and pop over. Can I bring wine or something?"

"You're kidding, right? Wine with dinner made in a crockpot?"

After brief consideration C.J. said, "I'll bring cheap wine and plastic glasses. That should fit the crockpot theme."

"The plastic glasses are fine, but if I'm going to drink wine, I'd prefer something...tastier than the boxed swill we drank out of Dixie cups behind the barn in high school."

"Got it. Nothing in a box." C.J. got a sly grin. "I saw some wine in aluminum cans."

Pam slid out of the booth. "A bottle of red wine. Travis was cutting up beef."

C.J. put her hand on Pam's shoulder. "Yanking your chain is almost as much fun as poking Floyd."

"I never come back with a politically incorrect response."

"Yeah, I do miss that about Floyd. I always wondered if he was really that oblivious to the sexual innuendos he threw out, or if he did it just to get a rise out of us?"

Pam stopped at her car, parked just outside the restaurant door. "Floyd was sharp. He knew he was pushing the envelope. On the other hand, he also knew we'd moan and groan about his off-color remarks but would chuckle about them later."

Nodding, C.J. added, "And we wouldn't file a harassment claim against him or the department." With her keys in her hand, she paused. "Floyd's kidding was nothing compared to what I've heard on the job, or the names I've been called."

Checking the area around them, Pam leaned close. "I'll tell you about the drunk who wanted to marry me some time."

"He wanted to marry you?"

Pam waited for a restaurant patron to pass. "When I refused his proposal, he called me every profane and derogatory name I've ever heard, and a few I think he made up."

"The drunks I can deal with. It's the comments I've gotten from other cops and attorneys that really got under my skin. I've almost blown up a couple of times, then I realized that was what they wanted. Now I just smile and say, 'Have a nice day.'"

"You zinged Ole at the tire company."

"That was nothing compared to what I say about some jerks after I get inside my car."

Chapter 8

Pam was walking into the courthouse when her cell phone buzzed.

"Deputy Ryan?"

She glanced at the caller ID. "Kurt Olson, thanks for calling me back."

"What can I do for the Pine County Sheriff's Department?"

Stopping just outside the entrance with no one around, Pam replied, "I'm investigating a suspicious death that looks like a murder. The victim is the owner of Askov Tire Company, and all his employees are federal parolees."

"Yeah, Bartlett is one of the few local people who'll hire paroled convicts. I hope his partner will continue that practice." Olson paused. "Do you think one of my guys was involved in Bartlett's death? I thought he died in a hunting accident."

"Like I said, his death is suspicious and we're investigating the possibility he was murdered."

"What do you need from me?"

"Can you access parolee phone and internet records without a search warrant?"

"In general, yes. The parole terms usually restrict the guys from specific activities. Any violation of the parole terms means an immediate return to incarceration for the balance of the sentence. For most parolees, that would mean a few more years in prison, so they are usually religious about compliance with their parole restrictions." Olson paused. "What are you looking for?"

"Bartlett's partner was in Las Vegas at the time of the murder. I'd like to make sure none of the tire shop's employees were in contact with Callahan in the days prior to Roger's death. It'd also be interesting to know if Igor/Aleksandr Lianin has been in contact with his cronies or trying to operate a new sex business."

"I can put your mind to rest about Igor contacting his former associates. If they knew where he was, they'd kill him. Since he's alive, it's safe to say he hasn't been in contact with his old buddies."

"Do you monitor his computer use?"

"They live communally, and the house doesn't have Wi-Fi, only cable television. Each of them has a basic cell phone without internet access and I get a monthly printout of their calls. I'll look at the most recent report, but they work for Bartlett and Callahan. I'd be surprised if there aren't calls between my guys and both Bartlett and Callahan."

"Bartlett's daughter is convinced that Callahan is responsible for her father's death."

Olson laughed. "I remember being young and naïve; thinking whatever I believed was the honest truth. This job, working with dozens of convicts who may or may not be going back to the straight and narrow has jaded me. I assume everything I hear is a lie, and that every one of them will be back in prison sooner, if not later. I'm right over half the time."

Pam blew out a breath. "And I thought I was cynical."

"Deputy Ryan, I passed the cynical mile marker years ago. I now have contempt for the entire human race. Everyone's bad. Some people do something egregious, get caught, and go to prison. Lots of people cross little lines and skate through life with an occasional speeding ticket and a guilty conscience. Others are masterful social outcasts who get away with crimes for years; evading detection and outsmarting the cops and/or the court system."

Pam walked into the courthouse as they spoke. "You make the world sound like a terrible place."

"It's okay most days, but keep in mind who I deal with on an everyday basis. The parolees were criminals before they went to prison. What they didn't know before, they learned behind bars. Don't get me wrong, some guys get out, have jobs, marry, and raise families. They're the exception. I also have the other extreme, the psychopaths, who have no consideration for others. None. Everything they do is for their own satisfaction. They have no reservation about pushing someone aside—or killing them, if that person blocks the psychopath from what he wants."

"I'd like to think there aren't many psychopaths out there."

"I'd like to think that too, but in reality, they make up about one percent of the population. The smart ones can pretend to be nice people. Others have no ability to color inside the lines."

"Which category covers the guys in Askov?"

"The jury's out on most of them."

"Not all?"

Olson paused. "Be careful around Igor."

"Is he more psychotic than the rest?"

"Let's say he's not particularly in tune with social boundaries and political correctness."

"That'd be my thought, too. We toured the Askov tire shop and I felt like Igor undressed me with his eyes."

"Yeah. Call me if he undresses you with anything other than his eyes."

"Trust me, he won't get close enough to touch me."

Olson sighed. "He's a master of sleaze. Never turn your back on him."

"That's not a problem. I don't intend to encounter him again."

"Did you replace Floyd Swenson?"

"Not directly. C.J. Jensen is the sergeant who took his position on patrol."

"Can you give me her phone number? We're exercising a federal arrest warrant in Markville this afternoon. We usually want an officer from the local agency with the fugitive task force."

"Markville is nothing but a cemetery."

"That's the address we have for our fugitive."

Pam gave Olson C.J.'s number. "We've only got one other deputy on patrol today, so she may decline your invitation."

"I'm just making the notification. It's up to your department whether you want someone on hand or not."

"Who are you picking up?"

Olson paused. "I'm not at liberty to provide the fugitive's name until after the arrest."

"Ah, it's one of those federal things: We tell you our information, but you won't share yours."

"Listen, if it was up to me, I'd tell you we're arresting Scott (Scooter) Juntunen. My boss would have my ass on a platter if that information leaked out."

"Kurt, you're something else. As far as anyone here knows, you refused to identify your fugitive. Why are you arresting him?"

"There's security camera video of him holding up a Wisconsin liquor store. He's a convicted felon, in possession of a firearm, who fled interstate to avoid capture and prosecution."

"Hang on for a second," Pam said as she opened a search on her computer. "We had a similar holdup here, but the guy was wearing a ski mask."

"Check the store security image and see if your guy has a heart tattoo on his right wrist, his gun hand."

"You're kidding. Who would be stupid enough to cover their face, but not cover a distinctive tattoo?"

"Well, there is no intelligence test for being a felon. I'm sure he thinks that robbing a Wisconsin liquor store makes him immune from arrest in Minnesota."

"Do you really think he's that dumb?" Pam asked as she searched for the holdup video.

"He probably grew up watching *Smokey and the Bandit* so he thinks cops won't chase a criminal across a county line, much less a state line."

"Hang on, I've got the Bruno bar security video loading on my computer. Okay, I'm watching jerky images of a guy wearing a ski mask coming into the store and approaching the liquor counter. He's holding a black automatic pistol in his right hand..." Pam laughed. "And he's got a heart-shaped tattoo on his wrist."

"You can notify your county attorney we've made an arrest of your robber later this afternoon. We'll book him in Minneapolis. Your county attorney and the US Attorney can negotiate on who tries him first. Most counties prefer to have the feds prosecute because it saves them time and money." Olson paused. "You're welcome to join the arrest party too."

"Thanks, but no thanks. I've had my fill of simple arrests that've gone south. I'd be perfectly happy not dusting off my bullet-proof vest and staying here to work on my other cases."

"It's your loss," Olson said.

"That's okay. I'll let C.J. represent Pine County this time."

* * *

C.J. was cruising the shore of Big Pine Lake, in the southwest corner of the county when her cell phone rang. She pulled into the driveway of a vacant cabin and answered on the fifth ring, just before it rolled over to voicemail. "Sergeant Jensen."

"Sergeant C.J. Jensen?"

Glancing at the screen, she was surprised to see USPO on the caller ID. Her

115

first thought was that the call was coming from the US Post Office. "Yes, it is."

"I'm sure my caller ID has you baffled. This is Kurt Olson, the federal parole officer for east central Minnesota."

"Oh, hi. Pam Ryan was going to call you about some parolees working for the Askov tire company."

"We've spoken about that. I'm going to get phone records for her. I have a different topic for you. We're doing a federal fugitive arrest this afternoon and I'm notifying you, as the Pine County officer in charge. I used to notify Sergeant Swenson, but I understand you've taken over his role in the department."

"Um, yes. So, I've been notified. Is there anything I need to do?"

"You're welcome to join the arrest team. We're meeting at 13:00 in the Rock Creek Log Home company parking lot to go over planning for the arrest. You can join us there."

"Who are you arresting and where are they located?"

"I never told you this, but the fugitive is Scooter Juntunen, and our informant told us he's living in an old house in Markville."

"Markville? I'm relatively new to the county, but I've never heard of Markville."

"According to Pam Ryan, it's a cemetery. I looked at the area on Google

Earth and there are two houses where I assume downtown Markville existed."

"I've been there. I guess I didn't realize it was a town. There's just a sign at the graveyard entrance that reads, 'Markville Cemetery'. There are a couple really old houses there."

"Our target and his girlfriend live in the most northerly of the two structures."

"Why are you arresting Mr. Juntunen?"

"He's an interstate fugitive and felon in possession of a firearm."

"Do you want me to be part of the entry team?"

"No. You're there out of courtesy. We have US Marshals from the fugitive apprehension task force who will be in heavy body armor."

C.J. breathed a sigh of relief. "Okay. I'll see you at one." After ending the call, she checked the time display on her cell phone. Picturing the drive to Markville and estimating the time it would take to drive there, she pulled out of the driveway and drove toward Finlayson. "I wonder what soup Crazy Mary's Café has today?"

After backing into a parking spot that faced the café's windows, C.J. walked in and checked out the pies in the cooler behind the cash register.

A young waitress rushed out of the kitchen and froze after seeing C.J.'s uniform. "Um, is something wrong?"

"Not if you've got hot coffee, soup, and maybe a piece of banana cream pie."

The young waitress tucked a stray hair behind her ear. "Um, sure. Sit where you like. I'll bring you a cup of coffee."

C.J. chose a table near the windows, facing the door. The retired men at the table next to hers nodded as she passed. One slid his chair closer after she sat down. "I think you scared the living daylights out of Autumn when you walked in."

"She seemed a little uneasy."

"You'll have to cut her some slack. Her boyfriend got ticketed for a DWI last week when they were driving home from The Floppy Crappie Saloon. She's a little down on cops right now."

The waitress brought a steaming cup of coffee and a menu to C.J.'s table as the retiree slid his chair back to his friends. "The special is a hot turkey sandwich with mashed potatoes."

"What's your soup?"

"Um, I think it's Mojakka."

"I'm not familiar with Mojakka. What is it?"

The waitress wrinkled her nose. "I'm not sure. It has carrots, beef, and celery."

The retiree leaned over again. "It's a fancy Finnish name for vegetable beef soup. It's pretty good."

"I'll have a bowl of soup," C.J. said, handing the menu back to the waitress.

"You don't look old enough to be drinking at the Floppy Crappie."

The waitress blushed. "Who told you I was drinking?"

Smiling, C.J. said, "It's a saloon. People drink beer and booze in saloons."

"I just had Coke."

"If I ever see you in the Floppy Crappie, Autumn, I'll check your ID closer than the bartender."

"But..."

"I can spot a fake ID from a mile away."

The waitress turned and scurried away. C.J. slid her chair over to the table with the retirees, who had all finished their meals and were nursing cups of coffee. "I think Autumn has a guilty conscience."

The men all smiled and nodded. The man who'd told C.J. about the Mojakka put out his hand. "I'm Hank Harju. I own the car dealership in town. Ted Kestrel is the guy with the beer belly, Paul Porter is the bald guy, and Roger Asgard is the guy who dyes his hair black."

Shaking hands, C.J. introduced herself. "I'm the new kid in the department."

Roger inspected C.J.'s stripes. "They don't hand sergeant's stripes to rookies, and you look a little more experienced than half the Pine County Sheriff's Department."

"I like that I'm experienced, rather than old. I spent a few years with the Cloquet PD before I moved down here."

Hank smiled. "I like my cops, doctors, and pilots to have a bit of gray in their hair. I'd rather have someone with experience show up if I've got a sudden and unexpected problem."

Autumn brought a bowl of soup, and C.J. was ready to return to her own table when the retirees slid their chairs apart. Hank patted the table. "The sergeant is eating with us, Autumn, and I'm paying her tab."

"I appreciate the offer, but..."

Hank leaned forward after the waitress left. "I don't want you to feel like we're buying you off or bribing you. I'd be honored if you'd let me pay for your soup."

"You understand a bowl of soup doesn't buy a *get out of jail free* card. If I catch you speeding, you'll get a ticket like anyone else."

The men all laughed as C.J. unfolded a napkin and spread it on her lap.

Roger, with the jet-black hair, nodded. "We're happy to have a deputy drive through town once in a while. It makes us think we're getting something for the property taxes we pay."

Paul nodded. "That, and you're a lot cuter than old Floyd Swenson."

"Some people might view that as a sexist remark, Paul."

"It's a statement of fact. I meant nothing by it."

C.J. smiled and wiped her mouth with the napkin. "I like to keep my relationships professional and asexual. I'm just a cop here to protect and serve, like any of my male colleagues."

Hank nodded to the other men. "She's not going to take any shit from any of us old farts."

Ted slapped his hand on the table, startling all of them. "That's it! You're the deputy with the farting basset hound the sheriff was talking about."

C.J. clenched her eyes shut. "What did he say?"

"John said his new female deputy brought her basset hound in and the damned thing nearly drove everyone out of the building. He said he thought someone had delivered a cadaver."

The men all laughed and C.J. couldn't stop herself from joining in. "Her name is Bailey and she's a sweet old hound with a bit of a gas problem."

The men started swapping dog stories and a piece of pie appeared at C.J.'s elbow as soon as she'd finished her soup. "Thank you, Autumn."

"It was the last piece of banana cream, so I set it aside when you said you wanted it."

"Thank you."

Autumn handed her a fork. "You wouldn't really ticket me for underage drinking, would you?"

"I'd probably take you home to your mother the first time. The second time, you'd need someone to bail you out of jail."

"My mom would kill me."

After the men stopped chuckling, C.J. nodded. "My mom would've grounded me for a month if a cop had dragged me home from a bar. It would've been far worse than any punishment a judge would've handed down."

Nodding, Autumn tore off C.J.'s bill and handed it to Hank. "I'll top off your coffee."

Hank pulled out his wallet and folded a ten-dollar bill inside the bill. "I think you're pretty smart, for a rookie."

"That's about the nicest thing anyone's said to me today."

Ted cocked his head. "Have you spoken to anyone other than us today, C.J.?"

"Not really."

That brought another round of laughter to the table.

Hank handed Autumn the bill and told her to keep the change, then she poured coffee in all their cups. C.J. waited until the waitress stepped away, then she leaned forward. "I was told there's a woman going door-to-door selling orthopedic braces to senior citizens. In return for an order, she promises to bill Medicare and give them fifty dollars when the Medicare payment is received by the brace company. Have any of you heard anything about this?"

The men looked at each other, shaking their heads. Ted spoke up, saying, "I haven't heard about anyone going door-to-door. I get a call about some Medicare or car warranty scam every other day, but no one ever shows up at my house."

"My source told me she claimed to be working for the Finlayson Brace Company."

Hank frowned. "There's no company making braces here."

"I didn't think there was, but a guy from Henriette got scammed out of his Medicare number, and he lives close enough he should've known whether the Finlayson Brace Company was real or not."

"Have you got a business card, C.J.?" Ted asked. "I'm an insurance agent and I talk to dozens of people a week. I could ask around to see if anyone's heard of this company or about a woman who's selling door-to-door."

Hank gestured for a card and read it while he thought. "I can guarantee you one thing. She's not going to be selling in another month. No door-to-door salesmen are walking the streets around here when the temperature drops below zero."

C.J. stood and shook hands with all the retirees. She checked the time again as she left the restaurant, estimated the drive time to Rock Creek, and decided she would probably pull into the Log Home Company parking lot about ten minutes before the fugitive task force would arrive. She stopped at the cash register, surprising Autumn.

"Can you make up a dozen cups of coffee to go?"

"Um, sure."

Autumn was pouring coffee into Styrofoam cups as C.J. checked the bakery goods under the cash register. "Do you have a dozen doughnuts?"

Without turning around, Autumn said, "There might be two or three, but most of them sold with the breakfast crowd."

"Put a couple dozen cookies in a bag for me with whatever doughnuts you've got left."

Autumn put the coffee cups in paper caddies, then arranged the baked goods in two white paper bags. "Anything else?"

"Not today," C.J. said, handing over her debit card.

"Are you hosting a party?"

"Not really a party, but I plan to make a bunch of cops very happy."

Chapter 9

There were two black SUVs and an unmarked Dodge Charger in the parking lot when C.J. pulled in. She carried the trays of coffee and the paper bags to the group of officers dressed in heavy body armor, all bent over a map on the hood of the nearest SUV.

"I hope everyone's happy with black coffee," she said, offering cups to the nine people who looked up at the sound of her voice. "Crazy Mary only had a couple doughnuts left, so you'll have to fight over them. The rest of you get cookies."

A stocky man wearing a vest marked "US Marshal" took a cup of coffee and passed the bag of pastries on without taking any. "I'm Cal Silver. You must be Sergeant Jensen."

"Call me C.J." she said, offering her hand.

"You sure know how to make an entrance. There's hardly a thing you could've done to etch yourself into the memory of this group that would've been more effective than showing up with coffee and doughnuts."

The others, a mix of marshals and county deputies from several local agencies, laughed and dug through the white bags. A dark-haired female marshal elbowed two deputies aside. "I get one of the doughnuts. I didn't get lunch, unlike you locals."

Silver put up his hand, stopping conversation. "Meet C.J. Jensen. She's our liaison with the Pine County Sheriff's Department."

Every officer nodded and held up their coffee cups in thanks. The female marshal walked over with her cup in one hand and a half-eaten doughnut in the other. "Nice to meet you C.J. I'm Emily Crockett, from the Minneapolis office. I'm happy to see another woman here. I was choking on the testosterone."

Her comment brought a round of chuckles from the other officers. A hulking blond man walked up and offered his hand to C.J. "I'm Kurt Olson."

"You look like a lineman for the Minnesota Vikings," C.J. said, shaking his hand.

Emily Crocket held up her finger while swallowing a bite of doughnut. "He'd be an improvement over the Vikings line."

Olson grinned. "They tried to draft me, but I told them I'd rather be a parole officer."

Cal Silver nodded toward the SUV with a map spread on the hood. "I hate to be a party pooper, but we need to finish up our assignments." He explained where he wanted each pair of officers to be and how they'd approach the house. Silver was going to the front door with a Chisago County Deputy. The others were going through the back door or blocking the driveway to prevent a car chase. "Jensen, since you're in a light vest, I want you and Kurt to take cover behind his car. If this turns to shit, shoot at anyone sticking a gun out of a window or door until the rest of us can find cover."

The members of the fugitive task force checked each other's gear and seemed amazingly focused and calm. C.J. got in the passenger side of Olson's Charger. As they followed the SUVs out of the parking lot, Olson looked at her.

"You look nervous."

"This is a big operation and I've never been part of any operation with this level of planning and logistics."

"This task force has their shit together. They train together and make a lot of arrests. The plan is always to go in with overwhelming odds, make a lot of noise, unnerve the people inside the house, and drag them out in handcuffs."

C.J. tugged at her vest and checked her weapon. "Do these arrests go down without any shooting?"

"Usually."

"What do you mean, usually? Do they sometimes turn into shooting matches?"

"Not like the Branch Davidian thing in Texas. But, yeah, they get crazy once in a while."

"Do you know in advance?"

"I suppose we expect some to be easy and others to be hard. It depends on the person we're arresting. If they're a psychopath who doesn't want to go back to prison, and we don't get him separated from his gun, they sometimes turn into shooting galleries."

"How about this one? Do you expect this guy to come out shooting?"

"I'd say there's a fifty-fifty chance he'll be sitting somewhere with a gun within reach." Olson paused. "Have you ever fired your weapon anywhere but on the range?"

"I put down a deer that had been hit by a car."

Olson glanced at C.J. "That doesn't really count. The deer wasn't going to shoot back."

"Then, no. I haven't fired my weapon in the line of duty."

"Okay. There are two rules: don't freeze up if someone starts shooting."

"I don't think that'll be a problem. What's the other rule?"

"Don't shoot one of our people."

"You have to tell people that?"

Olson nodded. "It sometimes gets crazy. Keep your head in the game and make sure of your targets."

"Okay, like on the range. Take a breath. Let it out halfway. Then, squeeze the trigger."

"Oh, hell no! If someone is shooting at our folks from inside the house, shoot at any window or door with a gun sticking out, as fast as you can. Don't stop until you need to reload."

"Seriously?"

"Listen, this isn't the shooting range. People's lives are on the line, and they're relying on us to keep the criminals inside distracted until the good guys can get behind something solid. Got it?"

C.J. reached for the spare magazines on her belt, then reassured herself they were where she thought they should be and took a breath. "Got it."

They went from tarred road to gravel, and Kurt followed the dust plume a quarter mile. The SUVs made a sharp turn. One skidded to a stop on the cracked concrete sidewalk while the other cut across the lawn and disappeared behind the house. Olson stopped on the road and jumped out, taking cover behind the engine with his pistol pointed at the house. C.J. went behind the trunk.

Silver and three men rushed to the front door. "US Marshals," he shouted. He nodded to the man behind him who hit the front door with a battering ram. Silver threw something through the door and spoke into his mic as the four of them stepped away from the door.

The chatter on Olson's radio became intense in the seconds before the blinding flash inside the door. The task force members rushed inside as the concussion of the flash/bang grenade echoed off the trees. A second explosion came from the rear of the house.

Olson glanced at C.J. "If things are going to pieces, it'll be in the next few seconds."

Shouted voices came through the door along with the sound of feet pounding up the stairs. "Get down! Get down!"

C.J. held her gun at her side, resting her shoulder against the side of the car as she peeked over the trunk. The shouting continued, then everything became quiet. She started to holster her gun, but Kurt Olson put up his hand. "Wait."

Two shots rang out from somewhere upstairs. They were followed by a hail of gunfire. An upstairs window broke, spewing glass onto the porch. C.J. aimed her gun at the broken window while still keeping her finger off the trigger in case a friendly face looked out.

"Clear!" someone said over Olson's radio.

The next voice said, "We need an ambulance."

C.J. turned her head and keyed her shoulder-mounted mic. "Dispatch, I need an ambulance in Markville."

Olson nodded and relayed the news that the ambulance request had been relayed to the Pine County dispatcher.

C.J. stood, then realized she needed a deep breath. Her heart was pounding, and she realized her hand was shaking when she holstered her gun. Silver came out of the front door and waved at them. C.J. took a few more deep breaths, hoping to stop her shaking hands, then followed Kurt Olson to the front door.

Silver waved Olson past, then he stopped C.J. "We're going to need a Bureau of Criminal Apprehension shooting investigation team. It'd be best if that request came from the sheriff."

Pulling her cell phone out of her pocket, she dialed the non-emergency number and asked the dispatcher to page the sheriff.

John Sepanen's deep voice answered a few moments later. "What's up, Charlene?"

The sheriff was the only person who insisted on calling her by her first name despite her repeated requests to be addressed as C.J. "I'm with a US Marshal's entry team in Markville. They were attempting to serve a fugitive arrest warrant and shots were fired. The team leader asked that you request a BCA shooting investigation team."

The sheriff's chair creaked. "What's the situation?"

"I'm not sure. I was positioned to provide covering fire for the entry team. I heard gunfire inside the house. I had the dispatcher request an ambulance."

"You're uninjured?"

"I wasn't anywhere near the gunfire." C.J. watched through the door as Silver spoke with the team members. No one seemed excited. For them it appeared to be just another day at the office. "The entry team seems calm, so I assume none of the officers are injured. They'd be more agitated if there was an officer down."

She watched one of the marshals walk down the stairs. His helmet, goggles, and tactical vest were covered with splinters and sheetrock dust. Silver broke away from the other officers and took the marshal with the splinters aside. C.J. noticed a trickle of blood dribbling down from a scratch on the officer's face.

"Where are you?" The sheriff asked.

"We're at one of the two houses in Markville."

"I'll make the call to the BCA, then I'll jump in my car. Stay there until I arrive."

"Yes, sir."

The sheriff chuckled. "You can call me John."

"Sure, John. I'll be here until you arrive."

Marshal Silver walked onto the porch. "Did you contact the sheriff?"

"He's calling the BCA as we speak, then he'll drive out."

Silver looked around from the porch. Seeing no activity he said, "You can advise your dispatcher to cancel the ambulance. We'll need the medical examiner."

C.J. drew a breath, then nodded. She hit redial on her cell phone and advised the dispatcher of the change as Silver watched. After the call, she put her cell phone in her pocket. "Is there anything else I can do?"

"Are you qualified to act as a deputy coroner?"

"All of our deputies are trained to determine if a person is dead, but the death certificate has to be signed by a doctor or the medical examiner."

"You're a third party here. I need you to verify that the victim is deceased." Silver stopped at the bottom step. "Don't mess up the BCA's shooting scene. They get testy if there are fingerprints and footprints all over the evidence."

Carefully stepping around splinters and dust in the hallway, C.J. noted four bullet holes that had come from the room on the other side of the wall. They stopped at the doorway where a dozen spent brass cartridges lay spread randomly on the floor.

Silver put his arm across the doorway, blocking her entry. "Are you going to be okay with this? A puddle of vomit next to the body is messy and irritates the hell out of the BCA techs,"

Pulling on a pair of purple gloves, C.J. lifted Silver's arm. "I've got this."

A man's body lay twisted on the floor next to an unmade bed, his open eyes staring at the ceiling. The sheets, wall and window behind the bed were splattered with blood and there was a single bullet hole in the window glass. A black pistol and five spent pistol cartridges lay among the dirty clothes strewn on the floor. All of them in a slowly spreading pool of blood.

C.J. paused. "Did someone do CPR?"

Silver raised his eyebrows. "Normally we would've, but his chest looks like Swiss cheese. He'd bled out by the time my guys got to him."

"But..."

"The purpose of CPR is to circulate blood to the victim's brain. Look at the floor. He's empty. No amount of CPR would've pumped a drop of blood to his brain."

Hopping from one piece of clothing to the next, and avoiding the spent cartridges, and blood, C.J. approached the bed. To avoid stepping on evidence around the victim's body, she had to lean over and brace one hand on the edge of the bed.

The room had the coppery smell of fresh blood, but the area around the body smelled of sweat, urine, and feces. The victim was only wearing a pair of gray briefs, now stained yellow and brown, his muscles relaxing after death. His arms and torso were covered with tattoos, including the heart tattoo on his right wrist. He had a few days of beard growth, and his body was as hairy as any man she'd ever seen. She put her fingers on the victim's neck. Not feeling a pulse, she touched the man's eye with her gloved fingertip.

Pushing herself up from the bed, C.J. looked at Silver and shook her head. "He's gone." She hopscotched back across the room, again using clothing to avoid stepping in the pool of blood.

"You grew up deer hunting,' Silver said as he escorted her out of the room.

"What makes you say that?"

"I've never seen a doctor or coroner touch a victim's eye to determine if they're dead. I have seen a lot of hunters make sure their deer were dead by touching their eyes before setting their guns aside."

"I can thank my dad for that technique."

"Where did you and your dad hunt?"

"I grew up in Cloquet. My dad's family farm was down in Mahtowa, so we hunted with my uncle and cousins there." At the bottom of the stairs C.J. stopped and turned to Silver. "You don't care where I hunted. You wanted to get my mind off the dead guy to make sure I wasn't going to freak out or vomit."

Silver shrugged. "It worked, right?"

"I've been to a few autopsies. I wasn't going to throw up on your shooting scene."

"I didn't know that. It's better to be safe than sorry."

Two of the marshals chuckled. "Pay up. I told you C.J. looked like a veteran who wouldn't chuck her breakfast."

The other deputy took out his wallet and handed over a five-dollar bill. "She looked like a puker to me."

Kurt Olson's cursing distracted her from the marshal's kidding. "That sonofabitch has a computer, and it's hooked up to this black thing. It must be some sort of wireless modem that gets internet from...somewhere."

Silver shook his head. "I suppose he's piggybacking off the neighbor's Wi-Fi."

"There's no cable out here and it's not connected to the phone."

A young Isanti County deputy shook his head. "You guys are dinosaurs. That's a mobile hotspot. It connects through a mobile phone network. If you turn it over, it probably says which company is the provider."

"Damn it!" Olson said, slamming down the hotspot. "Internet use violates his parole."

The young deputy tried to hide his smile. "So, are you going to have the judge revoke his parole and put him back in prison?"

Olson's lips were forming an F when he noticed C.J. smiling and hesitated. "Screw you, Frank."

"I'm a big girl, Kurt. I've heard swearing before."

"Yeah, well."

Silver was smiling now. "Kurt threw a few too many effenheimers around our office. One of the administrative assistants, who is very religious, filed a complaint. Since his sensitivity training, he's more aware of his audience when he swears."

Olson made a fist and raised his middle finger to Silver.

"What time do you expect the sheriff and BCA?" Silver asked.

"The sheriff was in his office, so he's probably half an hour from here. As for the BCA, I doubt they were sitting around waiting for the sheriff's call."

"Do you have any more coffee and cookies, C.J.?" The youngest marshal asked.

"I brought a dozen cups. The extras and the bakery bags are in the backseat of Kurt's car."

The room cleared in seconds as the marshals hustled out to get a cookie and some coffee. Kurt was sitting on the couch with the laptop open.

"You're not having cookies?" C.J. asked, sitting next to him.

"You know, there's something about the smell in here that makes me nauseous."

"What are you looking at?"

Kurt turned the computer so C.J. could see the screen. "I was checking the browser history. He's been on this site three or four times a day for weeks."

C.J. looked at the screen, which was broken into rectangles meant to look like picture frames. In each frame was a smiling female face. There was no name on the screen, just a phone number with a Duluth prefix. "What happens if you click on one of the faces?"

Kurt glanced at her. "I'm almost afraid to find out."

"Hey, I'm not going to file a harassment complaint against you no matter what's there. Okay?"

"Fine."

Olson picked the face of a young woman with oriental features, then clicked the mouse. A new screen came up with a larger picture of the woman in lingerie. The text started with her name, Jasmine, and went on explaining the things she liked to do and her "turn ons". The last line said, "Call for hourly escort rates and availability."

Frowning, C.J. turned to Olson. "What escort is going to drive to Markville? It says hourly rates, and it takes over an hour to drive here from Duluth."

Olson blew out a breath. "Maybe that was why he was holding up liquor stores, so he could afford to hire an escort. Or maybe he was meeting them in Duluth."

"Back up and click on another face."

Olson moved the cursor around and clicked on a blonde with pigtails. Chloe's picture and profile appeared.

"Oh man," C.J. said. "Chloe looks like she's fourteen."

"Maybe she's fourteen, or maybe she's made up to look like she's fourteen."

C.J. got up, shaking her head. "You need to call the Duluth PD so they can trace the phone number. Maybe they'll run a sting or something."

"He's got other stuff on here," the parole officer said.

"I've seen enough. You deal with it unless you find something that involves Pine County."

The faint sound of a woman crying caught C.J.'s attention and she walked down a short hallway and opened a kitchen door. The room smelled like rotten garbage and cigarette smoke. The counters and stove were covered with dirty dishes, pots, and pans. A wastebasket was overflowing with bags and wrappers from every fast-food place within fifty miles. On the floor and on top of the pile were tiny plastic bags with a gray powder. On the stove were rubber tubing, a syringe, spoon, and cotton ball—the tools required for injecting heroin.

Emily Crockett was sitting next to a young redhead wearing a dirty men's t-shirt and very short shorts. Smoke curled up from her cigarette and one foot tapped at a frantic pace. C.J.'s stomach clenched at the sight of a young teen whose eyes looked like she'd seen too much for her age. Emily looked up, then nodded to a third chair at the table.

"C.J., this is Arlette. She's from Grasston."

C.J. smiled at the girl and sat. "Hi."

The girl nodded but refused to look at C.J. Needle tracks on Arlette's arms were exposed when she reached out to stub out her cigarette in the overflowing ashtray.

"Arlette and I were just discussing options."

"Treatment is a joke," the girl uttered. "Just drop me off in Minneapolis. I'll take care of myself."

Emily glanced at C.J., then back at Arlette. "That's not an option. You're not eighteen and we're obligated to provide care for you."

"I don't need a babysitter, and foster care isn't an option."

"Maybe C.J. has some local options I don't know about."

"Are your parents in Grasston?" C.J. asked.

"I don't know who my father is, and my mother is so far into a bottle of booze she wouldn't recognize me. That's why I was in foster care; the county removed me for my own safety." Arlette snorted. "Like that worked out so well. They tried to make me go to school and do homework. It was all bullshit. I'm not going back. If you take me back, I'll run away again."

C.J. assessed the skinny girl. She looked malnourished despite the piles of food packages around the kitchen. "*I suppose she's so strung out on drugs she doesn't care if she eats or not.*" C.J. thought to herself. "There may be an opening in the Minnesota Teen Challenge program. They'd provide you with room, board, treatment, and counseling. Would you like me to call them?"

Arlette finally looked at C.J. "What's the point? I don't want to go straight. I like drugs."

"Your boyfriend is dead."

"So what? Get me to Minneapolis and I'll have a new boyfriend before sunset."

C.J. stood and took her handcuffs out. "Stand up. You're under arrest for armed

141

robbery. You have the right to an attorney. If you can't afford one, an attorney will be…"

"What? You're arresting me?"

"Yes. You're going to jail for armed robbery."

Emily leaned on her elbows and clasped her hands, hiding her smile.

"I'm not eighteen. You can't throw me into jail with a bunch of old skags."

"Get up."

Arlette stood and picked up her cigarettes.

"Leave the cigarettes here. All jails are smoke-free."

"This is bullshit. You can't just arrest me."

C.J. rolled her eyes. "I can just arrest you. You've committed several armed robberies. Turn around and put your hands behind your back."

"No!"

"Listen, Ms. Arlette. You either put your hands behind your back and let me cuff you voluntarily, or I'll do it forcibly. One way or the other, you'll be in cuffs."

"That's police brutality!"

C.J. pointed to the camera mounted on her chest. "I guess we'll show this video to your attorney and the judge. It'll be pretty clear to anyone who sees it that you were resisting arrest and I used only the force required to put you in handcuffs."

Arlette broke into tears. "You can't! I'm just a kid."

"You're a kid on drugs who's been holding up liquor stores. You won't be the only one in whatever prison you are assigned."

"Nooooo," Arlette wailed.

"All right, then pick one of the other options."

Arlette sniffled. "I don't like your options."

"Too bad. They're the only options you'll be offered."

"Fine! Call that Teen Challenge place and hook me up with them."

"I can call and see if they can place you. If they don't have any openings, you'll have to go into another facility until they're ready for you."

Arlette's eyes could've bored holes through steel. "If you don't know, just bring me to Minneapolis. Better yet, put me on a bus to Chicago."

C.J. looked at Arlette's sweaty face and shaking hands. "You'll have cramps and nausea in an hour or so. Right now, you seem to be more focused on getting somewhere you might be able to find another hit of heroin than anything else."

Arlette wrapped her arms across her stomach and looked down. "You don't know anything about me or what I'm into."

"I'll call from the other room."

C.J. walked into the living room where two marshals were searching the furniture. A chrome-plated revolver sat on a coffee table next to the couch cushion that had hidden it. She pulled up her cell phone contact list and selected a number. The man who answered had a soothing voice. After identifying herself, C.J. explained Arlette's situation and the circumstances of her detention.

"We have an opening for a female client if you can get her to Duluth."

"She'll be there in about an hour."

"Based on what you've told me, she'll be in tough shape by then. I'll get the on-call doctor apprised of her situation and we'll be ready to deal with her."

Returning to the kitchen, C.J. nodded to the female marshal. "I've found an opening in Duluth. They'll be ready for Arlette in an hour."

Emily nodded. "Are you able to drive her there?"

Ready to reply, C.J. froze. "My car is in Rock Creek."

"Talk to Silver. He'll have someone drive her there."

Chapter 10

After making arrangements for Arlette's delivery to the drug treatment facility, C.J. looked for Kurt Olson. She found him standing next to his car talking to the sheriff.

John Sepanen waved C.J. over to join them. "It sounds like this was quite an operation. Did you discharge your weapon?"

"Kurt and I were out here, ready to provide covering fire if the marshals ran into something more than expected."

Nodding, the sheriff said, "Good. Good. You won't have to stay here to be debriefed by the BCA shooting investigation team."

"We didn't see anything but a breaking window from here, so there's really nothing Kurt or I could add to the investigation. The Fugitive Apprehension Team did all the heavy lifting."

After checking his watch, the sheriff nodded. "The BCA said they'd be here about 16:00. All the shooters will have to stay here until they're interviewed and cleared." Continuing to nod, the sheriff was obviously mulling something. "Be at the courthouse at four, C.J."

"Sure. I was probably going to go back to type up an incident report before going home."

"A news crew from Duluth will be in Pine City at four. I'm having a press conference to announce this operation, expressing dismay over the loss of life, but successfully arresting the suspect's accomplice and closing a dozen robberies."

"Shouldn't the US Marshal do that?"

Nodding toward his car, they walked away from the parole officer. "Charlene...er Sergeant Jensen, there's an aspect to your new job that Floyd Swenson understood well. As a sergeant, you need to know that your number one priority is law enforcement."

"I get that," C.J. replied.

"Your number two priority is getting me re-elected."

C.J. was stunned. "What?"

"This arrest, in my county, makes us all look good in the eyes of the public. You were the Pine County liaison to this task force, and as such, played a role in the execution of the arrest warrant. That being the case, I will announce that we, the Pine County Sheriff's Department, assisted the Midwest Fugitive Task Force, with the execution of an arrest warrant for an armed robbery suspect who was responsible for multiple holdups in our county and the surrounding area. You'll be standing next to me during the press conference."

"Really? I'm kind of rumpled and…I don't look like a recruiting poster."

"Go home and change into a fresh uniform if you need to, but I want you to be the face of the sheriff's department at this press conference."

"But…"

The sheriff put up his hand. "Charlene, you're an accomplished professional, and having you alongside me puts a face to the department."

"I'm your new female sergeant."

The sheriff smiled but didn't comment.

"I'd rather not."

"Think of it as an order, Sergeant Jensen."

"I need a ride back to my car."

"Kurt has offered to drive you back to Rock Creek. I'll see you at four."

* * *

The click of a dog's toenails in the hallway distracted Pam Ryan from the computer. Bailey, C.J.'s basset hound started whining and chirping when she saw Pam. Unable to hold Bailey back, C.J. let go of the leash and let Bailey dash ahead, where she tried to leap onto Pam's lap. Only half succeeding, Pam's office chair was propelled across the room until it struck a desk where she ruffled Bailey's ears but tried to keep the basset's slobber off her uniform.

"You brought Bailey!"

C.J. set her coat on a chair and sat across from Pam. "The sheriff asked me to be here for the four o'clock news conference and I have to pick up Bailey from doggie daycare before five."

Bailey got bored with Pam and crawled into the knee hole under the desk, where she'd spent her days when Pam watched her while on maternity leave.

"We have the same issue with Luke's day care. Luckily, Travis has a normal forty-hour-a-week job, so he can get Luke before the five o'clock deadline."

"I always wondered what the daycare people would do if we weren't there before the deadline."

Pam rolled her chair back to her desk and arranged her feet around Bailey. "One daycare provider told Travis they'd call the sheriff's department and have them pick up Luke. Travis said, 'Good. My wife is a deputy, she can pick him up at the end of her shift.' That seemed to be the end of that issue." Pam paused and cocked her head. "You're here for a news conference? What news conference?"

"The sheriff is going to announce the raid to arrest our liquor store robbery suspect."

"I thought the task force went to serve the arrest warrant."

"They did, but since it happened in Pine County, and since I was there, the sheriff is making the announcement."

Pam smiled. "You got the lecture about being responsible for his re-election?"

"I can't say I was pleased by it but, yes, I got the talk."

Bailey chose that moment to release a huge fart. Gasping, Pam slid her chair back. "What have you been feeding her?"

"She has gas no matter what I feed her."

"Are you sure Eddie's not sneaking in and giving her baked beans or hard-boiled eggs?"

"He doesn't have a key. So, no, he's not sneaking in and feeding her."

After waving her hand to disperse the odor, Pam asked. "Why doesn't he have a key?"

C.J. looked around to make sure no one was listening. "You know perfectly well that I'm not ready for that."

"Not ready for what?" The sheriff asked, walking in with his empty coffee cup.

"The news conference," C.J. replied. "You don't expect me to say anything, do you?"

"I only need you to look professional and confident," the sheriff replied, placing his cup into the coffee machine and starting a brew cycle. The coffee started, he sniffed the air. "Is there a dead mouse in here?"

Pam started laughing and C.J. shook her head. "It's just Bailey. I had to pick her up from the dog daycare before the news conference would be over."

"Can't you take her up to stay with your boyfriend in the morgue? People might not question the smell there."

"My friend, Eddie, is not exactly my boyfriend."

The sheriff pulled his coffee cup out of the machine after it stopped gurgling, then paused. "You're dating."

"We go out to eat together once in a while, but we're not really dating." C.J paused. "Who told you Eddie and I were dating?"

With a dismissive wave, the sheriff stepped into the hallway. "Half the department thinks you're dating, and the other half have started a pool on when you'll announce your engagement."

C.J. stood. "What?"

The sheriff turned back. "You're not eligible for the engagement betting pool."

"My personal life is that. Personal!"

Pam watched the exchange with amusement. "You know nothing is personal in a cop shop. Everyone knows every other officer's business. And if they don't, they'll start a rumor."

"You're the only one who knows I go out with Eddie. Who have you told?"

Bailey reacted to her owner's sharp voice and peeked out to see if she was in trouble.

"I haven't told a soul, but at least one other deputy and a jailer have seen you eating dinner with Eddie. Another deputy saw you meet Eddie at the morgue and leave holding hands."

"Unbelievable!" C.J said, throwing her hands in the air. "I go out to eat with a guy and hold hands, and that leads to a betting pool on my engagement."

Pam looked sheepish and shrugged.

"NO! You're not in the betting pool too, are you?"

"I've got Valentine's Day."

"It's not happening."

Pam counted off months on her fingers. "A lot can change in three months." She pointed to the clock. "It's 3:50. You'd better hustle up to the courthouse steps."

C.J. glared at Pam. "This conversation is NOT over."

Pam bent down and scratched Bailey's ear. "Help me out here. I'd really like to win the engagement announcement betting pool. Work with Eddie on a Valentine's Day engagement."

Bailey panted with her tongue hanging out. Drops of saliva spotted the floor as she watched C.J., who wasn't amused by the engagement betting.

"Why don't you take Bailey with you?" Pam asked.

"Why would I do that?"

"Well, if you put on a black cowboy hat you could look like Rosco P. Coltrane at the news conference."

The *Dukes of Hazzard* image popped into her mind. C.J. couldn't help but smile. "Sure, Enos."

* * *

Three camera crews were setting up on the east side of the Pine County Courthouse when C.J. walked through the doors. Several other print journalists were setting up recorders and preparing to take notes.

A young female reporter from a Duluth television station saw C.J and rushed over. "Do you have any comments before the news conference begins?"

C.J. paused, tempted to say something to the young woman who looked barely old enough to be out of high school, her hair so heavy with hairspray it looked like it would crack if struck with a hammer. "You'll have to wait for the sheriff to make his statement."

"What's your name?" the young reporter asked.

"I'm C.J. Jensen."

"Just initials?"

"Just initials."

"You're a sergeant, right?"

C.J. nodded and tried to step away.

The young reporter stayed beside her. "You're the deputy who was shot last spring right after I started, right?"

C.J. froze. "I was in a confrontation with an armed assailant."

"Sergeant, can you give me a break? I'm the new kid here, and my job really depends on me standing out among all these other...vultures. Can you tell me anything that we won't all hear?"

C.J. felt for the young woman and gathered her thoughts. "Okay. I used to be a Cloquet cop. I moved to the Pine County Sheriff's Department about a year ago, and I'm very pleased that the sheriff recognized my experience and expertise by promoting me to sergeant."

"Were you at the shooting this afternoon?"

The sheriff came through the courthouse doors, resplendent in his freshly pressed white shirt. He nodded to C.J., then signaled for her to join him next to the microphones.

"I was on the scene, but I didn't shoot the suspect."

The sheriff checked his watch. At exactly four, he stepped up to the microphones. "Ladies and gentlemen, members of my department assisted the Midwest Fugitive Task Force when they served an arrest warrant on a man responsible for a regional crime wave, including several armed robberies in Pine County. Sadly, the person named in the warrant fired at members of the task force. Protecting themselves, they returned fire and the fugitive was pronounced dead at the scene of the shooting. Sergeant Jensen, standing next to me, was with the task force. Her heroic efforts helped ensure the safety of the team members. I'm happy to report that only one law enforcement person suffered a minor injury. The Minnesota Bureau of Criminal Apprehension is on the scene and collecting evidence." The sheriff paused. "I have time for a few questions."

The young blonde's hand shot up and the sheriff nodded to her. "Sheriff, this isn't Sergeant Jensen's first armed confrontation. Is she the one you choose for particularly difficult assignments?"

Pausing to compose himself, the sheriff looked at C.J. "Sergeant Jensen has proven herself to be a trusted member of the department, exhibiting the professionalism that's expected of the sergeants in the department."

The blonde cut off another questioner. "But, sheriff, she was shot in a confrontation last spring, and you sent her into another potentially dangerous situation this afternoon. Is she the point person you choose when facing a tough situation?"

The sheriff cleared his throat. "Sergeant Jensen is extremely capable. I know I can count on her when the chips are down."

The blonde wasn't done. "Sergeant Jensen, how do you feel about being in that role?"

C.J. suppressed a grin as she sensed the sheriff's irritation. Sepanen drew a breath. "Perhaps you'd like to answer that question, Sergeant."

Stepping to the microphone bank, C.J. smiled at the crowd. "I'm proud to be a trusted member of this department. I'll do whatever is required of me to protect the residents of Pine County to the very best of my ability."

"But are you happy about being thrust into risky situations?"

"I'm not an adrenaline junky, if that's what you're asking. On the other hand, I won't shy away from a tough situation."

The sheriff stepped in front of C.J. Ignoring the blonde who continued to fire questions, he said, "Thanks for your time and questions." He turned and walked into the courthouse, leaving C.J. unsure if she should follow, continue to answer questions...or hide. She took a step toward the courthouse door, then felt a hand on her elbow. The blonde was next to her, and the rest of the reporters were packing up or making comments for their evening news, using the courthouse as background.

"I hope I didn't embarrass you, Sergeant."

"No problem."

C.J. felt something in the palm of her hand. "I don't get much airtime and if you could call me some time, I'd like to do an in-depth interview with you."

"I'm sorry, but my role is..."

"Sergeant, I'm Shelly Basch, from channel 7. I can be discreet. I can keep secrets. Or I can be a leak if you want to be an unnamed source. Keep my card."

"Shelly..."

"Just keep my card, okay?"

C.J. put the card in her pocket. "I've got it." She turned to walk into the courthouse.

"Sergeant..."

Putting on a professional smile, C.J. turned. "Yes, Shelly?"

"I think you're a great role model. There are girls out there who don't know what they want to be when they grow up. Your face on the news tonight will show them that there are women in law enforcement doing important things. You should be proud of that."

"Thank you."

C.J. walked into the courthouse wondering if she'd just been set up for future interviews, or if she'd just received the nicest compliment she'd ever had.

* * *

Bailey whined when C.J. walked into the bullpen, causing Pam to look up from her computer. "How was the press conference?"

"I felt like a token minority on a TV show."

Pam smiled. "You're a great face to put forward for the department."

Snorting, C.J. sat down. Bailey waddled to her and sat at her feet, passing gas, then looking at her tail like she wondered what had happened. "If the sheriff wanted a pretty face beside him, he should've asked you."

"You were the department liaison to the task force. In addition to that, you project an air of professionalism and trust. I'm sure that's why the sheriff wanted you there."

"He left the interviewers with the impression I'd been with the task force team during the shooting."

"So?"

"I wasn't. I was behind the parole officer's car. We were watching the front door."

"I doubt that slight exaggeration is material to his message."

C.J. scratched Bailey's ear. "One of the reporters asked a question."

"That's what they do."

"She asked *me* a question."

Pam shut down her computer and turned. "What did the sheriff do?"

"He asked me to answer."

"He let you speak during a news conference? What was the question and what did you say?"

"The blonde from channel 7 mentioned the shooting from last spring. Then, she asked if I was comfortable being chosen as the deputy assigned to risky situations."

"And?"

"I said I wasn't an adrenaline junky, but I was comfortable stepping up when asked to take on whatever situation arose."

Pam smiled. "I'm sure the sheriff was pleased with that response."

"He cut off the next question and ended the news conference. Shelly, the channel 7 broadcaster, cornered me afterward and gave me her card. She told me I should be proud to be a role model for all the girls out there who are trying to decide their future career choices."

"That was a very nice compliment."

C.J.'s cell phone rang before she could reply. "Hi Eddie."

"I just saw a leader for the early news. You're standing next to the sheriff during a news conference."

Blowing out a breath and shaking her head, C.J. put the phone on speaker before she replied. "I just put you on speaker so Pam can hear us. Yeah, about that news thing…"

Cutting her off, Eddie said, "I've never seen a deputy at a news conference before."

"I'm sure the sheriff chose me to be the token female department representative."

"I don't think so. The news leader said you were part of the team trying to serve an arrest warrant. A gunfight broke out and the robbery suspect was killed. One of the entry team members was injured. Are you okay?"

C.J. rolled her eyes at Pam, who smiled. "I was behind a car in the yard. A bullet may have flown thirty feet over my head, but that's as close as I came to being injured. My big contribution was determining that the guy was dead."

"I took a call about an hour ago. The Hinckley ambulance is delivering the deceased to us."

"I can save you some time. The victim died of multiple gunshot wounds to the chest leading to massive blood loss."

Eddie chuckled. "I'll tell Tony he can stay home tomorrow because C.J. Jensen has already determined the cause of death."

"You can add that the victim probably had heroin in his system. His girlfriend was downstairs, and she was in full withdrawal. I found a room for her at the Duluth treatment facility."

"If you come to Duluth after you get off, we can catch the news broadcast on a TV in a restaurant or sports bar."

Shaking her head, Pam walked to C.J.'s desk. "Hi Eddie. Come down to our house for supper and we'll all watch the broadcast together."

"I have to wait for the victim's body to arrive."

"We'll record the news conference and watch it whenever you get here."

"Gee, a home cooked meal with friends. I'm not sure my introverted personality is ready for that."

"Don't get too excited. Dinner is coming out of a crockpot."

"I'm sure it'll be wonderful. I'll see you when I get there."

The sheriff walked in just before the end of the conversation and stood quietly next to the coffee maker until C.J. ended the call. "My wife just called and said channel 7 ran a teaser for the five and six o'clock news with us standing on the courthouse steps. You should call your parents to make sure they watch the news."

"Oh geez, yes. Mom would kill me if she found out I'd been on television and hadn't told her."

"Was that your boyfriend on the phone?"

"It was Eddie Paulson, from the medical examiner's office. He called to tell me the shooting victim was being delivered to them."

Smirking, the sheriff said, "I didn't know Pam invited you and Eddie over for supper every time they got a body."

"It's not like that…"

Sepanen put up his hand, cutting off C.J.'s reply. "You were great at the news conference. Channel 12 called a few minutes ago with a follow-up question they didn't get to ask during the broadcast. Tina Fellows, their producer, said she'd previewed and edited their recording. Aside from thanking me for including them in the broadcast, she added that she was very pleased to see Sergeant Jensen on the steps. She said your comments were concise and well stated. You appeared professional and competent." The sheriff paused, apparently ready to leave. Then, he looked at C.J. "You did well today. You should be proud of yourself."

With the sheriff gone, Pam put on her jacket. "I feel like I should buy a bottle of champagne or something."

"Remember, I already said I was bringing wine. I'll be looking for something celebratory that goes with a crockpot meal."

After zipping her jacket, Pam looked at Bailey. "Your mom is a smartass. Did you know that?"

"Oh crap, I have to call my mother."

Chapter 11

Still basking in the glow of a dinner with friends, C.J. got in the county cruiser and announced that she was on duty at her house. The dispatcher acknowledged her but had nothing demanding her attention. Driving to the interstate, she reflected on her departure from Pam and Travis's house.

Hugs had been shared and she walked away holding Eddie's hand on one side and trying to control Bailey with her other hand. After letting Bailey sniff every flower and post, she'd finally peed next to the sidewalk. A bit tipsy, C.J. leaned her head against Eddie's shoulder and pulled him close. They'd stood silently as Bailey relieved herself, then were tugged apart when Bailey decided it was time to get in the car.

Leaning against the car, C.J. had looked at Eddie's contented expression and said, "It was nice of Pam to invite us over for supper."

"A home-cooked meal was a real treat. It was almost as nice as the company."

"The sheriff overheard our phone discussion. He called you my boyfriend."

"Yeah. Tony, who never notices anything social, actually kidded me about our dating."

"I've been telling people we're just friends going out for dinner."

Eddie nodded. "That's what we've been doing."

"I'm amazed that you've never made a pass at me."

Eddie stared at his shoes. "I'm a crusty old vet with PTSD and you told me you weren't ready to date. I think that leaves us as friends, not boyfriend and girlfriend."

C.J. reached out and squeezed his hand. "Thank you for understanding, and for being my friend."

"You seem to need a friend more than a boyfriend."

C.J. smiled. "I do."

Still daydreaming as she reached the interstate entrance ramp, she was pulled back to reality when her radar started beeping insistently. As a blue Buick flew past her, C.J. flipped on her flashers. With the Buick still pulling away, C.J. pushed the accelerator to the floor. The Buick zig-zagged through a smattering of morning traffic, apparently unaware of C.J.'s approach. Once past the pickup that was slowing traffic to near the speed limit, C.J.

turned on her siren, hoping to get the Buick driver's attention.

Brake lights flashed as C.J. neared the car's bumper while driving in the lane alongside the Buick. A glance at her speedometer showed she was going over 110 mph. The Buick slowed, but didn't stop as C.J. moved behind it, anticipating the driver's turn onto the highway shoulder.

"Dispatch, I'm in pursuit of a Buick at milepost 185." C.J. reported the license number and asked for backup, unsure of what had caused the Buick's driver to be virtually flying down the road and reluctant to stop.

A state trooper reported he was driving toward them from the south and asked if C.J. needed him to deploy stop sticks to end her chase. Something about the driver's demeanor made C.J. think she wasn't chasing a hardened criminal.

Pulling into the left lane, C.J. moved alongside the Buick, giving her a visual of the gray-haired driver. The annoyed woman glanced at her when they were side-by-side, and C.J. gestured for the woman to pull over.

The Buick finally turned onto the Hinckley exit ramp. C.J. turned off her siren but left the flashers on. They stopped at the red light at the top of the ramp as the dispatcher announced that the car belonged to Bernice Crowell, of Sturgeon

Lake. There were no outstanding warrants for the owner and no record of any traffic violations. Preparing to exit her vehicle, C.J. released her seatbelt when the traffic light turned green. The Buick turned left, with C.J. scrambling to buckle her seatbelt. She reported her location as they passed Tobies Restaurant.

The slow chase continued until the Buick stopped in front of a house built along the golf course. The driver got out and was walking up the sidewalk when C.J. caught up with her. "Excuse me, ma'am."

The gray-haired woman turned, apparently surprised to see someone behind her. "Can this wait? I'm late for cards."

"Ma'am, you were driving over 100 miles an hour."

"Yes," the woman said, obviously irritated. "I told you, I'm late for cards. Bonnie can be very testy if one of us is late." She pointed at the living room window where three other women were watching. "See, they're all waiting for me."

"Ma'am, I need your driver's license and insurance card."

"Not now. I'm late for cards. We'll be through about ten. Can you come back then?"

Struggling to maintain her composure, C.J. smiled. "I'm sorry to delay you, but I'm going to issue a citation for speeding. I need your driver's license and proof of insurance."

The woman sighed and dug in her purse as the front door opened and a woman stepped outside. "Bernice, you're partnered with Julie. We drew a card for you."

Pulling a wallet from her purse, the driver handed C.J. her driver's license, then an expired insurance card. "Now, write the ticket and bring it inside when you're done."

"That's not how this works. I need you to wait in your car until I complete the citation and you sign it."

The woman on the steps walked down the sidewalk. "Is there a problem officer?"

C.J. looked at the driver's license. "I need to finish dealing with...Ms. Crowell."

"There are three of us waiting for Bernice. It's terribly inconvenient for her to be delayed. She's already late."

"She may be late, but she was speeding and I'm going to issue a citation to her."

The woman from the house put her hands on her hips. "Don't you know who I am?"

Looking between the two women, C.J. clenched her teeth. "Please return to the house while I deal with Ms. Crowell."

"I beg your pardon, officer. I'm Bonnie Prescott. I write historical romance books set around the time of the Hinckley fire."

"Ms. Prescott, your writing credentials aren't material to Ms. Crowell's traffic violation."

"But I know people. The sheriff would be very upset if you continued to delay our bridge game."

"Why don't you give him a call while I write Ms. Crowell's traffic citation."

"Well!" Prescott huffed. "I will call him. Remind me who won the last sheriff's election."

"Sheriff Sepanen has won the last few county elections."

"I thought Robert Coyle won."

C.J recalled Robert Coyle's name but couldn't recall how many decades ago he'd held the sheriff's office. "Why don't you call both of them while I write up Ms. Crowell's citation."

Prescott stomped into the house and C.J. took Crowell's elbow. "Please sit quietly in your car while I write your citation. While you're there, see if you can find a current proof of insurance card or I'll have to add your lack of insurance to the citation."

"Fine. But you have to stop referring to me as Ms. Crowell. I've been married for over fifty years. I'm Mrs. Crowell."

"Okay, Mrs. Crowell, please sit in your car and wait for me."

With the citation nearly complete, C.J.'s cell phone rang. The caller ID showed that the call was from the sheriff.

"Good morning, John."

"What in hell are you doing?"

"I'm writing a traffic citation for a woman who was going more than 30 miles an hour over the speed limit and who refused to pull over in the ten miles I followed her. Oh, and her insurance has expired."

Sepanen's booming laugh came over the phone. "Bonnie Prescott, claiming to be my close personal friend, said some uppity female cop was holding up their card game. She asked me to intervene."

"So, you don't want me to issue a citation?"

"Issue the citation and tell my 'friend', Mrs. Prescott, that she's lucky because you're not arresting her for offering a bribe to a public official."

"She tried to bribe you?"

"She offered me a signed copy of her most recent book if you left and let her friend get on with their bridge game."

"Wow. I don't know how you could refuse an offer like that."

"Just give Mrs. Prescott's friend a ticket and let them get on with their card game."

"Yes sir. I'm on it, sir."

"Oh, cut the 'sir' bullshit, Charlene. Just be glad the women didn't recognize you from last night's news. Otherwise, I imagine

169

Mrs. Prescott would be calling the television stations about your harassment of her friends."

When presented with the speeding citation, Bernice Crowell handed C.J. a different insurance card. C.J. checked the expiration date, then said, "Thank you for locating the current insurance card."

After putting the speeding ticket and insurance card in her glove compartment, Crowell got out of the car. "I saw you talking on your phone while I waited for you. I hope the sheriff gave you an earful."

"Actually, he suggested I arrest Mrs. Prescott for trying to bribe him with a copy of her latest book."

Crowell smiled. "That's just like Bonnie, trying to impress people because she's written a *New York Times* bestseller."

"She wrote a bestseller?"

"Yes, *The Bread Also Rises* was a big hit in the 1980s. She's written a dozen additional baking-themed mysteries. *Dying for Hotdish* is her latest title. It's selling well in Minnesota, but people outside the state don't use the term hotdish for a casserole."

"Have a good day, Mrs. Crowell."

C.J. got in her car and tried to clear the thoughts of the card players from her mind. *"I told Pam I'd drive past the house where the Askov parolees live."*

Returning to the freeway, C.J. drove north to the Sandstone exit. She filled her gas tank at Chris's Foods, then got a to-go cup of coffee. Driving old highway 23, she passed old farms with dilapidated barns and a few pastures with mixed breed cattle trying to find grass in the snow.

"I can't imagine the first immigrants who tried to farm this land after the lumber companies cut the giant White Pine forests. Even after the Hinckley fire, the stumps must've been enormous, and once they got the land cleared, they discovered rocky soil that was nearly impossible to plow and a growing season too short for corn."

The Askov city sign showed a population of 364. C.J. had been assigned to walk the town during the previous Rutabaga Days Festival. An old-time resident had explained that the town had been established by Danish farmers who grew rutabagas, a favorite root vegetable related to turnips, as an alternative to potatoes. During the festival, it seemed like the entire population of the town had been in line for aebleskivers, an apple-flavored baked item that resembled a doughnut hole, and rutabaga sausage. In November, the town was nearly empty except for a few cars parked at the historical society, bar, and small grocery store.

C.J. turned off the highway and passed the Askov Tire Company, with nearly as many cars in the parking area as the entirety of downtown Askov. She continued on, reading the fire numbers, a system used by the fire department to locate burning buildings, in an area where street addresses didn't exist.

The old two-story farmhouse where the parolees lived had peeling white paint and a weedy yard. Aside from one pickup with a dust-covered windshield, parked near the back door, it appeared all the residents were at work. The windows looked like they hadn't been washed in at least a decade and an assortment of faded curtains, bedsheets, towels, and torn window shades hid the interior rooms from sunlight and prying eyes. C.J. stopped on the road and took a picture of the building with her cell phone.

"This place looks like a larger version of the Markville house where the Marshals tried to serve the arrest warrant," she thought to herself.

A bed sheet covering an upstairs window moved aside, giving the resident a view of C.J. and her cruiser while hiding the identity of the person peeking out. As quickly as the sheet had moved aside, it fell back. She parked on the road for a few more minutes to see if someone would come out to ask what she wanted, but the house remained quiet.

Turning around in a driveway a quarter mile farther down the road, C.J. drove slowly past the parolees' house again without noting any activity. The person watching from the upstairs window nagged at her. When she got to the driveway, she pulled in and radioed her location to the dispatcher. "Call me for a radio check in five minutes. If I don't respond, send the cavalry."

"Ten-four," the dispatcher replied.

With the hair on the nape of her neck bristling, C.J. knocked on the door. "Sheriff's department."

A chair scraped on the floor, and someone ran up the stairs. She knocked again and footsteps approached the door. The door opened to a Hispanic man, his dark hair tied in a short ponytail. His broad shoulders blocked the view past him so C.J. couldn't tell if there was anyone behind him. Then she looked in his eyes and sensed emptiness. It was like staring into a well, there was nothing, not hatred, welcome, or emotion. The two teardrops tattooed under his left eye rattled her. Some gangs used teardrops to signify the number of people the person had killed. The lower teardrop was inflamed, like the tattoo was recent.

"What?" he rasped.

"We had a request for a wellness check," C.J. said, throwing out the first excuse for knocking that came to mind. "Helen Jacobsen said her mother, Aggie hasn't answered her phone. Is Aggie here and well?"

173

"Ain't no one named Aggie here. You got the wrong address."

"I'd like to check. May I come in?"

"There's no Aggie here. Never been an Aggie here. You got the wrong address."

"I heard someone go upstairs. Was that her?"

The man shifted and C.J. glimpsed the mud room behind the door and a bit of the kitchen. "Listen, lady cop, there's no one here but me and you're trespassing. Leave."

"Are you the homeowner?"

"I'm the homeowner's BFF. He asked me to keep an eye on the place while he's working. Okay?"

"And you are?"

"Your worst nightmare if you don't shuffle your skinny butt out of here."

The incident the previous spring at a hunting shack flashed through C.J.'s mind. The menace in this guy's voice was primal, and the teardrop tattoos rattled her. With her hand on the butt of her pistol, she straightened up and met the man's eyes. "If you're not the homeowner, I need to know your name."

The sneer on the man's lips added to the menace. "My friends call me *La Serpiente*." He turned down his shirt collar exposing a cobra head tattoo on his neck. "My bite is worse than my bark."

"Can I see your driver's license?"

174

"Does it look like I'm driving a car?"

"I'd…"

The dispatcher's voice came over the radio, requesting C.J. to check her radio. Without taking her eyes off the man in the door, she backed down the steps to the sidewalk. "I read you five-by-five."

"Are you still at the same location?" the dispatcher asked as *La Serpiente* took a half step forward, then leaned on the door frame.

"I am having a conversation with a Hispanic man at this address who just told me he's called *La Serpiente*. Check again in two minutes."

"Do you require backup?"

"Not at this time."

C.J. was about to ask for the man's name again when he raised his hand and pointed at her car. "A lot of bad things could happen to a woman in two minutes. You should get in your car and leave."

"Did you just threaten me?"

"Just giving you advice." The man backed through the door and closed it.

C.J. walked to her car without turning her back to the house. A faded curtain slid aside on an upstairs window, exposing what appeared to be a woman's eye. C.J. waved, but the curtain fell back as quickly as it had opened.

After backing out of the driveway, C.J. told the dispatcher she was leaving that

175

location. She took a deep breath as she accelerated away. *"What in hell just happened?"*

* * *

After passing through downtown Askov, she parked next to the historical society building, located inside the old school. She punched in Kurt Olson's phone number, hoping he'd pick up. His phone rolled over to voicemail so C.J. left a message for him to call her about *La Serpiente*. Then she walked into the Little Mermaid Café, located inside the historical society building.

Marietta Johnson looked up from the book she was reading. Recognizing C.J., Marietta turned over a coffee mug printed with the Pine County Historical Society logo and poured coffee for C.J. Carrying the mug to a table along the wall she said, "If memory serves me, you prefer your coffee black."

"Yes please."

C.J. nodded toward a table far from the only other mid-morning customers—two women sipping coffee and sharing a cinnamon roll. Marietta poured herself a cup of coffee and joined C.J. at the small corner table. "Will you join me?"

"I think I can handle this crowd. Sure, I'd like to sit and gab for a minute."

176

Marietta settled into her chair and C.J. asked, "What do you know about the Askov Tire Company?"

"Roger Bartlett started it up quite a few years ago and ran it with his wife. A couple years ago he sold a half interest to some out-of-town guy. The word is that they were scraping by before Roger found this partner, but they're doing well now. Apparently, the partner has a Canadian source for the materials and because they buy old tires and supplies in Canadian dollars then sell the recapped tires in US dollars, there's an automatic twenty precent profit."

Stunned by Marietta's knowledge, C.J. set her coffee down. "How do you know all that? Are you pulling my leg?"

"I used to be their bookkeeper."

Sipping the hot coffee, C.J. nodded. "You were a bookkeeper before you started here, at the historical society?"

"I'm the historical society treasurer, too."

"I suppose there are lots of businesses and people who would like to hire someone, like you, to keep their books and calculate their taxes."

"That's very insightful," Marietta said, smiling. "I refuse work all the time. I try to keep a non-stressful job that pays for my winter travel."

"I changed the topic before you finished explaining the tire company's financial situation to me. They're making twenty percent margins just because of the Canada/US dollar differential. I'd expect the shipping costs to eat up most of that profit."

Marietta leaned back. "Let's just say that their books don't exactly balance. When I asked too many questions, they decided to let me go. Roger Bartlett's partner took over the payroll and bookkeeping."

"They're losing money?" C.J. asked.

Marietta shook her head. "They're making more than can be explained by their business activity. When I tried to get Joe Callahan to explain it, he fired me."

"I'm confused," C.J. said. "They're making too much money, so they fired you?"

"Their profits exceed what can be explained by their business activities. That's on top of a healthy profit from the recapping business."

"Are they in some other business?"

"Roger said they were vertically integrated."

"What does that mean?"

"The Askov Tire Company owns their Canadian suppliers. So instead of buying their recapping supplies from a different company, they own the suppliers. That way they get the supplier's profits and eliminate the profit of the distributor."

"That sounds like a shrewd business move. I assume that's legal."

"It's legal as well as being a good way to maximize your profits. But..." Marietta stood and brought a coffee carafe to the table. After topping off their coffee mugs, she continued. "But they're not accounting for all the cash flow. When I tried to put all their businesses on one balance sheet, Roger said that wouldn't work because their Canadian business is a different company. The Canadian wing of the company operates in Ontario and pays taxes there, then essentially deposits the net profits in a US bank."

"I assume that's all legal if they're paying the Canadian taxes on their operations there."

"Both Roger and Joe assured me that everything they did was above board."

"But you didn't think so?"

"It's probably okay, but I couldn't see what the books looked like in Canada. They had a local accountant handling their books and paying the taxes. All I saw was money coming in with no way to account for it on the books other than to call it offshore profit."

"I get the feeling you were troubled by the arrangement."

"Like I said, I couldn't get the books to balance. Joe and Roger weren't concerned. They finally got tired of hearing me ask to see the Canadian books."

"Did you smell a rat?"

Marietta smiled. "I smelled a whole cesspool."

"Did you report it?"

Marietta shook her head. "They were paying taxes and had a bunch of employees who depended on them. I had no basis for complaining to the IRS or state revenue department."

"What do you *think* is going on?"

Marietta leaned close. "I think they're laundering money. Why else would someone overstate their sales?"

The other couple waved at Marietta, and she walked over to check on them.

Sipping coffee, C.J. pondered what Marietta told her. *"Why would someone come to Askov to launder money? What money are they laundering? The bigger question is: does Marietta really know that they're laundering money? Or is she seeking retribution for her firing?"*

The ring of her cell phone jarred C.J. away from her musings. "Sergeant Jensen."

"Hey, C.J., you left me a message about *La Serpiente*. What's the context?"

"I saw movement inside the parolees' house. There weren't any vehicles around, so I stopped and knocked on the door. A hulking guy with teardrop tattoos under his eye answered the door. He said his friends call him *La Serpiente*, then he told me to leave."

Blowing out a breath, Olson paused. "That would be one of my previous parolees, Raul Sanchez."

"He's no longer on parole?"

"He finished his parole about nine months ago, so technically he's a free man. You said he was at the Askov parolee's house?"

"Yes, and I'm sure he wasn't alone. I heard someone run up the stairs before he opened the door. I'm sure a woman peeked from behind a second story curtain as I walked back to my car."

"That was probably Candy, his on and off girlfriend. The last address he had was her apartment in Cloquet. I haven't kept track of him."

"He's a piece of work," C.J. said. "I looked into his eyes, and they were empty."

"Yup. He's a total psychopath. That teardrop tattoo under his eye supposedly signifies he killed someone."

"He has two teardrop tattoos now, and one of them is new and still inflamed."

"Shit," Olson said. "I wonder if he's doing some contract work in Minneapolis. He was part of a gang, and he couldn't have contact with them while on parole. But now…"

"Maybe we should look at him as a suspect in the Bartlett case."

"It doesn't fit. Raul is a city kid. He'd be out of his element in the boonies. He barely copes with living in a city as small as Cloquet." Olson paused. "I'll talk to the parolees and see why Raul is at their house. I don't see him mixing well with the white-collar parolees. They're all non-violent offenders and Raul is a brawler."

"I had the dispatcher make a radio check on me. Then I told her to check again in two minutes. Raul said a lot of bad things can happen to a woman in two minutes."

"You went there without backup?"

"I was just going to drive by the house to see what it looked like. I didn't expect to knock on the door and run into a…killer."

"If you run into him again, make sure you have backup. If there's no one around, have your pistol out of the holster. No jury up here will convict you of shooting that…idiot if he takes one step toward you."

C.J. ended the call, finished her coffee, and left. She called Eddie from the parking lot and told him about the encounter with *La Serpiente*.

* * *

Pam was typing a report on the computer when C.J. walked in. She looked up when the coffee pot started gurgling. "Tell me about the parolee's house."

After hanging her coat over the back of a chair, C.J. carried her coffee to Pam's desk and sat in the guest chair. "The yard is overgrown with weeds, and they were apparently all at work."

"What do you mean, apparently?"

"Their vehicles were gone, but someone looked at me from an upstairs window, so I pulled in the driveway and knocked on the door."

Pam pushed herself away from the desk. "I didn't hear a call for backup."

"Yeah…about that. There was a bunch of scuffling noise inside then a guy who gave me chills answered the door."

"Igor's brother?"

"No. This guy made Igor look like a schoolyard bully. He had teardrops tattooed under his left eye. When I asked his name, he said his friends call him *La Serpiente*. He showed me a cobra head tattoo on his neck."

"You apparently escaped from *La Serpiente* unscathed."

"Dispatch paged me, and I asked Jodi to do another radio check in two minutes. *La Serpiente* told me a lot of bad things can happen in two minutes. I backed away and called Kurt Olson. The guy's name is Raul Lopez, a gang banger from Minneapolis. He completed his parole, so he's no longer supervised. Kurt is checking to see if he's allowed to have contact with the tire company parolees or not."

After making sure the sheriff wasn't getting coffee, Pam leaned close to C.J. "We always assume there's a potential for violence when we walk into any situation, but these federal parolees give me the creeps. They're several steps up the scary scale from our run of the mill jack pine savages."

"Jack pine savages?" C.J. asked.

"That's what the guys call the local kooks who are trying to live off the land on their forty-acre tracts. Most of them are goofy, but not scary." Pam leaned back so it wouldn't appear they were sharing secrets. "Did you learn anything else?"

"I had a conversation with Marietta, at The Little Mermaid Café. She did the tire company's books for a while and got fired when she started noting anomalies in their cash flow."

"I suppose they're under-reporting income to avoid paying taxes."

"Marietta said it's exactly the opposite. They're reporting income that's not supported by their sales. She thinks they're laundering money."

"I don't understand what you're saying."

"They've got a couple questionable things going on: They're buying their supplies and used tires from Canada, so they're saving money by purchasing supplies in Canadian dollars that are worth twenty precent less than US dollars. Some of that is lost in shipping, but still they're leveraging their low-cost supplies. But they've also got cash coming in from Canada. Joe Callahan said they're repatriating their Canadian profits, but Marietta thinks there's too much money coming in and their books don't balance."

Pam turned to her computer and keyed in some information. "Joe Callahan was busted for smuggling in illegal Cuban cigars when he was still a teenager. Maybe he's learned from the pros while in prison and perfected his smuggling expertise. If they're buying truckloads of Canadian used tires and supplies, maybe they're hiding contraband in the loads."

C.J. closed her eyes and tipped her head back. "I don't even know where to start investigating an operation like this. One misstep, and the whole thing could collapse, and we'd get nothing."

The sound of the gurgling coffee maker startled C.J., and she nearly tipped her desk chair over. When she opened her eyes, she was looking at the sheriff. He was leaning against the counter where the coffee pot sat with his arms crossed. "I have some thoughts on your next steps."

"*Oh great!*" C.J. thought to herself. "*I've just done exactly what Pam and Floyd said not to do. They told me to be careful about discussing cases when the sheriff is around. Despite his good intentions, the sheriff may have you chasing down wild geese. And there's no good way to tell him that his suggestions are stupid and will waste valuable time."*

Reading C.J.'s mind, Pam smiled. "What would you do, Sheriff?"

"Walk up to Tom Bakken's office and tell him what you overheard. Then tell him you'd like to get a search warrant to seize all the tire company's financial records." The sheriff removed his coffee cup from the brewer. "That should keep the two of you busy for weeks."

C.J. waited until she was sure the sheriff was really gone. "We can seize the records, but I don't understand the accounting well enough to be an effective auditor."

Nodding her agreement, Pam added, "And by the time we got enough information, Callahan would be long gone."

After steepling her fingers and pressing them against her lips, C.J. shook her head. "I agree with you. The sheriff's suggestion would be good in a couple weeks, after we gather more information. Serving a search warrant now would only tip our hands and send Callahan running."

"The problem is," Pam explained, "that you can't unhear what the sheriff said. And you can't ignore his suggestion."

C.J. leaned forward, pretending to be waiting for Pam's sage advice. "What do I do now, oh wise one?"

"Save the sarcasm for some time when we've got a beer or glass of wine in our hands."

"I was being facetious, not sarcastic."

"What's the difference?" Pam asked.

"The primary difference is that facetious uses all the vowels, in the alphabetical order."

"Oh great, now I've got an English major for a partner."

"Back to the sheriff's suggestion. How do I handle it?"

"Let's talk to the county attorney, as the sheriff suggested. We'll explain the situation, then we'll let him tell us why it's too early to get a search warrant. I'm sure he'll have a more realistic suggestion for our next steps." Pam picked up the phone and dialed a three-digit extension. "Hi, Tom. C.J. got some information from a confidential informant and we'd like to brainstorm the best approach for follow up."

C.J. gave Pam a thumb's up sign and smiled.

"Tom has half an hour for us right now."

* * *

187

Tom Bakken's suitcoat was on a hanger next to his office door. His sleeves were rolled up and his tie was loose. What voters had described as boyish good looks during his first election twelve years before, had turned into a face that was tired and lined. He looked up from his desktop when Pam knocked on the door frame, then slid his notes into a folder that hid the content. "What can I do for you, Pam?" Then C.J. walked in. "Uh oh, I'm being double-teamed."

C.J. closed the door, then took the guest chair alongside Pam. "We have a problem that may be an opportunity in disguise."

Bakken leaned back and gripped the arms of his office chair. "That sounds ominous."

After explaining her discussion with Marietta, C.J. took a deep breath. "The sheriff told us to get a search warrant so we can seize the tire company's financial records."

"That's the problem part of our discussion?"

Pam slid a sheaf of papers across the desk. "The top printout is Roger Bartlett's partner's Canadian record. At first blush, I'm inclined to believe he's still in the smuggling business. The rest of the files are printouts from the NCIC computer on the Askov Tire Company's employees. They're all on parole from the Sandstone Federal Prison."

Bakken flipped through files, nodded. "This is quite a crew. They're all white-collar criminals, so probably not a threat to the community." Bakken straightened the papers and slid them back to Pam. "What do you want from me?"

C.J. and Pam looked at each other. C.J. took the lead. "I think it's too early in the investigation to tip our hand by seizing the tire company's financial records. The IRS might be very interested in the tax implications of their financial information, but I...we believe the employees may be involved in Bartlett's murder."

Bakken rubbed his thumb across his palm, deep in thought. "John asked you to get a search warrant for the financial records, and you two think it would be beneficial to wait until you dig deeper into the murder and smuggling issues. Right?"

Both women nodded.

"Did anyone besides you two hear the sheriff's suggestion to get a search warrant?"

C.J. frowned. "No. Why would that matter?"

Bakken's smile made his face look ten years younger. "If there were witnesses, you'd be disobeying a direct order. If you're the only two who heard him, well, he might've suggested that you talk to me about the timing of a warrant versus the state of your investigation."

C.J. caught on quickly. "Yes, it was a suggestion. And here we are, asking for your input on the timing of a warrant to seize the financial records."

Bakken turned his chair to face his computer. He typed in a password and moved to the Pine County email server. "I'm sending John an email…" Then he stopped and turned back to the deputies. "An email creates a trail, and it might sound like you two were tattling on the teacher."

Bakken picked up his phone and dialed a three-digit extension, then activated the speaker function. The sheriff answered on the second ring. "Hi John. I've got Pam and C.J. up here and I wanted to follow up on their request for a search warrant. After listening to them, I think it's too early in the investigation to execute a search of the tire company financial records. I wonder if the partner or their questionable employees were part of Bartlett's murder? I think your deputies need to do more homework on the whole thing before I'd be comfortable approaching a judge for a search warrant."

"That's a good suggestion, Tom. The search warrant suggestion is probably just their eagerness to move ahead on the one big piece they have. You're right. Are you there, C.J. and Pam?"

"Yes, we are."

"Tom's spot on. Kick your murder and smuggling investigations into high gear, then go back to Tom when you've got some meat to hang on those clues."

Pam leaned close. "Will do, sheriff."

"Um…Tom."

"Yes."

"Thanks for helping set the investigation straight. As always, I appreciate your input."

Bakken rolled his eyes as he disconnected the call. "I think you two are off the hook."

C.J. stood and shook Bakken's hand. "Thanks. I'm surprised the sheriff was so effusive with his thanks."

Bakken smiled. "Always remember that John's a politician. Then keep in mind that the three of us were the only ones who heard him offer his thanks. I think he likes to pretend the relationship between the sheriff's department and the county attorney are frostier than they are."

"Why?" C.J. asked with her hand on the doorknob.

"It gives him plausible deniability if something goes to hell in a handbasket." Bakken paused and gestured for C.J. to leave the door closed. "To be clear, we are law enforcement partners. My door is always open for either or both of you and I'd much rather know about your concerns or misgivings behind the door than have them

191

pop up in front of a jury. I'm also the county attorney and it's my responsibility to advise you legally, with the best interests of the county in mind."

"Thanks," Pam said.

"Hang on," C.J. said. "Do you have any Canadian contacts I could call with my smuggling theory?"

"I think your best approach would be to call the Ontario Crown Attorney. I'll text you his phone number over our lunch break in the trial."

Chapter 12

"What next?" Pam asked as they walked away from the county attorney's office.

"You're the investigator, Deputy Ryan. You tell me what's next."

"You said we were partners."

"Unless I'm mistaken, *you* said we were partners."

"Whatever. That still begs the question of what to do."

After a moment of thought, C.J. said, "We've got a murder and smugglers. The murder has to be the highest priority, then the smugglers."

They waited for the elevator silently as people passed. Once alone in the elevator, Pam said, "I've got this inkling that they're all related."

"Kurt Olson is checking the parolees' phone records and internet access. I'll call him and ask for a progress report."

"Bartlett's partner, Joe Callahan should be back from Las Vegas this afternoon. I'll check on his expected return and interview him." Pam paused. "What do you hope to get from the Crown Attorney?"

"Callahan may be the target of a Canadian investigation. I don't know if they'll share that information with a sergeant from a tiny Minnesota sheriff's department, but they might open up if I tell him about Marietta's comments."

Pam seemed fixated on her smartphone as they walked back to the bullpen. C.J. glared at her, but Pam was totally absorbed by whatever she had on the phone screen. Unable to stand it anymore, C.J. said, "Are you checking Twitter postings?"

That got a glare. "Well, Sergeant Smartass, I happened to have my phone out while we were touring the tire company." Pam turned her phone so C.J. could see the photo of a semi trailer. "I held the phone next to my leg and took pictures everywhere we went on the tour. The guys were loading finished tires into this trailer, which happens to advertise Fort William Trucking Ltd. on the side. The Crown Attorney might be interested in having that tidbit of information."

Accepting the phone from Pam, C.J. enlarged the view of the truck. "I always see tires being transported in open trailers with tarpaulins over them, not enclosed semi trailers."

"We only see the ones with open beds. There could be a thousand tires a day

194

passing in enclosed trailers and we'd never know it."

"Or there may be some requirement unique to international shipments of tires. Either way, it's worth asking the Canadian authorities about the shipments." C.J. sat at her desk and stared at the ceiling. "We've got plans for investigating the murder and smuggling. Now all we need is something related to the Medicare fraud."

"The shooting victim was one of Kurt Olson's parolees. I'll ask him if he's got any information about the criminal activities of the others."

That caught C.J.'s attention. "Ask him about the hotspot and laptop computer the marshals recovered from the house they raided. He told me none of the parolees were allowed to use the internet, but technology may have leaped ahead of his monitoring. He spoke about the Askov house not having cable. He assumed that not having broadband limited their internet access. If they can buy a hotspot device from a cell phone company, they've got the internet."

Pam made a note to herself, then said, "There are also satellite internet providers."

"I think that requires a dish. There was a UHF television antenna strapped to the chimney, but there weren't any satellite dishes on the roof."

"I guess we're putting the Medicare fraud case on the back burner for the time being."

"I could ask one of the guys to canvass the houses around Henriette. They might find someone with a better description of the woman or her car."

"You don't want to destroy the good will you've built with the deputies by having them walking door to door asking about a woman who's promising the victims money."

C.J. leaned against Pam's desk. "You're probably right. They have been told that you're the investigator and they'll view that as your job. Let's be upbeat. We'll whip through the other cases, then we can chase down the Medicare woman."

* * *

C.J.'s phone rang while she was waiting in line to purchase air fresheners. She was surprised to see the county attorney's name on the caller ID. "This is C.J."

"I decided you'd get better service from the Crown Attorney if I called him and explained who you are and what you're doing."

"Thanks. I hope there's something we can work on together."

"I've got to rush back into the courtroom, but the Crown Attorney's name and number are coming in a text. I primed Ian for your call. He said he'd be in the office all afternoon."

As promised, Ian McMurtrie's name and phone number arrived in a text message just as C.J. reached the cash register. The matronly clerk gave C.J. a funny look. "Was there a chemical spill at the sheriff's office or something?"

"These are for personal use."

The woman nodded and scanned the bar codes. "We sell toilet plungers too."

"I've got one of those. Thanks anyway."

The card reader was extremely slow, giving the clerk time for further interrogation. "Did your refrigerator or freezer die, leaving you with a pile of rotten food?"

Still waiting for the card reader to indicate her transaction was done, C.J. was at the mercy of the nosy clerk. "I've got a basset hound with a gas problem, and I invited friends over for supper."

The clerk laughed. "That's a good one. Really, why are you buying so many air fresheners?"

Snatching her debit card out of the reader, C.J. reached for the bag, but the clerk held it out of reach. "All right. The deal is this; a drunk puked all over the backseat of my car last night and I need to freshen it up."

Smiling, the clerk handed C.J. the bag. "I figured it was something like that."

C.J. drove to the back of the parking lot and dialed the Crown Attorney's phone number. She was surprised when he answered it on the first ring. "McMurtrie."

"Hello, this is Sergeant Jensen, from the Pine County Sheriff's Department. I understand Tom Bakken told you I was going to call."

"Yes, Sergeant Jensen. I recognized the 218 area code and thought it might be you calling. How can I be of assistance?"

"I hate to tie up your valuable time. Would it be more productive if I spoke with one of your assistants?"

McMurtrie laughed. "To be frank, my time is no more valuable than yours. Please go ahead with your call. I may choose to bring in one of my assistants after I understand your issue."

C.J. explained the tire company, the parolee employees, Joe Callahan being a co-owner, the Canadian suppliers, and Marietta's take on the bookkeeping issues. McMurtrie interrupted a few times for clarification, but mostly listened quietly. "The former bookkeeper was fired when she asked too many questions about the repatriation of Canadian profits and the company's financial books not balancing."

"I have to agree with your bookkeeper. This all sounds suspicious. Did she mention the names of any Canadian suppliers?"

"I'll have to follow up with her. She may or may not remember the suppliers. My partner and I recently toured the tire company, and she took a picture of the truck being loaded with freshly recapped tires. The name on the trailer was Fort William Trucking Ltd."

"I'm not familiar with the firm, but I'll take a look at their ownership and legal filings. I am familiar with Mr. Joseph Callahan. He's been in a bit of trouble since his childhood, and we've been rather surprised to have not dealt with him for almost three years. We'd actually speculated that he'd been killed and fed to a polar bear. It makes sense now to hear that he's been in the United States."

"His partner in the tire business was killed last week in what appeared to be a hunting accident. Mr. Callahan was conveniently out of town at the time of the shooting."

Sighing, McMurtrie paused. "One of my assistants suggested that the next level of Callahan's escalating crime career might involve a murder."

"We haven't been able to tie him to the actual murder yet, but there's something fishy about all the tire supplies coming here from Canadian sources. That and the sums of cash coming in from the Canadian subsidiaries."

"Sergeant, can you give me a day to dig into Mr. Callahan's dealings and the Fort William Trucking Company?"

"Certainly! I'm pleased that you're willing to assist us at all."

McMurtrie laughed. "There's a dotted line on the map that separates our countries, but we're all concerned with the rule of law. We all like to see the bad guys put into prison."

"How should I address you, sir?"

"My given name is Ian and that's what most everyone calls me except for defense attorneys."

"My name is Charlene, but I prefer to be called C.J."

"Very well, C.J. I'll dig around and get back to you."

* * *

By Pine County standards, Joe Callahan lived in a mansion. The house on the shore of Big Pine Lake was over 5,000 sq.ft. and included four garage stalls. The lake view was stunning. Having checked the address out on a real estate app, and Google earth, Pam thought the house and view were even grander in person.

A white Land Rover SUV was parked outside a garage stall, giving hope that Callahan had returned from Las Vegas. Joe

Callahan's Facebook page showed his birthday was 1968, making him roughly 54 years old. He'd come a long way since his cigar smuggling arrest as a young man. His arrest photo showed open contempt. His eyes were narrow, his nose wide, and cheekbones high. The long scraggly blond hair looked like it hadn't been washed or seen a comb in days if not weeks.

Pam rang the doorbell, expecting some older version of the man in the picture. Instead, she was met by a cute woman who might've been Joe's daughter. The woman was momentarily stunned by Pam's uniform, but she regained her composure quickly. "Can I help you?"

Putting on her best professional smile, Pam asked, "I'm Deputy Ryan. Is Joe Callahan home?"

"He's upstairs unpacking his bags. Come inside while I find him." Pam watched the woman, who never introduced herself, walk up a staircase built behind the entrance atrium. The woman wore sandals and short shorts, making Pam think she was from somewhere other than Minnesota where it didn't snow in November.

Joe Callahan, looking like he's been pulled out of a shower, came down the stairway wearing a pullover sweater and jeans. His hair was damp and dishevelled from a quick towel rub. "How can I help the Pine County Sheriff's Department?" He asked as he stepped off the stairs, still in bare feet.

"Could we sit down for a bit?"

Concern swept Callahan's face as he gestured for Pam to follow him into a formal living room with huge windows overlooking the lake. A field-stone fireplace took up nearly all of one wall and there was a crackling fire warming the room. Pam sat in the chair farthest from the entry door. Callahan took a chair next to the fire.

"I understand you've just returned from Las Vegas. I was dispatched to notify you of your partner's death."

Callahan was either a good actor, or the news stunned him. He stood without speaking, then placed another log on the fire. "I...No one called to warn me that something had happened to Roger. Did his high blood pressure do him in?"

"He was involved in a hunting incident. He was shot sometime on the opening day of deer hunting season."

"Shot by another hunter?" Callahan asked, returning to his chair.

"His single gunshot wound looked accidental. His hunting party reported him missing when he didn't return from his hunting stand after sunset. His body was found the next day inside a cabin where he'd apparently sought shelter."

Callahan put his face in his hands, then took a deep breath. When he looked up, there were tears on his cheeks. "You make it sound like he didn't die quickly."

"He hiked miles in the dark after he was wounded."

"Shit."

The young woman who answered the door appeared with a tray. She set the coffee carafe, mugs, and a plate filled with chocolate chip cookies on an end table, then sat on the arm of Callahan's chair. "What's wrong?"

"Roger died in a hunting accident while we were in Vegas."

The woman, who Pam estimated to be in her early twenties, patted Callahan's back. "Are you going to be okay, honey?"

"Yeah, I'll be fine in a moment."

The woman stood, then poured three mugs of coffee. "How do you take your coffee, Deputy Ryan?"

"Black is fine, thank you."

"By the way, I'm Katie," the woman said as she handed Pam a steaming mug with one hand, offering the plate of cookies with the other hand. "Be careful of the chocolate chips, I just took the cookies out of the oven and the chips may still be molten."

A timer dinged in the kitchen and Katie dashed off. Pam ate a cookie, getting chocolate on her fingers. She let the silence work on Callahan as she wiped her fingers on a paper napkin from the coffee tray. With her mug in hand, Pam leaned back in the chair, staring at Callahan.

"What a fucked-up trip. I lost my shirt at the tables, then you show up when I get home to announce that my partner is dead."

"Do you know anyone who disliked Roger enough to kill him?"

Callahan was reaching for a coffee mug, then froze. "You don't think Roger's death was an accident?"

"We're exploring that as one of the options. It's also possible he was shot on purpose." Pam paused as Callahan poured a dollop of cream into his coffee and stirred. "As I asked, is there anyone who disliked Roger enough to shoot him?"

"I…ah…don't think so. I mean, we staff the tire company with federal parolees, but they're all pretty mellow. Plus, they can't own guns. They're all felons."

"Disgruntled customers?"

"Pfft. We don't deal directly with our customers."

"Is there an unhappy supplier who got paid late?"

"We own most of the suppliers. They're part of us and most are Canadian."

"There's not a disgruntled Canadian employee?"

"Not *that* unhappy. Who would drive down from Canada to shoot Roger?"

"Was Katie with you in Las Vegas?"

"She doesn't get off on watching me play blackjack for hours. So no, she wasn't along" Callahan paused. "Katie didn't kill Roger. Hell, I don't think she even knows how to shoot."

Katie walked back in with a platter stacked with warm cookies. "I don't know how to shoot, and I don't want to learn. I went to the range with Joe a couple times and his pistols scare the hell out of me."

Pam reassessed Katie. After watching Katie for a few seconds, Pam was convinced that she was no more than thirty years old. By looking at his hands, Pam estimated that Joe was over fifty. His facial skin was taut, like his plastic surgeon had taken out a little too much skin when he did Callahan's face lift. Were they having a May/December romance? Did Katie find a sugar daddy? Checking Katie's ring finger Pam noted the one carat diamond on a pair of rings. *"Trophy wife."*

"What guns do you own, Mr. Callahan?"

"I've got a couple pistols for self protection and a shotgun for goose hunting."

"No deer rifles?"

"Roger took me deer hunting once. The drinking and smart talk were fun. But, I really have no interest in shooting a mammal that weighs as much as I do."

Katie wrinkled her nose. "Venison tastes bad. So do the geese Joe brought back from North Dakota. I told him to donate them to someone up there."

Callahan shook his head. "Katie likes chicken." He paused and asked, "How's Caroline?"

"She's rattled. I've seen a lot of widows hear that their husbands are dead. Her reaction was right in the middle of the pack, some tears and shock. Some denial."

Katie picked up a cookie, broke it in half, then she nibbled at it like a rabbit sampling a strange piece of lettuce. Something was on her mind besides baking cookies, but she wasn't sharing.

Callahan took the other half cookie from Katie's hand and ate the whole thing in one bite. "Make up a plate of cookies for Caroline. We should go over and pay our respects." Callahan stood, signaling the end of their discussion. "If we're done here, Katie and I are going over to Bartlett's house."

Pam stood up and put her tiny notebook in her back pocket.

Katie went to the living room door, waiting for Pam. Callahan picked up the cookie plate and carried it to the kitchen. With the doorknob in her hand, Katie stopped Pam. "Take a closer look at Caroline Bartlett. I hate to speak ill of the dead, but we're sure she was having an extramarital affair."

"Do you know her lover?"

Katie shook her head. "Caroline never confided in me. She treats me like an unruly teenager, but Roger confided in Joe at the shop. I don't think Roger ever caught her with anyone, but he was suspicious. I guess she'd been driving to the Cities and Duluth for long shopping trips."

Katie opened the door and held it for Pam. "Here's my card, Katie. If you think of anything more, please call me."

Katie palmed the card and slipped it into the front pocket of her tight shorts. "There's more, but Joe will come looking for me in a second."

Walking to her car, Pam tried to process what she'd been told. *"Caroline Bartlett may have been having an affair. With whom? What bearing does that have on anything?"* In the car, Pam turned the heat up before driving out of Callahan's driveway. *"Katie says there's more but is unwilling to speak with Joe around. Hmm. Who owns the tire company now? Did Bartlett have a life insurance policy that made him more valuable dead than alive?"*

Pam set her cell phone on the console and selected C.J.'s number from her contacts list. "What's up, partner?"

"I just spoke with Joe Callahan and his wife, Katie. She dropped the bombshell that Caroline Bartlett was having an affair. She didn't have any names, but Caroline has

207

been going on a lot of out of town shopping trips."

"Does she inherit half the tire company?"

"I don't know. I'm also curious about Roger Bartlett's life insurance."

"Curious as in 'is there a new, very large policy?'" C.J. asked.

"Exactly. I don't know how to check on any of those things without asking Caroline. I expect she'd be less than candid about anything that looks suspicious."

"I'll call Eddie to see if they acquire that information as part of their cause of death investigations."

"Good idea," Pam said. "How do we find out if she's having an affair?"

"I suppose we could subpoena her credit card transactions to see if her out of town shopping trips included a dinner for two and/or a motel room. I could call our new BFF, Tom Bakken, and ask for guidance."

"Why don't you just ask her when you talk to her this afternoon?"

"What?" C.J. asked. "I don't recall a re-interview of Caroline Bartlett being on my to do list."

"You notified her of Roger's death. You said her son was there, so you didn't really question her. Besides, if she's lying, you might catch her changing her story. I might not catch a subtle misstatement. You could use the autopsy report as a door opener, saying that you want to tell her what the ME discovered."

"I haven't seen anything on Bartlett's death from the ME's office."

"You haven't? I thought your boyfriend would call you the instant he had something to report."

"Just stop that boyfriend stuff, okay. I know you're just trying to prod me, but please stay away from that one topic."

"Have you heard from…Eddie about Bartlett's autopsy?"

"I guess I'm busted on that one," C.J. replied with a sigh. "Eddie sent you an email with the autopsy report a few minutes ago. As suspected, Roger Bartlett died from blood loss after being shot with a high-powered rifle. There wasn't any powder stippling on his coat, so the shooter was more than a few feet away. His blood alcohol level was zero, and aside from diverticulitis, he was a healthy fifty-year-old man."

"What about the guy the marshals were trying to arrest?"

"Massive chest trauma from multiple gunshot wounds. His heart was shredded, and he was legally dead when he hit the floor. In addition to that clinical diagnosis, Eddie said the guy was covered with crude gang tattoos, probably done in prison. They compared the robbery security photos with the tattoo on the guy's hand and they're ninety-nine percent sure it's the tattoo visible on the videos. We got the right guy and solved a string of robberies.

"And I called the Crown Attorney."

"You actually got someone to talk to you?"

"Yeah, strangely enough, the number Bakken texted me was the Crown Attorney's direct line. Ian McMurtrie answered the phone himself. I told him about the apparent money laundering, and our suspicions about the Canadian suppliers."

"Then he passed you off to his admin assistant or some fresh out of school lawyer."

"No, he was amazingly cooperative and said he would follow up on your photo of the shipping company painted on the side of the semi trailer. He also told me that Joe Callahan's criminal record is not as clean as it appears. I got the impression Joe might not want to cross back into Canada."

"As in, he'll be arrested at the border for outstanding warrants?"

"Ian didn't say that outright, but I was left with that impression," C.J. replied.

"If we crack this case, they might make us honorary Mounties."

C.J. snorted. "Gee, that would be almost as satisfying as having a degree from a mail-order university."

"Don't rain on my parade. I was visualizing my look in a Mountie uniform."

"I think their riding breeches make a woman look like she's got a big butt."

"Their breeches might fit better than my uniform pants until I get rid of the pounds I put on while I was pregnant." Pam paused. "Thanks, this banter is what I miss the most since Floyd retired."

"Is that what you were up to by calling me Rosco P. Coltrane and kidding me about my boyfriend?"

"Gee, I'm sure I'm not clever enough to come up with those digs intentionally."

"Sure, Enos."

"All right. Yes, I was trying to get a response out of you. And it worked. You rose to the bait every time I threw it out there." Pam got serious. "Will you talk to Caroline Bartlett? I'd like to know how she's handling Roger's death now that the original shock has passed."

"I'm trying to find a way to bring up the topic of infidelity. I can't come up with anything short of 'I heard you were having an affair. Who is the guy? Do you think he killed Roger to get him out of the way without a messy divorce? How big a life insurance policy did you have on Roger and when did you buy it? Are you half owner of the tire company now?'"

"Those are the questions I'd like answered. But you're right, they sound kind of heartless."

C.J. slowed as she passed a flock of wild turkeys. Having written a report on a car/turkey collision the previous week, she knew that a turkey was heavy enough to break the windshield of a car being driven at highway speeds.

* * *

Bartlett's house was much less opulent than Callahan's mansion. The house sat on a neatly trimmed lawn with flower beds on both sides of the steps. The flowers, now dead in November, were brown stalks.

Caroline Bartlett answered the doorbell herself. Her hair was tied into a ponytail, and she wore a heavy knit sweater, jeans, and tennis shoes. Her eyes were red, apparently from crying, leaving C.J. feeling like a lioness about to jump on a wounded prey animal. "Mrs. Bartlett, I'm Sergeant Jensen. Could I come in for a bit? I have some information and it's a little brisk to be standing on the steps."

Caroline pushed the storm door open. "Come in. You call this weather brisk. I went to college in Texas. If this weather hit there, they'd be closing schools and warning people not to drive."

The entryway was a small landing with a coat closet on the left side. The living room was on the other side. Caroline led C.J. into the living room, then she added a log to the fireplace, knocking embers loose that swirled and flew up the chimney. The temperature in the living room was nearly eighty degrees but Caroline, already dressed for winter, pulled a wool blanket across her lap after sitting on a sofa.

C.J. took off her jacket and laid it across the arm of an overstuffed chair before sitting. "I spoke with the coroner's assistant. Roger bled to death after being shot with a deer rifle."

Looking at her feet, Caroline's only response was, "Oh."

"I understand your grief and how painful the next weeks will be. I lost my husband two years ago and it still hurts when I think about him. Because Roger's death was caused by a shooting, we need to complete a full investigation."

Caroline took a tissue from a box on the coffee table and blew her nose. "But you thought it was a hunting accident."

"The Medical Examiner has to assign a cause of death before he'll sign the death certificate. He's not willing to call Roger's death accidental until we gather more information."

Dabbing at tears leaking from her eyes, Caroline seemed unable to form a word.

213

She nodded, showing her understanding of the situation.

"Do you know if Roger was having an affair?"

Caroline locked eyes with C.J. "That's a cruel question at this point in time."

"I'm sorry, but we really need to know about all of Roger's life situations to complete his death investigation."

Picking an invisible piece of lint from her jeans, Caroline shook her head. "I'm not aware of another woman in my husband's life. He comes home when I expect him. He doesn't go out drinking with his friends. Most evenings we eat supper, then watch television and go to bed after the news. Unless he was sneaking out for noon trysts, I don't see how he had time for an affair."

Making notes, C.J. nodded. "Are you having an affair, Mrs. Bartlett?"

Caroline shuddered like she'd been hit with a bat. "I fail to see..."

"Because Roger's death is suspicious, I have to investigate all possible motives. Most murders involve the victim's spouse. A spousal affair is a big murder motive."

"I go shopping with a girlfriend every couple of weeks. We have a nice dinner, then go to a concert or play. If it's too late, we share a hotel room and drive home the next day. Cindy and I are not in a relationship, we're just old friends whose husbands are not into shopping or cultural events."

"What's Cindy's last name? Does she live nearby?"

"Smith. Cindy Smith. She lives in Pine City."

"So, when we check your bank and credit card records, we'll find gas, restaurant, and hotel charges."

Caroline sat up and pulled the blanket to her shoulders. "You're checking *my* banking records?"

"It's all part of our unexplained death investigation."

Huffing, Caroline glared at C.J. "Yes, you'll find charges for all those expenses on my AmEx card. Cindy is a Walmart clerk and can't afford tickets to the Guthrie or Orchestra Hall, so I usually treat her to the tickets. In exchange, I have a pleasant companion for a few nights a year."

"Cindy is only a friend..." C.J. let the comment dangle, hoping Caroline would become inpatient with the silence.

"Yes, that's what I said. She's my friend and nothing more."

"Does Roger have life insurance?"

Caroline drew a deep breath and blew it out. "Of course he had insurance. I don't work, so we had enough insurance and a few investments to carry me through the rest of my life. I won't be rich, but I'll be comfortable."

"Have those policies been in place for a long time or were they taken out recently?"

"I resent the implication posed by that question."

"If there's anything that looks suspicious, you might as well tell me now because I will get that information before the medical examiner signs the death certificate."

"Fine," Caroline snapped. "We went to a financial planner last spring. She suggested a retirement plan that included whole life and term insurance policies on both Roger and me. The term insurance is intended to pay off our existing debts if either of us dies before we hit full Social Security age, and the whole life policy builds a nest egg for the future while protecting my financial situation if Roger precedes me..." Caroline choked off the rest of her response. After composing herself, Caroline finished the sentence. "In case Roger died before I did."

"So, those insurance policies are new?"

"Like I said, we set them up after consulting with our financial planner. That was last spring, around Memorial Day. I can look up the details of the policies and the date they were issued if need be."

"Great. That'll help the medical examiner see the whole picture." C.J. took out one of her business cards and wrote Eddie's email address on the back. "You can email that information directly to the ME's office at this address."

Caroline accepted the card but handled it as if it was covered in manure.

"Are Roger and Joe equal partners in the tire company?"

"Roger retained the controlling interest when he sold part of the company to Joe. I don't know the exact details, but I think Roger said they had a 60:40 ownership split."

"What happens to Roger's share of the business now?"

"Our financial planner set up a family trust account. Our share of the tire company, this house, and a Texas condo are all in that trust. I became the trustee when Roger died. The trust ownership transfers to our children upon my death."

"What are your plans for the tire company? Do you plan to actively participate in the day-to-day operation?"

"Good god, no. I can't think of anything that would be more distasteful than spending my days in that dusty, stinking building. I asked Gary to resign from his job at Cargill and take over as the tire company CEO. He made it abundantly clear that managing the tire company is not a part of his future. Our daughter said much the same thing."

"How would Joe Callahan feel about a family member taking over the operation?"

Caroline shrugged. "I don't care how Joe feels about our plans. I inherited the majority of the company, and I can appoint whomever I want as the CEO. As of now, I think Joe is probably the best choice since he's developed the vertical integration plan and has negotiated all the Canadian contracts."

"Vertical integration?"

"He's buying suppliers and shipping companies to control his supply chain, and to get the profits from each of those entities."

Closing her notepad, C.J. took a deep breath. "I'm sorry about the timing of these questions. If Roger's death is anything other than a tragic accident, we need to move quickly to find his killer. I sincerely apologize for having to put you through this questioning, but I'm sure you want us to diligently look at every possible means and motive."

Caroline stood and folded the blanket she'd been under. "I appreciate your dedication, Sergeant, but I think your time would be better spent looking at the sleazy convicts Roger and Joe hired to operate the tire company equipment. Aside from the smell and dust in that building, I get goosebumps every time I talk to the parolees."

They walked to the door with C.J. nodding. "Pam Ryan and I got a tour of the recapping operation and I agree. Some of your employees made us uneasy."

From her car parked in front of Bartlett's house, C.J. typed Cindy Smith, Pine City into the computer on her console. Getting no hits, she changed the search to Cynthia Smith and immediately got an address and car license number, along with a short list of traffic violations, mostly for speeding. C.J. was entering Cindy's phone number into her smartphone when she happened to look at Bartlett's house. Caroline paced back and forth across the living room, going in and out of C.J.'s view. She held her cell phone to her right ear and gestured emphatically with her left hand, like she wasn't hearing the responses she wanted from the person on the other end of the call.

"Hmm. Guilty conscience? Needs to tell someone what she's said to me, so their stories match?" C.J. mused. Struck by an obvious reason to call someone so soon after her departure, C.J. hit the call button and waited to be connected to Cindy Smith's phone number. After a few seconds of dead air and clicks, C.J. was prompted to leave a message after the tone.

C.J. disconnected the call and watched Caroline Bartlett. When Caroline's call ended, C.J. hit the redial button and Cindy Smith's phone started ringing. *"Coincidence? I think not."*

"Hello."

"Ms. Smith, this is Sergeant Jensen from the Pine County Sheriff's Department. I'm following up on leads related to Roger Bartlett's death. Do you have a moment to answer a few questions?"

"Um, sure. But I really don't...didn't know Roger that well."

"I thought you were close to the Bartletts."

"I've known Caroline since grade school, but I've never been part of their social circle in Askov."

"Are you still close to Caroline?"

"We get together a couple times a month for a girls weekend in the Cities. We go out for a nice dinner then go to a concert or play. If it's too late, we get a Minneapolis hotel room and drive home the next day."

"How does your husband feel about your girls weekends?"

Cindy laughed. "He's happy about it. He hates driving to the Cities, he'd rather eat fast food than have a nice dinner, and I'm sure he'd feel like he'd entered the first layer of purgatory if I dragged him to a concert."

"Have you spoken to Caroline recently?"

The pause that followed was overly long. "I...ah...called her as soon as I heard about Roger's death. So yes, we spoke a couple days ago."

"But she hasn't called you today?"

"Um, no. Can we end this call? My dog is scratching at the door, and I need to let him out."

"Just one more quick question. We'll have to look at Caroline's credit card records. I assume we'll see ticket purchases and hotel charges. Does she always pay when you go on a girl's weekend?"

"Um…yes. She usually uses her card, then I reimburse her in cash."

"Thank you, Mrs. Smith."

"Any time."

C.J. ended the call, then watched Bartlett's house. Within a minute, Caroline was talking on the phone and pacing back and forth. C.J. punched the redial feature, dialing Cindy's phone. After a few clicks, she got a prompt to leave a message. C.J. smiled. "Gotcha," she said to herself.

Chapter 13

Pam's computer chimed, announcing the arrival of an email. Looking for an excuse to break away from the parolees' arrest reports, she clicked on the email icon. The subject line was simple: phone records. The sender was Kurt Olson, the federal parole officer. The files were line after line of incoming and outgoing calls made to six different phone numbers. Many of the calls showed the caller's ID. It appeared that the Pizza Pub was a favorite among all the parolees. The other identified outgoing calls were to relatives, the tire company, Joe Callahan, and Roger Bartlett. The incoming calls were from the same numbers. Troubling, or worthy of follow-up, were the calls to and from phones only identified by their number or marked 'Private Caller'.

Pam picked up the phone, planning to leave a message for Kurt Olson. She was surprised when he answered the phone himself. "Hey, Kurt. Thanks for the phone records. They're interesting, but I didn't see any smoking gun."

"Yeah, I was looking for the caller ID from Ima Killer. She apparently is one of the unlisted numbers."

"Do you recognize any of the numbers without caller ID?"

"About half of them are to or from my federal phone. It blocks the caller ID. I assume the others are to friends and relatives who can't afford anything but pay as you go phones. I plan to talk to the guys about those calls. If they've had calls from the prison, or to inmates living elsewhere, it could be a parole violation." Olson paused. "I'm surprised you didn't ask about two of the calls that set off bells and sirens for me."

After looking through the list again, Pam clucked her tongue. "Nothing jumps out at me."

"One is from Amazon customer service."

"Okay, I see it. Why is that a problem?"

"They don't have internet access, so they can't order from Amazon. Why would customer service be calling them?"

"Amazon has become such a big piece of our lives that I didn't even blink when I read that line. What's the other thing I missed?"

"There were two calls to a 900 number."

"I guess I don't know the significance of that."

"The 900 numbers are reserved for pay-per-call or pay-per-minute calls. The only ones I'm familiar with are for phone sex, horoscopes, and psychic readings. I'm not going to call any of those numbers from my work phone because the IT watchdogs would notify my boss before the first ring. My personal guess is that they're not calling for psychic readings, horoscopes, or weather reports, which leaves numbers that might be a parole violation."

"Ouch, a stupid horny phone call could cause a parole revocation."

"There's one other thing of note; something that's missing."

Pam leaned back and studied the phone records. "Again, I'm missing it."

"There are seven parolees living together. Only six of them have logged any calls."

"Who's not calling their mama?"

"Igor has never made a call from his phone. My guess is that he purchased a pay-as-you-go phone and is calling from it rather than using the phone I can trace."

"What are you going to do about that?" Pam asked.

"Technically, Igor is supervised by the US Marshals because of his witness protection agreement. I left a message with my contact in the program. When you called, I thought the call was probably coming from that contact, not you."

"I'm hurt. You'd rather talk to a guy from the marshal's office than me?"

"The 'guy' in the marshals office is a woman. And yes, I'd rather talk to her. She and I have to share a lot of information. You're just a pleasant diversion from my stressful job. We'll get through this case, and you'll be gone. I'll still be working with Annie for years."

"Well shit. I thought we had a thing going on here," Pam kidded.

"Um, no. You're a newlywed with a little kid. That puts you on the do-not-disturb after hours list. On the other hand, if C.J. offered me her phone number…"

"Don't scratch that itch, Kurt. C.J. is a recent widow who's told me repeatedly that she's not ready for a relationship."

"Damn. All the good women are taken."

"Which groups of women fall into the not so good category?"

"Drug users, parolees, drunks, chronic gamblers; pretty much anyone who can't control their urges. I just don't need that kind of shit in my life."

"There must be some good and available women out there."

"Pam, if you find one, feel free to give her this number." Olson paused. "I have to go out to the parolees' house to talk with them about the phone calls and to verify that they don't have an internet access gadget of some kind. Would you like to ride along and ask questions about your case?"

"I probably should, even if the thought of dealing with those guys makes my skin crawl. And telling me about the calls to the 900 number hasn't reduced that icky crawling feeling."

"Can you meet me at Banning Junction at 4:00? We can leave your car parked there and drive to Askov in my car. That'll give us a little time to strategize extracting information from the guys. On the return trip, we can compare notes. I'm going to focus on the phone and internet issues. You can listen to side conversations and be another set of eyes and ears."

"I'd be happy to back you up, Kurt."

"Let's hope it doesn't come to that."

Pam was reaching to hang up the phone when she heard the sheriff behind her. "Kurt the parole officer needs backup?"

"He doesn't think so. He offered to take me along when he interviews the Askov parolees. He thinks I might hear or see something he might miss."

Sepanen put his coffee mug into the machine without comment. When the coffee started dribbling into the cup, he turned. "Be careful. Those guys are hardened criminals. Don't take any chances around them."

"They're not allowed to have guns, but you heard what happened when C.J. went along with Kurt to arrest one of the parolees."

"I'll be careful, but I doubt going to their house is much riskier than serving court papers on people with outstanding county tickets and warrants."

"Funny you'd mention that. I don't want you serving our county court papers without backup either."

"You make it sound like the wild west."

Taking his mug out of the brewer, the sheriff walked over and sat in Pam's guest chair. "There is an air of the wild west right now. You're petite and people tend to underestimate you. Because this county is spread over 1,400 square miles, your backup might be an hour away. I don't want another incident like C.J. had last spring. Understood?"

"I'll be careful."

"No, you'll call for backup before you step out of your car. On second thought, you won't get out of your car until backup arrives."

"That seems a little excessive."

The sheriff stood. "I think it was Chuck Yeager who said, 'There are old pilots and there are bold pilots. But there aren't many old bold pilots.' I want you around to take care of your son."

Pam nodded. "Understood."

After the sheriff walked away, Pam dialed her cell phone. "Hi, Floyd. Do you have time for a cup of coffee?"

"If you're buying, I'm available. When and where?"

"I have to be in Askov at four o'clock. Let's meet at The Whistle Stop Café at three."

"That sounds great. The last time I was there they had sour cream raisin pie. I'm going to call and have them set a slice aside for me."

"Floyd, is there any restaurant in Pine County you don't like?"

"They all have hot coffee and comfortable chairs. Those are my only requirements." He paused, then asked, "Is there something special on your mind?"

Two of the jailers walked past, so Pam paused. "Not anything I can discuss over the phone."

"Then I'll see you at three."

* * *

Cindy Smith was stunned when she opened her door and saw C.J. standing on the step. "Can I come in Mrs. Smith?"

"I'm busy. Could you come back in…say half an hour?"

"As long as I'm here, I think we should talk now. Do you have any coffee brewing? I could use a warmup."

Cindy sighed and opened the door. "I'll make a new pot. Follow me into the kitchen."

A basket of clothing sat on the living room couch. Fresh from the dryer, C.J. could smell the cotton flower scent of the dryer sheets. Smith's small kitchen was neat, the countertops clear of dishes. Four wooden chairs circled a round oak table that took up most of the free space in the kitchen.

Without waiting for an invitation, C.J. sat in a chair where she could see both the back door and the hallway leading to the front door. She looked around for the dog Cindy reported wanting to go out, but saw no dog, water bowls, or dog hair. "Your children must be grown. Do they live nearby?"

"Our daughter works for an insurance agent in St. Cloud, and our son is the city manager for Brooklyn Center, down in the Cities. It's pretty quiet around here with only Hank and me banging around inside this old house."

With the coffee pot gurgling, Cindy took two mugs out of the cupboard and carried them to the table. "Do you use cream or sugar?"

"I love the coffee, but I don't need the extra calories from the cream and sugar. Thanks anyway."

"What brings you to my doorstep?"

"I wanted to look you in the eye when I asked you a few questions."

"I don't understand," Cindy said, glancing at the coffee pot.

"Tell me about your trips to the Cities with Caroline Bartlett."

"We've already discussed that on the phone. She and I go on shopping trips a few times a year. We go to a concert or play and have a nice dinner. If it's late, we spend the night in a hotel and drive back in the morning."

The coffee pot gurgled, signalling the end of the brewing cycle. Cindy retrieved the carafe and poured coffee while C.J. watched silently. When it was clear Cindy wasn't going to say anything more, C.J. asked. "What do you shop for?"

"Um, mostly clothes."

"Do you shop in downtown Minneapolis, or do you go to the Mall of America?"

"We've been to both places. It kind of depends on what Caroline is looking for."

"When was your last trip and what concert did you see?"

Cindy froze. "I don't recall the date. It was a few months ago."

C.J. pulled out her notebook and flipped through a few pages. "Caroline said you saw *Wicked* at the State Theater. I heard it was wonderful."

"It was okay. I prefer productions with music I can sing along with. I didn't know any of the songs in *Wicked.*"

"Where did you go for supper?"

"I don't recall the name. It was just a few blocks from Orchestra Hall and near the hotel."

C.J. looked at her notes. "I've heard the Ivy Hotel is very luxurious."

"Yes, it's nice."

C.J. leafed through her notes and sipped coffee without saying anything. Cindy began to fidget as she stared at C.J.'s notebook. Setting the notebook aside, C.J. wrapped her hands around her mug.

"That's all bullshit, Cindy."

Smith's eyes went wide. "What is?"

"Your whole story. The play *Wicked,* hasn't been in Minneapolis for a couple years. You've never been to the Ivy Hotel. You're covering for Caroline."

"No…I just got flustered. We went to a classical music concert at Orchestra Hall and stayed at the Hilton."

"I heard the words, but there's no conviction in your voice. What's Caroline hiding? Is she having an affair and using you for her alibi?"

Cindy's façade crumbled. "I think you should leave."

"Mrs. Smith, I'm investigating the murder of Caroline's husband. If you're giving her a false alibi and she was complicit in the murder, you'll be an accomplice after the fact and subject to the same penalty as the murderers."

Cindy stood and stalked to the counter where she braced herself. A second later, she turned and ran to the bathroom. C.J. poured herself another cup of coffee while listening to the woman vomiting. After a few moments, the toilet flushed, and water ran in the sink.

Cindy hardly looked like the same person when she stepped out of the bathroom. Her makeup was gone and her face was pale. Wiping her forehead with a hand towel, Cindy sat down across from C.J. "I can't throw Caroline under the bus. She's one of my closest friends."

"I've got news for you, Mrs. Smith. You're the one being thrown under the bus. Caroline is using you to create a false alibi for herself. Friends don't do that to each other."

Beads of sweat formed on Cindy's forehead. She wiped them away with the hand towel, then leaned back and crossed her legs. "I warned Caroline that I wasn't a born liar, like she is."

"Who goes with her on her shopping trips?"

"Joe."

C.J. nodded like she just got confirmation of information she'd already heard. It was an act and the news that Bartlett's wife was having an affair with her husband's partner was an unexpected twist. "Do they always go to Minneapolis?"

"I think they actually go to Canada more frequently than Minneapolis. Joe has lots of business in Thunder Bay, so I think they go there or Montreal at least quarterly."

"And Caroline's husband wasn't suspicious?"

"I think he wanted to believe that Caroline and I were in the Cities having fun. She would build these fake itineraries with details of what we were planning. She printed a copy for me just in case Roger ever called."

"Has Roger ever called you?"

Cindy blew out a breath. "Just once. They'd replaced some plumbing thing and it was leaking. He called me because Caroline's phone was rolling over to voicemail and he needed the name of the plumber who did the work. I told him Caroline was in the ladies room, but said I'd pass the information to her."

"How did you contact her if she wasn't answering her phone?"

"Roger always called, and she could see his number come up on caller ID. I texted her. I guess she told Roger she'd had her phone on airplane mode during the concert."

"How long have they been having an affair?"

"I think they started having clandestine trysts shortly after Joe became a partner in the tire company. At some point, they realized their activities were taking place too close to home, so they concocted these stories to camouflage their real plans."

C.J. closed her notebook and put it in her pocket. "Thanks for clearing this up."

Cindy followed C.J. to the door. "You're not going to tell Caroline I outed her, are you?"

"She's probably smart enough to know the information came from you."

"But..."

"No buts about it. Good friends don't ask you to cover for them when they're doing something illegal... or immoral."

"You don't think Caroline killed Roger, do you?"

"I doubt she pulled the trigger, but that doesn't absolve her from being part of the plan."

Cindy was crying when C.J. walked out the door.

Chapter 14

Floyd was reading the newspaper at a table near the kitchen when Pam walked in. Taking a chair across from him, Pam flipped over her coffee cup and signaled the waitress. "You've been here a while."

Floyd folded the paper and wedged it against the wall behind a sugar dispenser. "You're late."

The wall clock next to the kitchen was directly over Floyd's head. "We agreed to meet at three, and the clock says I'm ten minutes early. What time did you arrive?"

"It's hard to say. I stopped wearing my watch when I retired. My stomach said it was time for a slice of sour cream raisin pie. You should try it."

The waitress arrived with a coffee carafe and a menu. "Are you eating or just having coffee this afternoon?" Janice had been waiting tables at the Whistle Stop Café as long as Pam had been with the department.

Pam glanced at the chalkboard listing of the lunch special and pie options. "Janice, you are the devil incarnate. I'm trying to drop another six pounds of weight

235

gained when I was pregnant, and you're tempting me with pie."

"I am not twisting your arm, dear. I'm just giving you the option."

"Blueberry sounds good."

Tucking the menu under her arm, Janice smiled and asked, "Would you like that a la mode?"

"Just the pie is bad enough, thank you very much."

Janice winked at Floyd and picked up his pie plate. "There's one more piece of the sour cream raisin pie in the back. It looks kind of sad and lonely."

"Since it's been forsaken by its friends, I suppose the only humane thing to do is eat it." Floyd looked up and snapped his fingers. "Yes! Pam's buying so I will have that pie."

With Janice gone, Floyd leaned forward. "This is the second time you've invited me out for coffee this week. Is everything all right?"

"Things are mostly under control. We haven't solved the murder yet, but we've got some leads."

"I've been working the cafés. The consensus is that one of the convicts working at the tire company killed Roger Bartlett."

"Is that consensus based on facts and evidence?"

"Oh, hell no. It's the popular vote tallied in my head."

"Well, gee whiz, Floyd. With sound evidence like that, I should run right back to the county attorney's office and have him issue arrest warrants for the whole lot of them."

Returning with two slices of pie, Janice set a slice of blueberry pie in front of Pam. A large scoop of ice cream sat in a puddle on top of the crust.

"I said no to the a la mode, Janice."

"Whoops. My bad. Well, that piece of pie is ruined now so I can't put it back. I guess I can't charge you for my mistake."

Pam waved her hand. "I think you must've gone to smart aleck school with Floyd."

Janice smiled. "I was the class valedictorian." She paused, then added. "Seriously, the pie is on me."

Eyeing the ice cream and pie, Pam pushed the ice cream to the side and took a bite of pie. "It's like the whole world is conspiring to keep me from losing weight. Travis is making crockpot dinners full of potatoes or pasta; you insist on eating pie or caramel rolls when we go out for coffee. The sheriff brought a box of doughnuts in yesterday. I'm gaining instead of losing weight."

"Don't be so hard on yourself. It's only been a couple months since Luke's birth."

"You and Mary got married by the judge, but I thought you were planning a reception so we could hug and congratulate you two."

"We've balked because of the Covid thing. Most everyone is vaccinated, but with all the new mutant strains showing up, we've decided it's prudent to wait a bit so we don't make all our friends sick."

Surrendering to the call of the ala mode, Pam cut away a bit of ice cream and ate it with a bite of pie. "I do love ice cream."

"You didn't invite me out just to feed me pie. What's up?"

"The sheriff cornered me and said I shouldn't put myself into any risky situations without backup on the way. It made me feel..."

"He's just being overly protective. And to be honest, I was uneasy with some of the things you've done without backup in the past. You don't need to walk into a bar fight alone. You shouldn't stop a car filled with drug suspects on a dark back road."

"I shouldn't follow a teenage girl into a dark hunting shack when I think there's a stoner inside."

Floyd set his fork down and wiped his face with a napkin. "That was on the dispatcher for not following up with C.J. But no, she should've stepped back and waited for backup."

"C.J. and I have spoken about that a couple times. She really shouldn't have rushed into the dark shack and should've had her gun in hand even approaching the scene. But, we've been trained to be assertive and take control of situations."

Poking at his pie, Floyd thought. "Yes, you have to be assertive. But you also have to be smart and weigh the risks. These rural counties are getting more drug activity and crime than we've ever seen. I was happy to retire when I did because the job was no longer what I'd signed on for."

"But you miss it every day."

"Yes, but that doesn't mean I'm interested in dusting off my uniform and begging John to rehire me."

"Do you still have your uniforms?"

Chuckling, Floyd cut another bite of pie. "I wear them when I work on my truck and pull weeds. I don't want to get my dress jeans dirty."

Pam snorted. "What are dress jeans?"

"They're the cleanest, newest pair in the drawer; the ones I save for special occasions, like going out for coffee."

Janice topped off their coffees and slid the bill to Pam. "Can I get you two anything else?"

They both shook their heads. Floyd looked at Pam's coffee. "How much coffee do you drink a day?"

"Who are you, the coffee police?"

"I'm just worried about your health and well being. You must be unbuckling your duty belt a dozen times a day just so you can pee."

"This is what I miss. No one else makes politically incorrect comments as well as you."

"What's politically incorrect about worrying about you dropping your belt and breaking a toe?"

"Yeah, I'm sure that's what you are concerned about."

Chuckling, Floyd leaned close. "Back in the old days, I'd forgotten to snap the strap on my Colt .38 Special. It fell into the toilet when I pulled my duty belt up."

"Oh, geez. What did you do?"

"I had to fish it out. Then I field stripped it, then used several cans of bore cleaner and oil before reassembly."

"I'm happy to say that's never happened to me."

"Well, just be careful. It'd be just about as bad to drop a magazine full of 9mm shells or your handcuffs into the toilet."

Pam pushed her plate and coffee mug away. "How did we get into this discussion?"

"You needed a diversion from John's backup admonition."

"I suppose I did."

"What else would you like to talk about?"

240

Pam picked up the bill and took a debit card out of her pocket. "I wanted to see you and hear your voice."

Reaching out and patting her hand, Floyd said, "I've missed you too. I'll talk to Mary, and we'll have you guys over for supper some night. Mary's got a great pork chop recipe."

Pam froze. "You haven't mentioned Mary's cancer."

"It's still in the back of our minds, but Mary's decided that she's not going to let it define her life."

"I have to hustle. I'm meeting the federal parole officer in a few minutes. We're going to talk to the tire company employees about their phone and internet use."

"That's a place where you need to watch your back."

Pam shook her head. "They're all white-collar criminals. I doubt any of them pose a threat."

"Don't kid yourself. They're federal convicts and even if they went in for relatively minor felonies, they learned a lot while they were locked up. Being in prison changes men. It's like the guys come out with PTSD. They're all goofy and messed up."

Pam patted Floyd's arm. "I appreciate that perspective…and your concern for my safety."

241

Floyd pushed her hand aside and engulfed Pam in a hug. "Listen, I still consider you my daughter. You shouldn't be surprised that I'm expressing the same concern you'd hear from your own father."

After pecking Floyd's cheek, Pam said, "You're tactful compared to Dad. He told me he hoped I'd quit playing cops and robbers now that I had a kid to take care of."

* * *

Kurt Olson's car was parked in a corner of the Banning Junction parking lot behind the diesel pumps. He looked up from his cell phone when Pam pulled in alongside him. He pushed the passenger door open. "The guys are probably making supper about now. Don't be put off by the pigsty they're living in. This is the maid's week off."

"I'm a new mom with a husband who is willing to cook but isn't much into house cleaning or dishwashing."

Kurt cocked his head. "I heard you grew up on a farm."

"Yeah, in Southern Minnesota."

"Then you do understand the meaning of pigsty. I'm not talking messy, I'm talking food ground into the floor and dirty clothing strewn around on every piece of furniture. I carry a pack of wipes in the glove box. I wipe my hands off before touching the steering wheel."

Pam asked about life as a parole officer. Kurt shared anecdotes about the funny and scary things he'd encountered. Most of his job was a boring routine, talking to the parolees, following up on their job attendance, and occasionally rearresting the ones who violated the terms of their parole. The trip through Askov to the parolees' house flew by.

After parking among the beat-up cars and pickups in the driveway, Kurt paused. "Cold calls like this sometimes get confrontational. I'm going to question their phone calls and they won't like it, but hey, that's my job. Let me handle that. You hang back a bit and keep an eye on the guys who are watching. I'd like to know about furtive glances that might mean there's more than the answer I've been given, or that hit close to the target, and are making the guys nervous. Don't let them lull you into a sense of security, and don't let any of them get behind you. Got it?"

"You make it sound like we're going inside the prison," Pam said as she opened the car door.

"We're only one step away from the prison here. I think of the parolees as animals that have been partially tamed in the zoo and released in the community.

243

They're still wild and may turn on you if the circumstance is to their advantage."

"You live through this every day?" Pam asked as they walked up the steps.

"Welcome to my world."

Kurt knocked but didn't wait for a response before opening the door. "It's your local parole officer. Pretend to act nice, I brought a friend along."

Five men were sitting around a rectangular table that looked like it had been recovered from a landfill. They seemed unsurprised by Kurt's arrival and continued eating what appeared to be stew out of chipped stoneware bowls. They glanced at Kurt, then saw Pam, which caused the men to look back and forth with raised eyebrows.

Igor stood and wiped his mouth on his shirt sleeve. "If it isn't the pretty woman in the sheriff's department vest. Don't worry, we're not allowed to have guns. None of us will shoot you."

Kurt walked into the kitchen. "We're going to have a talk about phone privileges."

The men groaned, but Kurt pulled out his report and started questioning the men about the unusual calls. Hanging back, Pam noticed a blaze orange jacket hanging on a peg. She lifted the sleeve and inspected a smear that appeared to be blood on the cuff. She patted the pockets and found a pair of gloves and a pack of cigarettes, but no weapon or drugs.

Kurt was leaning over the table discussing phone calls when Pam carried the orange coat into the kitchen. "Who owns this?" The parolees looked at each other, but no one spoke up. "I find it interesting that you guys can't own guns, but you've got a deer hunter's coat with blood on the cuff."

Igor had drifted back from the group and stood leaning against the counter with his arms crossed. "Garage sale deal. Five bucks. It's funny about being out here in the boonies. Any coat that warm and waterproof is either orange or camouflage."

"If I took this to the lab, they'd tell me this is deer blood that's been on the cuff for years?"

Igor wrinkled his nose. "Hard to say." He pushed himself off the counter and smiled. "Tell you what. I've got a bag upstairs. You bring the coat up to my room and I'll help you package it up for the crime lab."

Kurt straightened up and stepped away from the table. "Down, Igor."

"Hey! I'm just trying to be helpful."

Kurt picked up the stack of phone records. "Explain why everyone else has a page or more of calls, but your phone has never been used."

"The battery died," Igor replied.

"Empty your pockets on the table, Igor."

Igor raised his hands. "What?"

"Just empty your pockets. If you have a different phone, you'll be in violation and the marshals will pick you up."

"The marshals gave me a phone, you know, for personal business." Igor removed a flip phone from his pocket. "It's a hot line to the US Attorney's office."

Gravel crunched in the driveway and Pam realized her back was to the door. She stepped aside and leaned against the wall. She looked at the men sitting around the table and saw concern on their faces. One of them looked at Igor and nodded toward the door. Igor bent his wrists, signalling everyone to stay sitting.

The outside door thumped open and someone stepped in with the sound of crinkling paper shopping bags. "It looks like a cheap used car lot out there. Which one of you smartasses bought the used cop car?"

The man who walked into the kitchen was a decade younger than any of the parolees and dressed in a name brand coat with the logo embroidered on the chest. His right arm was wrapped around a shopping bag. His left hand pulled a young woman behind.

The silent room stopped him in his tracks. Pam, just out of his peripheral vision, reached back and wrapped her hand around the handle of her pistol.

"Who the hell are you?" the young man asked Kurt as he pulled the waif-like teenager into the kitchen. She was dirty, fidgety, anorexic, and probably strung out on crack.

Igor shook his head and glanced at Pam. The man wheeled toward Pam, tossing the bag at her as he yanked the girl's arm. The heavy bag hit Pam in the chest and nearly knocked her over. It fell to the floor with the sound of breaking glass. Kurt lunged for the man, but a foot shot out, sending him sprawling on the floor.

With her gun drawn and pointed at Igor's forehead, Pam sidled past the bag, now sodden with booze and beer. "Nobody move," she said as the outside door slammed.

Kurt scrambled to his feet, trying to determine who'd tripped him. Failing that he stepped toward the door. "Come on, Pam," he said as he rushed past.

Pam eased toward the door, keeping her gun leveled at Igor's chest. "I'm right behind you," she said, backing through the mud room, but keeping her gun on the men in the kitchen.

Once past the door, Pam holstered her gun and ran for Kurt's car. A gray pickup truck bounced down the driveway. Tires squealed as they bit into the tar of the road.

Kurt's car was in motion before Pam had the door closed. "What the hell is going on?" she asked as she buckled her seatbelt.

The heavy police special suspension bounced over the rough driveway, accentuating the potholes. "I assume we interrupted this evening's entertainment." Kurt flipped a switch lighting red and blue flashers in the grille of the car.

Turning her head, Pam activated her radio mic. "Dispatch, we're in pursuit of a gray four-wheel-drive pickup. I'm in a police vehicle with a federal parole agent. We will be in Askov within a minute."

The dispatcher relayed the information on the state-wide police frequency. "What's the reason for your pursuit?"

Pam looked at Kurt. "Prostitution?"

"Human trafficking. That girl didn't look like she was even fifteen."

Pam relayed that and announced that the pursuit was now moving south on Highway 23, through the town of Askov.

Aside from a half dozen cars at the Highway 23 bar, the town was dark and apparently unoccupied. Kurt glanced at Pam. "What are your pursuit rules?"

"We have to break off when approaching a residential area."

Shaking his head, Kurt accelerated through town, his speedometer quickly passing seventy, eighty, and ninety miles an hour. "I don't think a deserted ghost town counts as a residential area, do you?"

"It's irrelevant, we just passed the city limits."

The dispatcher requested an update as they passed Banning Junction. The pickup crossed over I-35 and made a looping turn onto the southbound entrance ramp. A state patrol trooper announced his approach from the north, behind Kurt and Pam as they raced down the entrance ramp, the pickup two hundred yards ahead of them. C.J. was coming from the other direction, driving home at the end of her shift. Kerm Rajacich, another Pine County Deputy, announced that he was leaving the courthouse parking lot and would be northbound on I-35 in a few moments, which put him almost ten miles behind C.J.

Being pressed back into the car seat by the acceleration, Pam watched the pickup's taillights get closer. "We're going to be on his bumper before anyone else is near us."

"Is that a problem?"

"I guess that depends on your plan."

Olson chuckled. "What plan?"

"I was afraid of that. If we stay behind him, C.J. might be able to deploy stop sticks."

"Can you read his license plate?"

Pam called in the license number. "I wonder if it's stolen, or if that guy runs a string of on-call girls?"

Olson stopped talking, concentrating as the pickup wove in and out of a convoy of semis, all going one-mile-an-hour under the speed limit, then slowed when he caught up to an aging RV slowly passing a semi.

"What's your bet?" Olson asked, wiping his damp palms on his pants.

"What bet?"

"Does the pickup take the left shoulder, the right shoulder, or just hang back until the RV gets past the semi?"

"Hey," Pam said, "the semi just speeded up and flashed his lights. He's blocking the right lane for us."

The left shoulder was narrow, and after flashing his headlights at the RV and pulling his left wheels onto the shoulder, the pickup steered to the right lane, then onto the shoulder. Olson followed a few car-lengths back.

"We've got company."

"Oh shit," Pam said, bracing herself. "The semi's squeezing him off the shoulder."

The semi braked as he drifted across the rumble strip, forcing the pickup into the ditch. Bucking through the rough grass the pickup's driver struggled to maintain control of the vehicle. Steering left, to climb the shoulder and regain traction on the road, the pickup teetered on its right wheels for what seemed like a minute before it pitched onto its right side and flipped across the ditch, rolling two and a half times before skidding to a stop on its roof.

The trooper behind them called in the location of the accident and requested emergency services as Olson's car slid to a stop on the shoulder of the road. Bounding out of the car, Pam sloshed her way through the watery ditch, and threw herself down next to the passenger's window with Olson a step behind her.

"Wait!" Olson yelled, "He might have a gun."

Pam shined her flashlight in the passenger's window, the beam reflecting splatters of blood that obscured her view. Olson pulled on the door handle, but the cab had buckled during the rolls, jamming the door.

After a few seconds of trying to see into the cab, Pam heard the trooper sloshing through the ditch. "The Sandstone rescue squad and ambulance are coming. What's the situation?"

Pam squirmed ahead and shone her flashlight into the spider-webbed windshield. A moment later she rolled away and stared at the sky. "They didn't have seatbelts on," she said to no one in particular.

"I don't know what you mean," the parole officer said. He took Pam's flashlight and shone it into the cab. "Oh Geez." He looked at the trooper but couldn't get out a thought. Sitting next to Pam, Olson rested his arms on his knees and hung his head. "We were trying to save the girl."

The trooper put his hand on Olson's shoulder. "Who are you, sir?"

Olson removed his P.O. credentials from his pocket and handed them to the trooper as the flashing lights of the rescue squad crested the hill behind them. "This is one of the unintended consequences we sometimes encounter."

C.J. raced across the ditch and saw Pam lying on her back. Pam's forearm covered her eyes. "Pam, are you okay?"

Letting out a sigh, Pam pushed herself up. "I'm fine. Well, fine except for killing the kid we were trying to save."

C.J. pulled Pam to her feet and they walked to the fence farthest from the ditch. "Take a breath and tell me what happened."

The police and fire radios were alive with chatter, people announcing their ETAs, others requesting more assistance, and a trooper diverting traffic in Hinckley. Pam drew a breath, then bit her bottom lip. "It's that damned Igor's fault."

"That's Igor in the truck?"

"No, it's Igor's buddy. The guy showed up with a girl and a bag of booze. He freaked when he saw my uniform and made a run for it."

Clenching her jaw, C.J. looked at the firemen trying to extract the bodies from the

252

pickup cab. "I don't suppose we can prove any of that."

"I'm not sure what burden of proof is required to prove that Igor violated parole. We may not be able to implicate him in whatever this guy was into, but maybe Kurt Olson can get Igor's parole revoked. He'll finish his sentence behind bars."

They watched Kurt talking with a trooper. Kurt's dark expression reflected his emotion over the sad outcome. The trooper made notes and nodded. When the parole officer saw C.J. and Pam staring at him, he trudged through the deep grass to them. "They're through with me. I said our pursuit ended when the trooper showed up. That seemed to satisfy the question of our role in the crash."

"If you're free to leave, take me back to Banning Junction so I can retrieve my car."

After surveying the massed emergency vehicles, Kurt nodded. "I think I can squeeze through behind the fire truck."

C.J. put her hand on Pam's arm. "Coffee at Peggy Sue's tomorrow at eight."

"I…Luke has to…"

"I'll call Floyd as soon as you guys leave. He'll meet us there." As an afterthought, C.J. looked at Kurt. "You're welcome to join us."

"I'm going to have so many calls to make and reports to fill out, I'll be stuck at my desk for a week. I'll take a rain check."

Kurt wound through the emergency vehicles and pulled into an opening in the traffic. Pam entered a number in her phone. "Hey, honey. I've been at the scene of a fatal accident and am tied up. Can you put Luke down for the night?"

Making a U-turn at an emergency crossover, Kurt accelerated north, towards the origin of the evening's activities. "I apologize for getting you into this mess. On the other hand, I'm not sure things would've played out well if I'd been alone with Igor, his buddy, and the rest of my parolees. I'd like to believe the other guys would've stayed out of it, but there's no way to be sure."

"Yeah, what happened to you? You turned toward the door, then I got hit with the bag. When I got my balance, you were face down on the floor."

"I think someone tripped me. I can't say that for sure, or even guess who might've done it, but I'd like to think I'd be able to turn and take a step without doing a face plant."

"I assume you used to be athletic."

Laughing, Olson glanced at Pam. "Thanks. I used to be athletic?"

"Sorry. Were you a college athlete?"

"I played football, basketball, and baseball at Hamline University."

"I thought athletes specialized in one sport?"

"I lived to be on the field. There was no way I could play one sport and sit out the rest of the year."

"I take it you weren't good enough to turn pro."

"I couldn't name the last Hamline player who got drafted into the big leagues. We all hang up our cleats when we graduate or play in community softball leagues."

"So, if you didn't trip over your feet, someone didn't want us to catch the guy and girl."

"Honor among thieves," Olson replied.

Flashing back to the house and chain of events leading to the chase, Pam froze. "Let's go back to the house."

"I plan on talking to the guys tomorrow during the day. They'll all be agitated tonight. I'd prefer to let them settle down, then talk to them one at a time."

"I want to pick up the orange hunting coat. There were blood stains on the sleeve."

"Don't you think the garage sale story holds water?"

"We'll never know if the blood is from a deer or Roger Bartlett if we don't test it."

"I thought the killer wasn't near Bartlett when he was shot."

"The shot came from more than a few feet away, but that doesn't mean the killer didn't have contact with Bartlett after the shooting." Pam thought back to the inventory of Bartlett's belongings that were recovered from his clothing. "There wasn't any money in his wallet."

Olson turned onto the Banning Junction exit off the freeway. "Everyone uses their debit card all the time. Lots of people don't carry much cash."

"He had no cash. Not one single dollar bill. I think the killer couldn't resist the temptation of the cash, even if he didn't steal the credit and debit cards." Olson passed the parking lot where Pam's car was sitting. "Hey, you passed my car."

"You're not going back to the house alone. I'll advise the guys that I'll be back to interview them tomorrow, we'll talk about the booze and girl, and you can pick up the orange coat."

"Are you planning to tell them about the crash?"

After a sigh, Olson nodded. "I'm sure a fatal crash will be headline news by morning. There's no point in sugar-coating it."

The only light was in the kitchen. After backing in close to the back door, Olson led Pam up the back steps. They walked in without knocking and found Iggy, the tire company office manager, working on a Sudoku puzzle. There was no evidence of the bag that had been thrown at Pam other than the slight aroma of beer and a clean spot on the floor.

Kurt leaned on the table. "What happened to the booze?"

Iggy nodded toward the sink. "We poured it down the sink. The bottles are in the garbage if you want to check."

"Your breath smells like Jack Daniels."

Iggy smiled. "I spilled some on my shirt. Do you want to sniff it?"

"Who was the guy with the girl?"

Iggy's eyes went back to the Sudoku. "No clue."

"So, a guy just walks in with a bag of booze and an underaged girl and no one here knows him?"

Iggy filled in a number. "Happens all the time. People get addresses wrong."

The orange coat wasn't on the peg where Pam had last seen it. She pulled other coats and jackets aside but didn't find it. "Where's the deer hunting coat?"

"I don't know what you're talking about."

"There was an orange coat here earlier. When I asked about it, one of the guys said it was from a garage sale."

"I've got no idea what you're talking about."

Kurt pulled out a chair and sat at the table. "Iggy, you've got the most to lose out of this bunch of cons. Three months and your parole is over. If you don't answer our questions, you can spend those three months behind bars. Hell, if there's something else going on, you could be charged as an accessory or with obstruction. Where's the coat?"

Iggy looked up at the parole officer, then checked the living room. "It might be outside, under the steps. The wind might've blown some leaves over it."

Pam walked out while Iggy and Kurt continued their discussion. She pulled the flashlight off her duty belt and shined it under the steps. A square of orange reflected from among a pile of damp leaves and twigs piled under the wooden steps.

Opening the door, Pam found Kurt in the mud room holding a pair of steel-toed work boots. "Iggy says the coat's owner may have been wearing these boots, too."

* * *

Olson's phone rang as they pulled out of the driveway. He pulled to the shoulder and took it out of his pocket. Pam listened to the one-sided conversation that consisted mostly of Kurt saying, "okay." Ending the call, he pulled back on the road and drove toward Askov.

"That was one of the deputy marshals. The license plate on the rolled pickup belongs to one of Igor's associates from Detroit. They traced his charge card to a motel near the Mall of America where he's rented two rooms. They've got the rooms under surveillance while they get a search warrant and find a magistrate to sign it. The manager said the rooms were rented to two guys with three girls and they've been on the move day and night for almost a week."

"Some sort of sex trafficking?"

"That's Igor's thing. So, yeah, that's what they're using to justify the search warrant."

"What happens to Igor?"

"Good question. The guy who showed up with the booze and girl seemed happy to see Igor. On the other hand, he may have been putting on a show. Igor is persona non grata in Philly and Detroit after rolling on his associates. This guy may have been just the point man to verify where Igor was so his associates could take him out."

"There was going to be a hit? In Askov?"

"Who knows?"

Chapter 15

Peggy Sue's Diner was nearly full when Pam walked in. The owner nodded toward the row of booths and Pam spotted C.J. and Floyd sitting in the back corner booth. C.J. slid over and signaled Peggy for a coffee refill.

Floyd's smile disappeared when he saw Pam's tired face. "It looks like you didn't get much sleep."

Peggy rushed down with an empty mug and a coffee carafe. "We've got cinnamon rolls today," she said as she poured a mug full of coffee for Pam and topped off the other two cups.

After glancing at the remaining crumbs from the roll Floyd had eaten, Pam nodded. "A cinnamon roll would taste good."

Peggy smiled at C.J. "Are you going to continue to resist the temptation?"

With a nod, C.J. said, "You are a devil, Peggy. Bring me a roll."

Floyd leaned across the table and whispered to Pam, "What happened last night is not your fault. That dipshit decided to flee and what happened after that is not on you."

Pam closed her eyes and nodded. "Maybe if we hadn't pursued them."

"You don't know what would've happened. That pickup might've raced all the way back to Minneapolis and crashed in heavy traffic there. Or they might've lit up someone's radar and been chased anywhere else down the road. You don't know what might've happened."

Pam looked up. "But I know what *did* happen. There's a dead teenage girl."

C.J. leaned back as Peggy set cinnamon rolls in front of them, the frosting oozing over the edges of the plates. "Are you ready for another, Floyd?"

With a smile, Floyd said, "As tempting as that is, I'll pass. Thank you."

C.J. leaned close as Pam spread a napkin on her lap. "I spoke with Eddie this morning. The crash victims were delivered to them last night. Eddie and the ME are doing the autopsies this afternoon. I know it's no consolation, but it appears the girl was thrown against the windshield and died almost instantly of massive head trauma."

"You're right," Pam said, peeling a piece of roll off. "It's not much consolation. She should've been home sleeping, maybe dreaming about playing soccer today. Instead she got dragged around like a piece of meat and died in a bloody police chase."

"Easy, Pam," Floyd said. "C.J.'s just trying to put the best light on a bad situation."

"I know. It's just that..." Pam put a piece of roll in her mouth. "This job sometimes sucks."

Floyd leaned back and nodded. "It does. Sometimes it's wonderful and you feel like you're making a difference. Other times bad stuff happens, and it eats your guts. But someone has to do it, and you're very good at it."

"Thank you. That means a lot."

Smiling, Floyd turned to C.J., "And you're pretty good too."

C.J. chuckled. "Is that why I make the big bucks?"

"I'm sure the raise you got when the sheriff promoted you to sergeant put you in a new tax bracket."

"Yeah, right. It's more like I can afford better dog biscuits for Bailey."

The gloom was broken, and Pam smiled. "Can you find some that don't cause flatulence?"

"I think passing stinky farts is a basset hound feature, like the floppy ears."

Floyd threw up his hands. "My work here is through."

"What?" C.J. asked.

Floyd slid across the bench and stood. "Everyone's head is on straight, and you're joking around. Go solve that murder."

Pam watched Floyd walk out. "I don't know how he does it, but I always feel better about myself and the job after we talk."

"Some people are like that. They exude confidence." After signaling Peggy for a refill, C.J. popped the last bite of roll into her mouth, savoring the cinnamon and frosting. "So, what are we doing today, madam investigator?"

"I've got an orange coat from the parolee's house that may have human blood on the sleeve. I've got to ship it to the Bureau of Criminal Apprehension lab for testing. After that, I thought I'd talk to Kurt Olson. I'm curious about Igor and his status after the chase and rollover."

Waiting until her coffee was topped off, C.J. watched Peggy walk out of earshot. "I'm going to dig into Raul Lopez's past. If he's working and living locally with his girlfriend, I'd like to keep an eye on him for a while."

"What about the partner's affair with Caroline Bartlett? Doesn't that make you just a little suspicious?"

"The affair and life insurance both intrigue me. But I doubt those are the reasons Bartlett was killed. I'll follow up with the Crown Attorney to see if he has any more information about the trucking company that's transporting recapped tires back and forth across the border and

Callahan's vertical integration suppliers." C.J. snatched the bill out of Pam's fingers. "I'll pick up coffee since I'm making so much more as a sergeant."

* * *

The Canadian Crown Attorney's phone rolled over to voicemail. C.J. left a brief message requesting a call back. Then she did an online search for Raul Lopez and *La Serpiente.* Lopez's file in the National Crime Information Computer database ran several pages.

Pam slid her desk chair over to C.J. "Are you looking up Raul Lopez?"

"He's been busy. There is a sealed juvenile file in Houston. Then an arrest and conviction for assault with a deadly weapon in Dallas. He disappeared for a few months, until a drug arrest in Kansas City, followed by an assault on a DEA officer in Omaha that sent him to federal prison."

"Is that how he landed in Sandstone?" Pam asked.

"No, he was in Yankton, South Dakota until he was accused of stabbing another inmate." C.J. looked up. "That would be his first teardrop tattoo. There was some question about who the actual murderer was because none of the prisoners were willing to snitch, but Raul got moved to Sandstone, apparently for his own protection. The stabbing victim was an

Asian gang member and they probably promised retribution."

"He's just a peach of a guy. Just the person you'd want to bring home to meet Mom."

Lifting the phone, C.J. said, "Let's call Kurt to fill in the blanks."

Kurt answered before the phone rang. "What's up, C.J.?"

"What can you tell me about Raul Lopez?"

"You mean, aside from saying his nickname is The Snake, *La Serpiente*?"

C.J. activated the speaker function. "Pam Ryan is here with me."

Leaning close to the phone Pam said, "I'm looking at his NCIC information. He was taken out of Yankton and moved into isolation in Sandstone after an inmate was killed. Can you provide more background?"

"It's all there in his file. He was approved for parole last January and spent six months working at the tire factory. Once his parole was over, he packed his bag and moved in with a woman who'd been his prison pen pal. The parolees in Askov have avoided him. They consider him more of a drug and gang guy than a white-collar criminal."

"There's a hierarchy of prisoners?" Pam asked.

"Oh yes." Kurt replied. "Child molesters are on the bottom rung of the ladder."

"The white-collar guys are the top?"

"Hardly. The toughest, with the biggest posse, are the top. The white-collar guys are usually segregated from the gangs and predators for their own protection."

C.J. leaned forward. "I assume Igor would be near the top of the heap."

"Most federal prisons are somewhat different. We have more of the white-collar guys and fewer of the murderers and rapists. There are a couple federal supermax prisons that are tougher, but people joke about a lot of the low-security federal facilities as country clubs."

"Country club prisons?" Pam asked.

"They're called that because there's less intense supervision and a more relaxed atmosphere. The prison cells are more like dorm rooms and there are fewer hard-core criminals."

"It's bad, but less bad," Pam said.

"Something like that."

"You skipped the question about where Igor fit in the pecking order," C.J. said.

"He's big and scrappy enough to keep himself safe, but he's not a leader."

"How does he fit in with your other parolees?"

The pause after the question was overly long. "He's not one to go along and get along."

"What do you mean?" Pam asked.

"He likes to pick at people. He perceives weakness, then tries to take advantage of it. He thought Charlie looked like an easy mark when he first showed up. Igor nipped at him until Charlie dumped a pot of steaming vegetables in Igor's lap."

"I don't see that going well," Pam said. "Igor's twice Charlie's weight."

Chuckling, Kurt said, "You're thinking of a boxing or wrestling match where there are rules. When people like Charlie fight, anything goes. They claw, bite, kick, and knee until one of the fighters gives up or gets knocked out."

"What happened with Igor and Charlie?" Pam asked.

"I wasn't there, and the parolees all claimed they didn't see the fight. Charlie had a gash on his forehead that didn't heal well for a couple weeks and Igor still has a limp. I suspect Charlie went for Igor's knees."

C.J. decided to move the conversation back to Raul. "Where would we find Raul if we wanted to talk to him?"

"He's no longer on parole, so he doesn't report in anymore. You could try his girlfriend's apartment, but she may have seen the light."

"Seen the light?" Pam asked.

"Some women like bad boys and being pen pals with a convict is fun and safe...until he gets free. She may have

267

found out just how bad Raul is and packed her bags and left. Or, they may still be together. I don't know."

Pam wrote the address from Kurt's records and thanked him. C.J. was ready to disconnect the call when Kurt had one last word. "Neither of you go to visit him alone. If you're planning to knock on the door and talk to Raul, have backup."

"Kurt," Pam said with her pen poised over the notepad, "what's his girlfriend's name?"

Chuckling, Kurt said, "He called her Candy Cane."

Exchanging a glance, C.J. and Pam frowned. "That sounds like a stage name. Is she an exotic dancer?"

"I have no idea. That's just how he referred to her."

Pam rushed to the computer as C.J. thanked the parole officer. Typing in Candy Cane, resulted in no known addresses in Cloquet. Typing in the address Kurt had supplied, offered hundreds of names, associated with unit numbers. "It's an apartment building, but there is no one named Cane living there recently.

C.J. looked at the names on the screen and pointed to the K section. "There. She's C. Keane. I bet she pronounces her last name, 'Cane'. Try searching for Candace or Candice Keane."

Re-entering the search gave a series of addresses for Candice Keane. "She moved from Cloquet five months ago. Here's a more current address in Kerrick Township."

"Have you ever seen Aaron Lane?" C.J. asked.

"I think it's a dead-end road off Palon Road." Pam walked to a county map mounted on the wall near the coffee maker. She put her finger on a thin red line near the northernmost edge of Pine County. "It's here. There appear to be three houses there."

"Have you ever driven down that road?"

Pam shook her head. "I've never taken a call there. So, no, I've never driven down that road. As I recall, it's dirt and not quite two cars wide."

"I think I'll cruise by," C.J. said, stepping away from the map.

"Oh, no. Neither of us is going there alone," Pam replied. "Give me two minutes to log off the computer."

* * *

As predicted, Aaron Lane was barely a car wide, with underbrush grown up to the edges of the road. Pam turned onto the road and announced their location to the dispatcher. After chattering the whole drive, C.J. was suddenly quiet.

"What's wrong?" Pam asked.

"Nothing. It's just that this looks a lot like…"

"I get it. There's no hunting shack at the end of the road and there's no drug-crazed kid who's going to shoot you."

"My head knows that," C.J. replied, "but my gut still clenches."

A driveway with a fire number matching Keane's address turned to the left. Pam slowed, then turned. Ahead was a rusty white trailer house with two cars parked near the wooden steps. After parking so Pam's cruiser blocked the cars, they climbed the steps. C.J. knocked on the door and Pam stood aside, near the hinges. After a second knock, shuffling noises came from deeper inside the trailer.

The door opened a crack and a woman glared at C.J. as the smell of tobacco and day-old garbage drifted out. "What?" The woman's brown hair was flattened on one side, like she'd just got out of bed. The dark rings under her eyes hinted that she might've had a late night.

"We'd like to talk to Raul Lopez. Please ask him to come to the door," C.J. said, trying to peek behind the woman.

"He's not here," the woman said, tugging at the hem on the men's white t-shirt she wore as a nightie.

"His car's here. Please ask him to come to the door."

After pausing a second to squint at C.J., the woman yelled over her shoulder, "Hey, Raul. There's a cop here to see you."

A man's voice came from the other end of the trailer, "Tell him to go away."

"He doesn't want to talk to you. Go away."

"Can we come in?"

"The place is a mess. Just go away."

Pam stepped closer to the door, surprising the woman who'd been focused on C.J. "Does Raul have any guns in the house?"

When the woman took a second too long to answer C.J. said, "He's a felon and prohibited from owning a firearm. How many guns are in the house?"

The woman stepped into the doorframe, pulling the door closed behind herself. "Listen, he'll kill me if…"

Pam put out her hand, "Come with us. You'll be safe."

"I'm with him. I'll be okay if you just leave."

C.J. put her hand on the woman's shoulder and gently guided her down the steps. "If he's in possession of firearms, it's a federal crime. He'll be back in prison for a long time."

When her feet hit the dirt, the woman stopped and looked at the trailer where a dirty drape was pulled aside exposing a man's eye and beard. "You don't know what he's capable of."

Pam pushed the woman toward her car and C.J. drew her pistol, holding it at her side as she backed away, shielding Pam and Candy Keane as they ran toward the cars. The trailer door flew open just as Pam pushed Candy into the back seat.

Raul wore striped boxers under his stained wife-beater t-shirt. He raised a black pistol and aimed it at C.J. as she ducked behind one of the two beat up cars parked in front of the trailer. "Bring Candy back and drive away."

C.J. leaned on the car's trunk, supporting her pistol in both hands. Car doors slammed behind her and Pam called dispatch, requesting backup. "Drop the gun, Raul."

"Leave Candy and drive away, bitches, and I'll let you live to see your kids again."

"Put the gun down or I'm going to shoot," C.J. yelled, lining up the Glock's sights on Raul's chest as he squared himself on the wooden landing outside the door.

The report of Raul's pistol was masked by the sound of the shattering windshield of Pam's cruiser. Startled by the breaking glass, C.J. flinched and pulled her shot right, breaking the window in the storm door. Raul dashed right and C.J.'s second shot was behind him. She could see Raul running through the windshield of the car she was using for cover.

With things seemingly in slow motion, C.J. moved behind the car she was using for cover. Pam took two shots from behind the cruiser, but not until Raul had fired wildly at C.J.: one shot flying over her head, the second shattering the driver's window slightly to her right. Raul disappeared behind the other beater car as Pam radioed the urgent message, "Shots fired! Officer needs assistance."

The dispatcher relayed the message over the state-wide frequency and police units responded with their locations. C.J. rolled her eyes as she realized the closest backup was in downtown Moose Lake, at least fifteen minutes away.

"Shit, somebody will be dead before another cop arrives," she muttered to herself before peeking over the trunk of the car shielding her. She saw the trunk of Pam's cruiser pop open, and assumed it was being used for cover.

"Candy!" Raul shouted. "Get out of the cop car!"

"She's locked inside," Pam replied. "Throw down your gun and put your hands up!"

Pam's order was answered with three shots that banged into the open lid of her car's trunk. C.J. couldn't see Raul, who was hidden behind the other car, but remembered Kurt Olson's admonition about providing covering fire when they were at the Markville arrest. She fired half a dozen shots into the windows of the car hiding Raul, hoping the glass would rain down and distract him from Pam and Candy.

With her ears ringing, C.J. registered the sound of pounding and saw Candy's fists pounding on the window of Pam's cruiser. Candy was yelling, but her pleas were muffled by the car. C.J. recognized the sound of Pam's shotgun pumping to chamber a shell and sighed in relief that Pam hadn't been injured in the exchange of gunfire.

Raul's gun appeared over the trunk of the Buick, firing wild unaimed shots that broke glass in the Chevy shielding C.J. As soon as they stopped, C.J. popped up and leaned on the Chevy's trunk, aiming her gun at the Buick and awaiting Raul's next move.

Raul sprinted toward Pam's cruiser and C.J. fired as he ran, but all the shots flew behind him. She held her fire as he stood next to the cruiser's door where Candy was cursing and pounding on the window. He yanked on the locked door, screaming a stream of Spanish expletives while waving his pistol.

Pam scurried from the back of her cruiser to the side away from Raul and pressed her back against the door opposite Raul. "Where is he?" she shouted to C.J.

"Opposite side of your car. He's trying to open the door."

With horror, C.J. watched Raul raise his pistol and point it at Candy. "NO!!!"

The window in front of Candy exploded and her head jerked back. C.J. fired through Pam's windshield until her Glock's slide locked open when the magazine was empty. She desperately yanked a spare from her duty belt, ejected the empty magazine, slapped the new one into the butt of the gun, and chambered a round. When she looked up, Raul was out of sight.

"Cover me!" Pam yelled as she rolled onto her stomach, aiming the shotgun under the cruiser.

The shotgun blast was muffled by the car, but Raul screamed in pain. Pam pumped the shotgun and fired again as C.J. raced around the front of Pam's cruiser.

The scene was gruesome. Raul was on his back, writhing in the dirt, his right foot twisted at a ninety-degree angle to his body. His ankle was a shattered mass of bone chips, muscle and sinew. A piece of his thigh muscle, the size of a softball, was gone, like a bear had bitten if from his leg muscle.

In obvious pain from his injuries, C.J.'s appearance gave him a jolt of adrenaline and he searched frantically for his pistol, which was just out of reach. Only feet away, C.J. leveled her gun at his chest and drew a breath, waiting for his fingers to touch the gun.

Pam dashed from the rear of her cruiser and stepped on his wrist, while pointing the shotgun at his belly. "You're done."

Raul flopped onto his back, slamming his free hand against the car. "Shoot me! I'm not going back to prison. Just pull the trigger." He lifted his head and looked at C.J. Through gritted teeth he seethed. "You. Bitch. Pull the trigger. Do it!"

"I'd love to see you rot in hell," she said, edging around out of Raul's reach. She kicked his gun into the weeds. "But I think rotting in a stinking prison cell while hobbling around with only one foot is better."

Raul's eyes froze on her. "One foot?"

C.J. glanced at Raul's injured foot. "Your ankle is hamburger. I think I'll watch while the doctor cuts your foot off."

Lifting his leg to look at his foot took every ounce of Raul's energy. He looked at his ankle, not comprehending the sight. He flopped back and looked up at Pam. "Do it. Pull the trigger."

Pam raised the shotgun and held the butt against her hip. "Not today."

Grabbing desperately for Pam's foot, Raul pulled himself across the gravel. She danced back out of his reach. C.J. reached down and pulled his right arm behind his back and clipped a handcuff on it. When he resisted, she put upward pressure on his elbow until he relaxed so she could cuff his other wrist.

A siren wailed in the distance as the radio continued to announce the location and ETA of the Moose Lake Police, state patrol, and Deputy Sandy Maki who'd heard the request for assistance from the opposite side of the county.

C.J. stood up, then saw the broken car window to her left. "Candy!" She lunged to the car and looked inside. Candy was curled in a fetal position with her knees pulled to her chest, covered with tiny cubes of broken glass. "Are you okay?"

Opening her eyes, Candy looked at C.J. "Am I dead?"

"You're alive. Did the bullet hit you?"

Shaking glass fragments from her hair and brushing them from the T-shirt, she composed herself. "I don't think so."

Pam announced the situation and requested an ambulance as a Moose Lake SUV roared down the road, passing the driveway, then backing up. The officer jumped out, drawing his gun. "Are you guys okay?"

C.J. nodded. "All the good guys are okay." She nodded toward Raul. "He needs a ride to the hospital."

Pam helped Candy out of her cruiser. Standing next to the car, Candy realized that the t-shirt wasn't covering her butt and she tugged at the hem. "Candy, why did Raul try to shoot you?"

Crossing her arms, Candy shivered. "Probably because I know he was hired to kill Roger Bartlett."

Chapter 16

C.J. and Pam sat in the sheriff's guest chairs as he paced the floor with the door closed. He'd been pacing for several minutes without saying anything and C.J. wondered what was going to happen when he finally erupted. His cell phone ring interrupted whatever was coming. He grunted and sighed several times before thanking the caller and ending the call.

"That was the BCA shooting investigation team." Sepanen turned to C.J. "You're the only one who discharged a pistol, right?"

"Well, the suspect and me."

"Fine, the suspect and you. But not Pam. Correct?"

Pam nodded. "I fired the shotgun."

The sheriff put up his hand. "We'll get to that in a moment." He turned back to C.J. "The BCA guy said they've never seen that many spent cartridges at a shooting scene without two or three wounded people being carted off to the hospital. He asked when you'd last fired your pistol on the range."

"With all due respect, sir. The suspect was running, and I was providing cover fire for Pam…"

The sheriff put up his hand. "How many rounds did you discharge, Charlene?"

"I'm not exactly sure. I emptied one magazine, reloaded, and fired part of the second magazine."

The sheriff pinched the bridge of his nose. "And you never hit the suspect?"

"No, sir."

After blowing out a breath, the sheriff resumed his pacing. "Pam, why did you shoot the second shot?"

"I assumed the suspect was still armed and presented a danger to Sergeant Jensen and myself."

"This isn't a formal hearing. You can refer to Charlene by name."

"She prefers C.J., Sheriff."

"I know that! She told me her mother called her Charlene when she was in trouble."

C.J. lifted her hand. "In Deputy Ryan's defense, she was looking under her car and couldn't see the suspect's hands."

"I spoke with the Moose Lake ER doctor after he airlifted Lopez to Duluth. He's sure they'll amputate Lopez's foot, and the channel ripped through his quadriceps is ragged and will have to be cleaned up. He'll need skin grafts and months of therapy."

C.J. glanced at Pam when the sheriff tipped his head back and closed his eyes. "Are we in trouble, John?" C.J. asked.

"I told you two not to get into any confrontations without backup."

Pam leaned forward. "We were backing up each other."

Clasping his hands on his desk, as if trying to keep from throwing something, the sheriff tilted his head. "I think that's what irritates me more than anything." He looked up. "You did exactly what I've asked of you, and it almost got the two of you killed."

"We're fine, John," C.J. said. "There was a lot of shooting, but the only one who suffered a gunshot wound was Lopez. I think it went really well."

One corner of the sheriff's mouth crinkled upward, and he leaned back. "It did. You two were spectacular."

Pam threw up her hands. "Then why are you calling us on the carpet?"

"Because you could've been killed along with Lopez's girlfriend. You were very lucky."

C.J. shook her head.

"What?" The sheriff asked. "You don't think you were lucky?"

"John, we were good. Very good. We're well-trained, seasoned officers who know how to handle a difficult situation. We did exactly what we were trained to do, and the result was the rescue of a hostage and arrest of a murderer. That's one hell of a good day."

"It was a good result, but next time, could you please do it without all the drama? How about a nice quiet arrest? Cuff the suspect and bring him in for questioning without the shootout. Okay?"

"In our defense," Pam said, raising her hands, "that was the plan. But it's like the old quote from General Patton, 'the battle plan goes to pieces when the first shot is fired.'"

"I know."

They all turned toward the door when they heard scratching. A moment later, the door flew open, and a basset hound raced into the office dragging her leash. Bailey paused only long enough to identify C.J. before racing to her and trying to crawl onto her lap.

Travis, Pam's husband, walked in holding the baby. "Sorry, I couldn't hold Bailey back any longer."

The sheriff stood and put out his hand to Travis. "Your wife and C.J. had quite a day."

"I caught the radio news on the way down. They only said two Pine County deputies were involved in a shooting and a suspect was in custody."

"Pam can explain it to you over the next week while she's on leave during the shooting investigation."

Travis looked between Pam and C.J. "You're both okay?"

Pam took Luke and pushed Travis toward the door. "We're fine."

"Are you ready to go home?" Travis asked.

Pam looked at C.J. and the sheriff, "I need to interview Candy Keane. I think she's ready to throw Raul under the bus."

Travis shook his head. "I think you need to let some adrenaline burn off. Talk to her tomorrow."

Pam kissed Luke's head. "Candy might have a change of heart by tomorrow. I need to talk to her now, while the memory of staring down the barrel of Raul's gun is fresh in her mind."

Nodding, the sheriff stood. "Pam's right. She needs to talk to Candy before she has a chance to change her mind. Can you take Bailey, too? C.J. needs to stay here a while longer."

Travis bent down and picked up Bailey's leash. "I understand the need for an after-action debriefing. But, I also know that your two combatants are going to crash and need to recover."

"I agree, but they still have several irons in the fire."

Travis and Pam walked out. The sheriff closed the door behind them and turned to C.J. "Stay here a minute. I've got a message to call a guy from Immigration Customs Enforcement."

Pulling one of the guest chairs close to the desk, C.J. asked, "Did the message give you a reason for the call?"

"There's nothing on the message slip except a name, the agency, and a phone number." After dialing, the sheriff switched the phone to speaker mode.

"ICE, Roy Pollack."

The sheriff introduced himself and explained he was on the speakerphone with Sergeant Jensen.

"Perfect, I was planning to ask permission to borrow Sergeant Jensen."

"Why do you need her?"

"I don't need her. I thought she'd like to be part of our operation at Pigeon River tonight."

C.J. leaned forward. "This is C.J. What's happening at the border?"

"You haven't spoken with the Crown Court?"

Digging out her cell phone, C.J. said, "Not recently. What's happening?"

"You probably have a message. We were contacted by the Ontario Provincial Police. They have a joint operation with the Canadian Revenue Agency tracking untaxed liquor. A truck loaded with untaxed booze is being filled with tires in Thunder Bay. Their informant says once the truck is loaded, it'll be crossing the border at Pigeon

River, en route to the Askov Tire Company. We plan to keep the truck under surveillance from the border to its final destination, Askov. I assume the load will be broken down and distributed there."

C.J. leaned close to the phone. "They're smuggling booze in the tire trucks? That hardly seems worth the risk."

Pollack laughed. "A liter of booze represents five dollars of federal and state taxes. The informant says they've loaded 1,200 cases of Canadian whiskey on the truck. That's $70,000 of untaxed booze. They're shipping two loads a month, so that represents nearly $1,500,000 a year in taxes."

"What do you need from us?" C.J. asked.

"Keep all your deputies away from Askov for the next twelve hours. We've got teams following the trucks. I'd like to meet with Sergeant Jensen. We need to find a location for a surveillance team to watch the tire company."

The sheriff leaned close to the phone. "This is Sheriff Sepanen. Let me make something very clear, Pollack. The Pine County Sheriff's Department will be part of this operation and our agency will receive credit for our contribution when it closes."

"Sheriff, we've been working this with the Canadian Revenue, the Crown Court, and the Ontario Provincial Police for over a year. This is purely a courtesy call…"

"Pollack, Sergeant Jensen is investigating a murder involving the owners of the tire company."

"Okay, please step back from the investigation until we close this operation."

Smiling at C.J., the sheriff picked up the phone receiver and disabled the speaker. "Listen Pollack, if you want us to play nice, then we're either partners or we're going to pursue our murder investigation with vigor. Based on an arrest Sergeant Jensen made this afternoon, I assume we'll have enough evidence to arrest the owner of the tire company tonight." The sheriff leaned back and listened, smiling. "That's just fine, Pollack. But, we're either on your team, or we move ahead with our murder investigation and make arrests. It's your call."

C.J. watched the sheriff and thought, *"I've never seen anyone stand up to feds like this."*

The sheriff punched the speaker button. "Let's run through the plan with Sergeant Jensen."

Sighing, Pollack paused. "I'll leave Minneapolis in a few minutes. Let's meet somewhere close to Askov. From there, I'd like to drive around Askov in a vehicle that doesn't look like a cop car and find a location for our surveillance team."

The sheriff opened his desk's lap drawer and pulled out a key ring. He slid it to C.J. "We just seized a Range Rover from a drug dealer. I just handed the keys to Sergeant Jensen. Come to the sheriff's department entrance to the courthouse. You and C.J. can drive to Askov from here." After ending the call, the sheriff leaned back and laced his fingers behind his head. "Let's see what Pam gets from Raul's girlfriend. If she implicates Bartlett's wife, we'll have even more leverage with the feds."

Fingering the Range Rover keys, C.J. paused. "I'm not sure what role I'm supposed to play in this?"

"Carve a role for yourself. Don't let Pollack bully you."

Standing, C.J. looked sheepish. "A lot happened today. Are we okay?"

"Charlene, you...did very well today." Sepanen stood and put out his hand. "We're lucky to have you."

C.J. felt red creeping up her cheeks. "Thanks." She took a step toward the door. "My uniform's a mess and I'm sweaty."

The sheriff went to the filing cabinet in the corner of his office and opened the bottom drawer. He took out a tan knit shirt and tossed it to C.J. "There's a badge embroidered on the chest. I wear them when I dress casually."

Unfolding the shirt, C.J. looked at the collar. "This is a man's extra large."

"Do you want a clean shirt or not?"

"I do. Thanks."

"You can keep it."

Holding it up, C.J. looked at the shirt that was two or three sizes too large. "Maybe it'll shrink if I run the dryer extra hot."

With a dismissive wave, the sheriff said, "Whatever."

* * *

After pulling on the knit shirt, C.J. gathered the excess fabric and tucked into her waistband and smoothed the front. The bathroom door opened and Pam appeared in the mirror. "Be careful if you run into Igor today."

"Why?"

"That shirt makes you look like a woman."

C.J. snorted. "I'll wear my vest over it and no one will know I have boobs."

Pam's smile spread. "You should wear it when you go out with Eddie. I think he'd appreciate your look."

"I doubt that Eddie thinks of me as anything but his drinking buddy."

"Don't be too sure of that," Pam replied.

The ringing of C.J.'s phone interrupted the conversation, giving her a chance to exit the uncomfortable topic. "Sergeant Jensen," she said without looking at the caller ID.

"McMurtrie here with an update on Callahan's Canadian activities."

C.J. exited the bathroom and retreated to a back corner of the empty bullpen. "I had a message from US Immigration Customs Enforcement. An officer is coming up. We're going to look for locations he can use to watch the tire company."

"I'm glad they contacted you. The Ontario Provincial Police are following a semi that recently departed the Thunder Bay tire graveyard. Our informant confirmed that there's a load of untaxed whiskey hidden in the truck. We'll keep an eye on it until it passes US customs at Pigeon River, then it's your case."

"Thanks for the update. It sounds like ICE is going to allow me to watch their operation."

McMurtrie's chuckle surprised C.J. "I've heard that your federal agencies are rather parochial. If it's of any consolation, your name is on the top of my list of key collaborators in this operation. When we're done, your sheriff will receive a letter of thanks with a copy going to US Customs."

"That should frost their undies."

A hearty laugh followed. "What a clever turn of phrase. I've never heard that before."

"Sorry. I probably shouldn't have let that slip."

"Sergeant, your candor is refreshing. Good luck dealing with your Customs people. Let me know how the operation goes."

"I'm sure the ICE people will keep you informed."

"I imagine we'll get a formal announcement of the operation's success through the channels. I'd appreciate a phone call when you wrap things up."

"I've got your number on speed dial."

C.J. was about to hang up when McMurtrie added, "Sergeant, these are not nice people. Be safe."

"Thank you."

* * *

Google Earth's view of Askov was a satellite view taken during the summer some years earlier. Trees obscured much of the area around the Askov Tire Company, but the parking lot and buildings were visible, as were five vehicles behind the building and a semi trailer backed up to the loading dock. C.J. leaned back and studied the view.

Her concentration was broken when Pam looked over her shoulder. "You know, I bet you could look at a 1940 picture of Askov and it'd look the same."

"Yeah, the only changes would be the names on the mailboxes."

"I bet half of them are the same, too," Pam said, edging closer to the screen. "What are you looking for?"

Pointing out the tire company's building, C.J. said, "I need to find a place where the ICE agents can set up surveillance of the Canadian delivery."

"Engquist's barn is just east of the tire company, across their hay field."

Zooming in on the area, C.J. looked at the barn. "That's a forty-acre field away from the tire company's parking lot."

"A surveillance team is going to have a hard time finding cover anywhere closer. The bar on Highway 23 is always busy, so a team parked there will stick out like a beacon, and there are open fields in almost every other direction."

"I think we should set them up in the swamp, here." C.J. said, pointing to the dense cover slightly east and across the road from the tire company.

Pam stifled a laugh. "Sure, set them up in a swamp so they're knee-deep in muddy water. Then tell them they have to wear camouflage even though there will be deer hunters all around them."

With her eyes sparkling, C.J turned. "Do you think we could find a pair of antlers for one of them to wear? We'll tell them it'll make them blend in."

The sheriff cleared his throat as he placed his cup in the coffee maker. "You two are having too much fun with this."

"Don't you think it'd be fitting to dress up one of the feds in a deer suit while they're watching the tire company from the swamp across the road?"

The coffee machine gurgled as the sheriff shook his head. "As tempting as that may be…"

"I think we'll tell Engquists we want to use their hayloft as the surveillance location," C.J. said.

"That's probably a good choice. Old Arnie Engquist will love having that story to tell his buddies next week."

"Do you think he and his wife will be willing to keep it a secret until the operation is over?" Pam asked.

The sheriff nodded. "They're stoic old Danes. I'm sure they can keep a secret for a week. I can almost hear Arnie telling his buddies how the feds threatened him if he told anyone about them hiding in his barn."

Chapter 17

The dispatcher paged C.J. to the security door. After shutting down her computer, she walked to the back of the building and opened the door for a tall man dressed in casual clothing. His hair was dark, graying at the temples, and he was trim. "Sergeant Jensen?"

"Please call me C.J."

"I'm Roy Pollack."

"Would you like a cup of coffee?"

"Actually, I could use a restroom. I've been drinking Mountain Dew for the last several hours."

Pam watched C.J. lead Pollack to the restroom. "C.J., did you notice if he was wearing a wedding ring?"

Giving Pam *the look,* C.J. wrinkled her nose. "You know, if any of the guys said that to me, I'd file a harassment claim."

"I'm just trying to fill Floyd's role as the source of inappropriate and off-color comments."

Pollack exited the men's room and C.J. led him to her desk. "I've done some research," she said, pulling up Google Earth. "This is the tire company, with the loading dock here. There aren't a lot of places to put a surveillance team. Askov is a small town and any unfamiliar vehicle is going to stand out like a lighthouse beacon."

Squatting down next to C.J., Pollack looked at the satellite picture. "How about this wooded area across the road?"

Pollack looked at Pam when she snickered. "C.J. and I looked at that, but it's deer hunting season. Your team wouldn't be safe in that swamp unless they were wearing blaze orange coats."

"Ah," Pollack said. "That's the value of local knowledge."

"There's a barn across this field. It's a quarter mile from the tire company building, but it has an unobstructed view of the loading dock and parking lot."

"That could work. We'll set up Gail and Red with an infrared spotting scope and a sound dish. They'll be able to see people moving inside the truck and hear their conversation. Can you print out that view?"

C.J. punched keys to transfer the file to the printer and stood.

"I think the barn will work nicely. Red's a farm girl and she'll feel right at home with a cattle barn. Gail will complain about the smell but will tolerate it."

Pam looked over from her desk. "You have an all-female surveillance team?"

"Yeah, they're great. They have the patience to sit through surveillance. My entry teams are ex-athletes. Most of the guys prefer more action than surveillance."

Pam rolled her eyes at C.J. who quickly ushered Pollack to the door. "Shall we take a drive?"

"Sure. Have you found a vehicle that doesn't look like a police car?"

With the key ring from the sheriff in her hand, C.J. said, "There's no cop in this county who drives a Range Rover."

"Perfect! Let's go."

C.J. pulled on her coat and carried her vest to the parking lot. "When does your surveillance team arrive?"

"They're on the road and should be in Pine City in half an hour. How far are we from Askov?"

"It's less than half an hour to Banning Junction and another ten minutes to Askov. Can you tell them to bypass Pine City and meet us at Banning Junction?"

Pollack made the call as C.J. drove from the courthouse to I-35. "They'll meet us in forty-five minutes. Is that enough time for us to scope out the area and get back?"

"If you recall the satellite view of Askov, there's not much to the town. We can drive down every street in the entire town in ten minutes."

"Ah, I see what you mean about a strange vehicle standing out. I'm used to dealing with the Twin Cities where it's easy to be anonymous. A strange face may stand out if they're walking in a neighborhood, but most times, if we put an agent on the street with a dog on a leash and a cell phone to his ear, no one gives them a second look."

"Do you have dogs for your agents to walk?"

"We have dogs to sniff drugs, bombs, and people trying to enter the country illegally. All of them live with their handlers, so they're happy to walk around on a leash."

"I never considered that."

"The guys are loading their heavy body armor and loading the chase vehicles. The plan is to let the suspects transfer the booze to a truck. One team will track them to their delivery point and an entry team stays here to arrest the truck driver and whoever helps with the unloading."

"Your entry team are former athletes?"

"I like to have team members who control the scene. They're big, they come in loud, and the party's over."

"Gail and Red aren't on the entry or tracing teams?"

"They fit better in a surveillance role. I don't want them to get hurt if things get ugly."

C.J. grimaced and drove in silence for a mile. Pollack didn't seem to notice her anger.

"Have you always worked in rural law enforcement, C.J.?"

"I was a Cloquet PD officer for my early career. I was on the regional emergency response team for eleven years." Pollack nodded, apparently not registering C.J's tactical credentials and experience."

"We're driving quite a way. How big is Pine County?"

"The county is 1,400 square miles. It takes forty-five minutes to drive from corner to corner."

"Really? Pine County is larger than the entire Twin Cities."

C.J. nodded. "You've got two million people and we've got ten thousand swamps."

"Do you think we'll have a problem getting permission to use the barn for surveillance?"

"I think the Engquists will be delighted to have a story to tell their friends when the operation is over." C.J. paused. "I had a call from the Canadian Crown Court just before you arrived. The truckload of tires is on its way to the border. They've got people on it. McMurtrie said their informant confirmed that there's a load of untaxed whiskey in the back."

Pollack turned toward C.J. "The information about the contents of the load and the informant is extremely sensitive. I hope you..."

"I understand and respect the confidentiality of the information. I'm not a country hick who's going to blow your operation by bragging about it to my friends in a bar."

"Thank you."

* * *

The drive through Askov took less than three minutes. Pollack looked over his shoulder as they passed the bar at the north end of town. "That's the whole town?"

"That's it," C.J replied. "Keep your eyes open; we'll be passing the tire company in about thirty seconds. If you blink, you'll miss it."

Slowing slightly, but trying not to draw attention, C.J. rolled past the tire plant. A single yard light hung over the west parking lot and two lights lit the opposite side, over the loading dock.

"That's it?"

"Now look left, you'll see the swamp we talked about as a potential surveillance location."

"That's woods, and we're only a half mile outside town."

"You've seen it all. I'm going to turn around in the driveway ahead. We'll look like a couple 'citiots' who got lost."

"Citiots?"

"That's short for city idiot. It's what the locals call the people from the Twin Cities who rush around like whatever they're doing is the most important thing in the world."

"Huh. I'll have to remember that. What's the best way for us to blend in if we're up here for surveillance?"

"You'll be obvious unless you drive rusty pickups, dress in bib overalls, and wear dusty caps with a seed or tractor company logo."

Pollack stared at C.J. "You're not serious."

"Look quick, we're passing the tire company again."

"That place looks like it's made of metal sheeting nailed to two-by-fours."

"It's actually a pole barn. They drive long posts, like telephone poles in the ground and then build a frame around them." C.J. paused. "Where are you from? You've never heard of a pole barn?"

"It's not a thing in L.A."

"Take a look at the vehicles in the bar parking lot. If you want to fit in, that's what you'll need."

Pollack shook his head. "Older American cars and dusty pickups."

"Yes. People drive their vehicles for a long time. I don't know anyone who buys a new car or gets a three-year lease. You'll also notice a lot of Chevys, Fords, and Jeeps. It's a long way to the nearest Toyota or Jaguar dealer."

"We've got SUVs."

"Big shiny SUVs that look like they just came out of the car wash?"

"I suppose so."

C.J.'s cell phone rang as they got to town. She pulled into a parking spot on the deserted main street and answered while Pollack gawked at the closed stores. "Hi John, what's up?"

"I spoke with Marvel Engquist. They're expecting you."

"They're okay with their barn being used for surveillance?"

Sepanen laughed. "They're delighted. Marvel is making coffee and putting a pan of sweet rolls in the oven. The rolls should be ready by the time you get there."

"Well, that should just about blow Mr. Pollack's mind. Thanks for calling ahead." C.J ended the call and pulled back onto the road.

Pollack looked at her. "What's going to blow my mind?"

"The people who own the barn are making coffee and baking sweet rolls for us."

"Yeah, right."

Turning toward Pollack as they drove through Askov's small residential area. "We're guests. Act like you appreciate it."

"I enjoy country humor."

C.J. shook her head as she turned into Engquist's driveway. "You have so much to learn."

Marvel Engquist met them at the door and introduced herself. The aroma of fresh baked rolls and coffee drifted out of the house. "Come in. I've set out some cups and plates." She held the door open for them. "Arnie's out checking the barn and moving some hay bales in the loft so there's a place to hide while you look across the field."

Pollack wiped his feet on the doormat. "Actually, I'd like to look at the barn."

Marvel, wearing jeans and a t-shirt, looked younger than her seventy-eight years. "Have a cup of coffee and a roll while we wait for Arnie. He'll be just a few minutes and I'm sure he'll want to talk to you before taking you to the barn."

C.J. nodded toward the kitchen table where an aluminum pan held freshly frosted cinnamon rolls. "Have a roll."

C.J. poured coffee into three mugs while Marvel lifted steaming rolls out of the pan and slid them onto plates. The frosting ran off the warm rolls and puddled on the dessert plates.

"I have half and half if you want cream in your coffee."

"Black is fine," Pollock said, examining the huge roll C.J. had passed to him.

"I like to butter the layers as I peel them off." C.J. accepted the butter dish and passed it to Pollack. "My folks had dairy cattle when I was growing up. We always drank whole milk and Mom put butter on everything."

Marvel nodded. "We're spoiled. We never got into that margarine fad, and now the doctors think butter is actually healthier than that fake butter."

The back door creaked and Arnie Engquist stepped in. He nodded at the guests and pulled off a pair of knee-high rubber boots before slipping off a canvas Carhartt coat. "I see Marvel's already feeding you."

Pollack and C.J. stood and introduced themselves. "Thanks for letting us use your barn," Pollack said.

Arnie sat and poured coffee for himself. "I'm pleased to meet an actual federal agent. I always pay my income taxes and wonder where all that money goes. Now, here you are, spending my tax money." Marvel set a roll in front of Arnie, who looked like he'd eaten a lot of Marvel's good cooking, his buttons straining to contain his ample belly.

302

C.J. wiped frosting from her fingers. "I understand the sheriff called and asked if we could use your barn. How much did he explain to you?"

Marvel shook her head. "He only said that the sheriff's department was working with the feds on a sting at the tire company and that our barn might be a good place to keep an eye on their building."

Pollack's slight grimace indicated his discomfort with the amount of information the sheriff had shared. "I hope you understand that this is extremely confidential."

Arnie nodded. "Yup. The sheriff told me we couldn't say a thing about you guys being here until we read about it in the newspaper."

Placing her hand flat on the table, C.J. put on her most earnest face. "We're relying on your discretion. Any leak could ruin a big federal bust."

Marvel and Arnie exchanged looks. "We understand. If there's a leak, it won't be from us." Arnie sipped his coffee, then added. "We've got a line of sight from the hay loft to the tire company across our hay field, but it's a quarter mile away. Is that close enough?"

Pollack nodded. "We have optics and electronics that will function over that distance. We need you to go on with your usual day-to-day activities, just as if we weren't here."

Marvel nodded and lifted her eyebrows. "Are you two going to be the ones watching?"

"I've got two surveillance specialists on the way from Minneapolis. They'll set up their gear as soon as they arrive. That way they'll be in place before we expect anything to happen at the tire company."

Leaning his elbows on the table, Arnie addressed himself to Pollack. "It's those damn convicts they're using over there, isn't it? I mean, who runs a legitimate business and hires a bunch of guys fresh out of prison?"

Pollock finished his roll. "I'm afraid I can't get into the specifics of our operation."

Marvel smiled, her eyes twinkling. "See, Arnie. I told you they wouldn't be able to tell us anything about what they're doing."

Arnie waved Marvel off. "Are they smuggling in Chinese workers in those tire trucks? I see that they're coming from Canada and I read that Canada is taking in a lot of Chinese people."

"Like I said, I really can't comment on our specific operation."

"Leave him be, Arnie," Marvel said.

"You don't have to comment. You can just nod your head if it's a Chinese smuggling thing."

C.J. grinned as she watched Pollack squirm and try to deflect the conversation.

"My team is arriving in a big Chevy SUV. Is there somewhere they can park their vehicle out of sight?"

"Oh sure. I'll move the tractor and they can park in the barn."

"The surveillance team is two of my very experienced agents, Gail and Colleen, who we call Red. They're totally self-sufficient, so please go on with your daily activities and pretend they're not even there."

Marvel frowned. "There's no bathroom in the barn. They'll have to come into the house."

Pollack put up his hands. "They'll be okay. Like I said, just ignore them."

That response was unacceptable to Marvel. "It may be okay for guys to pee behind the barn, but you tell your ladies to just slip in the house when nature calls." Marvel paused. "I've got a Thermos I can fill with coffee. They can..."

"Please," Pollack said. "They'll have everything they need."

"I don't want them having to pee in a bucket. That's just...un-ladylike. You tell them to come in here where it's private and warm."

Seeing no way to win, Pollack nodded. "I'll let them know that they're welcome to use your toilet."

Marvel nodded. "Will they come in for meals, or should I put together sandwiches that Arnie can take to them in the barn?"

Unable to contain herself, C.J laughed, then pretended she was coughing into her napkin.

"They'll have their own food and drink. You really don't need to provide them with anything. It'd be best if neither of you were seen going in and out of the barn during the surveillance."

Arnie frowned. "I thought you wanted us to carry on as normal. I have to go into the barn to put out hay and feed the cattle."

"That's fine if that's your routine. I just don't want any abnormal activity."

"Well, that may be a problem," Arnie said.

"What do you mean?"

"Cattle are curious. They might gather around the hay loft to check out your team."

Pollack closed his eyes, envisioning cattle gathered outside the barn, staring at the hay loft. "Can you move the cattle inside while my team is in the hayloft?"

Arnie rubbed his nose. "That wouldn't be normal."

C.J. decided to comment. "Let's just see how the cattle react. Maybe people at the tire company won't notice the cattle acting differently from a quarter mile away."

Pollack's cell phone rang, and he excused himself. He stood in the entryway, speaking softly, then he gestured to C.J. When she walked over, he handed her the phone. "Gail is in Askov and wants directions here."

Ten minutes later, Gail and Red, dressed in camouflage fatigues, were sitting at Engquist's kitchen table eating rolls and drinking coffee. Marvel was explaining her plan for discreet access to the bathroom and trying to talk them into a chicken dinner for their meal. Arnie eventually led everyone to the hayloft and the nest of hay bales he'd arranged to provide a discreet viewing location from the upper floor of the barn.

Arnie moved his tractor and Gail pulled the Suburban into the barn and they carried their equipment to the loft where Colleen and Gail set it up.

Pollack turned to C.J. as she drove out of Engquist's driveway. "Did I just witness 'Minnesota nice?'"

C.J. smiled. "Engquists are especially sweet people. Not everyone is as accommodating as Marvel and Arnie."

"They were warmer than most of my relatives," Pollack said. "I thought Marvel was going to hug me when we left."

"You wouldn't have gotten out of my parent's house without having a beer with my father. It's just not allowed."

"I need a place to stage my other teams. What do you suggest?"

C.J. considered the question. "I think you need to have them gather somewhere out-of-town. They'll stand out anywhere in Askov. There's a grocery store in Sandstone. I think they could gather in Chris' Foods parking lot and not spook anyone in Askov."

"Take me there…please."

C.J. smiled. "I'll have you saying 'ya sure, you betcha,' before you leave."

"I sincerely doubt I can reproduce that mild *Fargo* accent Engquists have."

Chapter 18

The rest of the ICE team arrived in the empty grocery store parking lot. The four vehicles gathered near the car wash. As Pollack had suggested, the young men unfolding themselves from the two cars and two SUVs looked like they'd all been high school or college athletes. Pollard stepped out of C.J.'s cruiser and handed her a radio. "Yell if something breaks at the farm or with the team following the truck.

With Pollack gone, C.J. keyed the mic. "Hay loft team, this is Pine County. How are you doing?"

"C.J., our hosts are killing us. Arnie's been out twice to make sure we're okay. The second time he brought coffee and two sweet rolls. We're struggling to stay awake after the sugar rush fades."

"The team from Minneapolis is here and staging. These guys are beefy."

"As much as we'd like to be part of the takedowns, I'd rather have one of those young bucks dodging bullets and wrestling people to the ground."

"Roger that," C.J. responded. "Is there any activity at the tire company?"

309

"Negative. It's as quiet as a morgue."

A male voice came over the radio. "This is tag team red, our target vehicle just exited. I have to pass and team blue will pick them up" There was a pause, then, "What the hell? They turned right at the top of the exit. I thought they were going on Highway 23?"

"This is blue. Maybe they made us. They've turned south at the T. Where's that go?"

"Pine County here. They've either missed the turn, or they're cutting through Sandstone, then looping back to Banning Junction to check for a tail. Either way, I've got to reposition our entry team."

Starting her cruiser, C.J. pulled ahead to the tactical team and rolled down the passenger window. "Change in plan. The tire truck turned the wrong direction. They'll be driving through Sandstone and will pass about a block from here. Move all the vehicles behind the grocery store."

Pollack got in with C.J. "What's with the change in plan?"

"I think they're checking for a tail. Nobody would knowingly follow them into Sandstone this time of night."

"Thanks for the local knowledge. I would've been poring over a map trying to figure out what was going on as they drove by."

C.J. followed the ICE teams behind the large grocery store and turned off her engine. "Your team tailing the truck is going to stick out like a flare. I hope they pulled off."

"If they did, we might lose the truck."

"I sincerely doubt that. Unless they're planning to take a dirt road to Wisconsin, they'll be driving past us in a few minutes."

"There's no one to pick them up here."

"Tell your other team to go through Askov. Have them park in the bar parking lot. They shouldn't look out of place there, and they'll know if the truck turns toward the tire company."

"How about the following vehicle, team blue?"

"Tell them to turn off at Sandstone and gas up at the exit. We'll watch from behind the building. I can pull out after they're nearly out of sight and follow without headlights until they're on the Interstate."

"Shit, if they don't turn north, we'll be scrambling resources to figure out their next move."

"Don't panic yet. I see headlights."

Moments later, the Canadian semi lumbered out of Sandstone. C.J., parked behind the car wash, watched them pass, then followed when they were out of sight.

Pollock was anxiously clenching and unclenching his fists. "This is the worst part. Any little thing can mess up a year of work."

Gail's voice came over the radio as C.J. followed the semi's taillights. "A white van just turned into the east tire company parking lot and a dark-colored sedan parked on the other side. Two people got out of the sedan."

Pollack drew a breath. "Let's hope that van is the pickup vehicle."

"Team blue. The tire truck just passed us and turned north."

C.J. turned right and doubled back toward Sandstone. She turned on her 4-way flashers as they sped through the deserted town.

"What are you doing?"

"There's a back road between Sandstone and Askov. If we don't hit a deer, we'll stop half a mile south of town and let the semi pass."

"If we don't hit a deer? Are you kidding me?"

"Not entirely. They're moving around this time of night."

Pollack leaned back. "I can see it now; I survived the L.A. gangs only to die in a collision with a deer in Podunk, Minnesota."

"We're in Askov. Podunk is near Fargo."

A skunk ambled across the road and C.J. braked to avoid hitting it.

"What the hell was that?"

"You've never seen a skunk?"

"Not in L.A. or Minneapolis."

C.J killed her flashers, then drove another mile before turning off her headlights and easing to the edge of the road.

"You're parked in the road."

"Don't get your undies in a bunch. No one's going past us at this hour."

Looking over his shoulder, Pollack looked behind them. "Please tell me no one will be barrelling down this road with their headlights off."

"Nah. Most of the drunks remember to turn them on…once they get out of town."

The lights of a semi cut across the road ahead of them and C.J. put the Rover in gear without turning the headlights on.

"Sergeant, I don't know whether to believe you or not."

C.J. smiled. "Gotcha."

"I've got them," Gail reported. "The semi is in the parking lot and backing up to the loading dock. And we have lights on inside the building. The loading dock door is opening."

C.J. pulled into the bar parking lot next to a blue Camry with two people inside. "I hope these are your people and not a couple from the bar getting it on in the back seat of the Camry."

"Really?" Pollack asked. "That happens?"

"The girls all look prettier at closing time. Determined people seem to be able to

313

make use of the smallest, most uncomfortable spaces."

"This is experience speaking?" Pollack asked.

"I've seen everything on the night shift after the bars close. I wish I could get some of those images out of my mind."

Pollack nodded to the agents in the Camry as C.J. turned off the engine. "Working the San Diego border, I've seen things that turned my stomach. I can't describe the inhumane things the coyotes do to those poor people trying to sneak across the border."

Gail's voice was back on the radio. "They're rolling tires into the building. It looks like there are four people going in and out of the semi trailer."

A gray Chevy Equinox parked alongside the Camry and waved. "I take it that's team red," C.J. said.

"It is. I need to put them somewhere inconspicuous where they can follow the van after it's loaded. Do you have a suggestion?"

"If you expect the van to travel south, you could put one car in the Banning Junction motel parking lot. There were a dozen cars there when we passed. Have the other car at the garden center at the Highway 23 west exit. They could jump on I-35 there or catch 23 west if the van turned there."

Pollack got out of C.J.'s car and walked to the two tailing teams. He explained C.J.'s suggestion to them. They were backing out before Pollack was back beside C.J. "Thanks for the local knowledge, again."

"We local yokels can sometimes be useful."

"I apologize if that's the way my demeanor came across."

"What's the plan for the tire company after the van leaves?"

"The entry team will storm the building and arrest whoever's inside and seize any booze that didn't get loaded in the van."

"They've switched from unloading tires to carrying boxes to the white van. This should wrap up in the next few minutes. Is the entry team staged?"

"We're a mile north of Askov, parked on the shoulder. Let us know as soon as the van is leaving, and we'll roll."

Pollack looked at C.J. "Do you want to be there for the fireworks?"

"Hell, yes. I'll grab my vest from the back seat."

Pollack laughed. "I was kind of hoping you weren't planning to breach the door wearing a golf shirt."

"I may not be a genius, but I'm not crazy."

"The van's closing up. They're on the move. Go time."

C.J. and Pollack hunkered down and watched the van pass the bar. When its taillights disappeared, C.J. started the car. She was backing up when the ICE team vehicles flew past.

The ICE guys were already breaching the entry door on the loading dock when C.J. pulled into the parking lot. A flash-bang grenade boomed inside the building a second before the team rushed in. She was nearly out of the car when Gail's urgent voice came over the radio. "We've got gunfire on the west side."

C.J. grabbed her radio mic, "Officer needs assistance. Gunfire at the Askov Tire Company. Dispatch an ambulance and rescue."

Pollack was running across the parking lot when the building lights went out and the parking lot went black. The dispatcher was announcing their situation on the state-wide frequency when Gail's voice came over the ICE radio Pollack had left on the seat. "We have people running across the parking lot to the dark sedan. More gunshots being fired."

That announcement was followed by the urgent call on the ICE radio, "Officer down! Repeat officer down. We need medical assistance."

C.J. had one leg in the Range Rover and the other out when the dark sedan sped past the east parking lot. With no one else in sight, she slammed the door, turned on her lights, and was buckling her seatbelt as she sped toward the parking lot entrance.

Once on the road, she picked up the radio mic, "Officer down at the Askov Tire Company." Announcing her unit number and use of the impounded vehicle, she added, "I'm in pursuit of a dark sedan, eastbound out of Askov. Request backup."

With the accelerator jammed to the floor, C.J. started gaining on the sedan, still a half mile ahead of her. The sedan's brake lights flared, then the car took a hard right turn.

"Shit, shit, shit," she uttered to herself. She picked up the mic. "The sedan just turned into the house where the parolees live."

The sheriff's voice boomed over the radio, calling C.J.'s unit number. "Do not continue pursuit until backup arrives. DO. NOT. CONTINUE. PURSUIT."

C. J. braked and slowed as she neared the two-story house. Two men got out of the car as she neared the driveway. One was hobbling, and the other ran to the steps, leaving the other behind.

"Nice honor among thieves," she said to herself. She stopped, blocking the driveway, then called in the fire number of her location. Lights came on in every window and shadows moved against the blinds. There was a flash in an upstairs window, followed by the sound of a gunshot.

"What the hell is going on?"

A second window flew open, and a man was climbing out as a flash lit the room behind him. He hung, halfway out the window, for a second, then he tumbled out, landing without trying to catch himself.

She picked up the mic. "Gunfire inside the residence at my location. A shooting victim just fell from an upstairs window."

Another shot flashed in an upstairs window and a body fell through the glass and tumbled to the ground. Inside the house there was shouting followed by the sound of a gunfight.

C.J. turned into the driveway and raced to the parked cars. With her pistol drawn, she stepped out as the sheriff repeated his order for her to wait for backup. She bounded up the steps and had her hand on the doorknob when the door burst open. The momentum of the person running out slammed the door into her face, propelling her backwards off the steps. Sprawling on the ground, she saw the flash and heard the report of a shot from inside the house. To her right, she saw Charlie stagger. Three more quick shots sent him twisting to the ground.

Igor stepped onto the steps, ejecting an empty magazine, and slamming a new one into the butt of his gun. C.J. patted the ground around her, trying to find her pistol while Igor walked down the steps and shot Charlie in the forehead. C.J.'s frantic search for her gun caught Igor's attention.

He spun, then smiled. "The older lady cop. And she hasn't got a gun. How sad." Holding the gun by his side, he walked toward her. His smile sent a cold shiver down C.J.'s spine.

Crab-walking backwards, C.J. edged closer to the steps as a siren approached in the distance.

Igor sensed her interest in the siren and laughed. "Whatever's going to happen between you and me will be over long before your friends get here." In three long steps Igor was reaching down and started ripping open the Velcro straps on her vest. She batted at his hands as she crawled away, but he loomed over her. Lifting her by the last strap, Igor dropped his pistol and grabbed her by the waist.

Focusing and using the momentum of Igor's pull, C.J. twisted and plunged her right thumb into Igor's eye. Momentarily stunned, Igor let go of C.J. and let loose an inhuman howl as he grabbed his eye socket. The fall knocked the wind out of C.J., but she rolled away. Feeling something hard under her shoulder, she reached behind herself and grabbed the barrel of her pistol. Leaning back as she spun the gun, she pointed it at the center of Igor's chest and pulled the trigger over and over until the slide locked back on the empty magazine.

Igor seemed more confused than injured by the fusillade of 9mm bullets that hit him in the chest. He reached down for C.J. grabbing her shirt and lifting it. With all her strength, C.J. slammed the pistol into Igor's temple while he continued to lift her.

Fixated on his bloody eye socket, she slammed the gun against his head again. In slow motion, she started to fall, her face inches from Igor's mouth, now bubbling bloody froth.

The crush of Igor's body seemed smothering as she pushed and kicked at him. Suddenly, the burden of his weight was gone and she was staring at Kurt Olson. "Are you okay?"

C.J pushed herself up on her elbows. "I think so."

"You're covered in blood. Are you sure you weren't shot?"

"I think it's all from Igor."

Chapter 19

Pam walked into the interview room with Raul Lopez's girlfriend, who was still dressed in the clothing she'd been wearing when they'd pulled her out of the car after the shootout at her trailer. Candy Keane had dark rings under her eyes and the night in jail had aged her a decade.

"Would you like a cup of coffee or a glass of water, Ms. Keane?"

"The cup with the jail breakfast tasted like floor sweepings. Do you have a Starbucks nearby?"

"There's no Starbucks in the courthouse but let me see what I can find."

Thinking that a good cup of coffee might build trust, Pam walked to her desk and took a Starbucks pod out of a box she kept hidden in the bottom drawer of her desk after depositing Candy in the interview room. She popped it into the brewer and watched it gurgle into the paper cup.

The sheriff's bass voice startled her. "What's your plan for today?"

"I'm getting Raul Lopez's girlfriend a cup of coffee, then I'm going to hit her with questions about her knowledge of Lopez's activities."

The gurgling was followed by the sound of steam spitting out the last drops of coffee from the pod. "Do you think a hardened con like Lopez actually shared anything with her?" The sheriff snorted.

After removing the paper cup from the Keurig and picking up two sugar packets, Pam shrugged. "The worst-case scenario is that she doesn't know anything."

"She might be complicit in what happened. That'll either shut her up or have her leading you down a rabbit hole of lies." The sheriff put his cup into the machine and took out the Starbucks pod. He stared at it a second, then looked at the array of coffee pod options on the counter. "Where'd you get the Starbucks pod?"

Smiling, Pam replied, "That was the last one." She walked away wondering if the sheriff bought her white lie.

Candy looked up when Pam entered the room with the paper cup. "I found one Starbucks pod in the office." She set the coffee and sugar packets in front of Keane.

After ripping open the sugar packets and pouring them into the coffee, Lopez's girlfriend lifted the cup to her nose and inhaled deeply. "I love the smell of fresh-brewed coffee."

Pam let her savor the aroma and two sips of coffee before going on. "How long have you and Raul been together?"

"I actually met him through the mail. My boyfriend was convicted of transporting Meth from California, and I went to the Sandstone prison to see him. He was being a jerk and went on a rant, trying to get me to find a better lawyer to appeal his case. Raul was at the table next to us having a quiet conversation with his lawyer. Our eyes met and…there was like a connection. When I got home, I looked him up on the prisoner database, then wrote him a letter."

"Did Raul respond?"

"Yeah. I put my address and phone number in the letter. He called me like three days later. I could tell he was a bad boy, but there was something about him…"

"How long was that before his release?"

"I guess it was like three months that we talked and sent letters back and forth. He said he wanted to stay close to the prison after he got out, so I quit my job in the Cities and moved to Cloquet. I got a job in the paper mill and rented an apartment near the library."

"One of our deputies used to be a Cloquet cop. She said it's a nice town."

Keane sipped her coffee and shrugged. "It was okay. I mean, the people were nice enough, but I kind of like the anonymity of the Cities. People were always talking to me like they knew me, and it was kind of creepy. I mean, a neighbor asked me over for a drink. He was like sixty and I think he was hitting on me."

"What happened after Raul got out?"

"Oh wow. It was like a dream. He was really into me, and we were having sex like two or three times a day. I've never felt so appreciated and loved."

"How long did that last?"

"You know how honeymoons go. He couldn't keep his hands off me for about two weeks, then he started calling his buddies in the Cities. He'd be gone for a couple days, then he'd be back demanding that I cook and clean better. Then he hit me one night. I mean, he said I'd provoked him, and he apologized afterward. But every time he got drunk I had to hide or make sure I didn't do or say anything to anger him."

"When did he get in with the parolees in Askov?"

"I don't know. He'd talk to people on the phone, then he'd be gone for a day or two. He never told me where he was going. If I asked, he'd get mad."

"But you eventually knew he was in contact with the Askov parolees."

Keane stared into the coffee without answering.

"What's the matter?"

"I don't think I should talk about that."

"Why not? Do you feel threatened?"

After drinking the last of the coffee, Keane set the cup on the table and bit her bottom lip. "Raul said he would kill me if…"

"Raul's going to prison for a long time. If or when he gets out, he'll have a prosthetic foot and only partial use of his other leg."

"You don't understand. It's not just Raul. He has friends." Keane looked up. "Am I under arrest?"

"You're in protective custody. I can move you to a home for battered and abused women. They'll help you transition to a different life."

"Raul would still find me." Keane clasped her hands and stared at them. "What happened to Igor?"

"Is Igor one of Raul's friends who scares you?"

"He…he's scarier than Raul."

"Igor is out of the picture."

Keane looked up. "I don't understand what you mean."

"There was a federal bust last night and Igor was killed."

The woman searched Pam's eyes for any hint of prevarication. "You're not lying to me, are you?"

"No, Igor is in the Duluth morgue awaiting an autopsy."

Keane relaxed. "Raul took me to Askov. After a few drinks, he told me to go upstairs with Igor."

Pam drew a breath and steeled herself. "And you went?"

"I, ah…couldn't argue with Raul when he was drunk. He's killed people."

"What happened?"

"Igor is an animal. Use your imagination."

"Did he hurt you?"

Keane tipped her head back and stared at the ceiling. "It was worse than a nightmare."

Visions of depravity flashed through Pam's mind, taking her back to watching videos of a teacher who'd taken movies of his students and sexual conquests. She quickly shut down that line of thought. "Did Raul ever talk about the people he'd killed?"

Keane shook her head. "He made it clear that I would be the next teardrop tattoo under his eye if I ever left or disappointed him."

"He had a fresh teardrop tattoo. Do you know about that?"

When the woman looked up, her expression became hard. "Can you offer me a deal?"

"What kind of deal?"

"I can explain Raul's teardrop, but I need immunity."

After studying Keane's eyes, Pam nodded. "I'll talk to the county attorney. Would you like another cup of coffee?"

Keane slid the paper cup across the table to Pam. "Tell him I know about the tire guy's murder."

* * *

Pam held the door to the interview room for Tom Bakken, who carried in a cardboard drink caddy with four huge paper cups of coffee. Pam set a bakery bag and napkins on the table as Bakken slid a third chair to the table. In an attempt to look non-threatening, Bakken left his suitcoat in his office and shed his tie.

Keane eyed the coffee suspiciously. Then her eyes locked onto the bakery bag,

After sliding her chair up to the table, Pam opened the bag and slid it across the table. "I heard you didn't like the jail breakfast."

Keane peeked into the bag as the county attorney pulled the coffee cups out of the caddy, setting one in front of each of them. "There's no Starbucks in town, but Nicoll's makes good coffee and baked goods."

Keane removed an apple fritter from the bag and took a paper napkin from the stack on the gray metal table. She bit into the pastry and closed her eyes. "If I didn't know better, I'd think you guys had brought me a last meal before my execution."

Bakken removed the plastic lid from his coffee and took a sip. "There's no execution. Deputy Ryan was kind enough to make a dash into town for treats while I excused myself from court. She said you needed to talk to me."

Keane washed down a bite of pastry with coffee, eyeing Bakken with suspicion. "I didn't say I needed to talk to you. I told the deputy I had information I would share if she guaranteed I wouldn't be prosecuted."

"That's the message Deputy Ryan delivered to me. I'm the one who can authorize a deal for you, but only if your information is more valuable than a case against you."

Candy took another bite of apple fritter, apparently weighing Bakken's words while she chewed. "I want to talk to Deputy Ryan alone."

"She's not authorized…"

"Alone," Keane said.

Bakken stood. "I'll be outside the door if you need me."

When the door closed, Keane wiped her fingers and set the remaining half of her fritter on a napkin. "I'm not sure I can trust him."

"Tom's a straight arrow. He's never lied to nor tried to manipulate me. I trust him."

Keane didn't look convinced. "Every man in my life has used me."

"I can't imagine what you've been through," Pam said, digging a chocolate-dipped doughnut out of the bag. "I've had some crappy boyfriends, but their bullshit is nothing compared to your dealings with Raul and Igor."

Pam took a bite of doughnut, hoping the woman would open up. When she didn't, Pam added, "What's your concern about talking to Bakken? Are you afraid he'll renege on a deal if you tell him you've been on the fringes of a serious crime?"

"I didn't pull the trigger, if that's what you're asking."

"But you know that Raul did?"

Picking up the fritter, Keane took a bite off the end. "Between us girls, let's say I know exactly what happened to the tire company guy."

"Okay."

"Would that put me in prison?"

"Depending on your knowledge and involvement, it might make you an accessory before or after the fact. Those are serious offenses when we're dealing with a murder."

Keane pushed the rolls aside and reached her shackled hands across the table. Pam's instinct told her to lean away, but something in the young woman's hard eyes made her reach out. "First of all, call me Candy. Okay?"

"Okay. I'm Pam."

"Make me a promise, Pam."

"My powers in this situation are limited…"

Sighing, Candy squeezed Pam's hand. "Promise me that if I agree to tell that guy something, you'll swear that you heard him tell me I won't go to prison."

"Tom won't renege on a deal."

"No, I want *you* to promise *me* that you'll swear in court that we had a deal."

"If it comes to that, Candy, I swear I will testify to whatever deal the county attorney makes with you."

Candy nodded and leaned back. "Go get him."

* * *

After a vague discussion of the evidence Candy could provide about Roger Bartlett's murder, Bakken left the room, promising to return with a document offering Candy immunity from prosecution in matters relating to the death of Roger Bartlett in return for her information and future testimony in Raul's trial.

Pam stood when Bakken walked to the interview room door. Candy looked up. "Pam, can I use the restroom? I really need to pee."

"Sure, I could use a relief stop myself."

Pam was drying her hands when Candy exited the bathroom stall, tugging at the waist of her jeans with her shackled hands.

Candy looked at Pam in the mirror while washing her hands. "You're wearing a wedding ring. Do you have any kids?"

"I've just returned from maternity leave after having my first child."

Candy shook the excess water from her hands and pulled a paper towel out of the dispenser. "I wanted to have a kid, but I've never been with a guy who I thought would be a good father."

"Maybe you'll meet a nice guy after this gets settled."

Candy walked out of the restroom ahead of Pam and said, "I don't know how to meet a nice guy. I mean, I kind of like bad boys who make my adrenaline flow."

"I outgrew that and decided I wanted someone who'd hold me while we watched an old movie on TV."

"Isn't that kind of boring?"

Pam chuckled. "I have plenty of excitement on the job. I want to be bored when I get home."

"Maybe that's it. All my jobs have been boring, so I crave excitement when I get home."

"There's excitement that doesn't involve getting beaten or handed around to your boyfriend's buddies."

"Yeah, I never see that when we're in the honeymoon stage. It's later when things get out of control."

331

"You need a better screening plan before the honeymoon stage," Pam said, holding the interview room door.

"Or a gun."

"Um, a gun isn't a good option."

Candy shrugged. "I might kill the next sonofabitch who hits me."

"No. Make sure you never get to that point. Walk away if you have to, but don't kill the guy."

Candy stopped alongside the table and looked at Pam. "It's hard to walk away when the guy's telling you he'll kill you if you leave."

"*Oh man, am I lucky to have Travis,*" Pam thought to herself.

Holding up her hands, Candy asked. "Since I'm not under arrest, can you take the handcuffs off?"

The door opened as Pam unlocked the second cuff. With his hands full of colored folders and pens, Bakken hesitated until Candy was seated. They talked through the immunity agreement and the stipulation that Candy would testify if Raul was tried. He explained that Raul might agree to a plea agreement that would release Candy from that obligation.

Holding the pen, Candy looked at Pam. "If Raul ever gets out, I'll call you for protection."

Pam looked at Bakken who nodded. "Raul may not live through his prison sentence if he's convicted of premeditated murder. Is that what we're going to talk about?"

Candy nodded as she signed the agreements, then watched Bakken countersign them. She pushed the forms to Pam.

"Deputy Ryan doesn't need to sign them," Bakken explained.

Candy's eyes were pleading. "You will sign them, won't you, Pam?"

Turning the papers toward her, Pam scrawled her name across the bottom. "Done."

As Bakken gathered the papers and slid them into a folder, he turned on a small recorder and nodded to Candy. "In your own words, tell me about Roger Bartlett's murder."

The next half hour was Candy's monologue about Raul's past, his gang connections, his murder of an inmate, and how she'd met Raul. Pausing, Candy looked in the bakery bag and took out a cruller. "Could I have more coffee?"

Bakken pulled out his cell phone and called his office. After a short conversation, he tilted the phone. "Would McCafé be okay? It's just across the road and will be piping hot."

"I'd kill for a café au lait." Realizing what she'd said, Candy stuttered. "Bad choice of words."

Bakken waved off her apology and relayed the order. Ending the call, Bakken leaned on the table. "Tell us about Bakken's murder."

Breaking the doughnut into bite-sized pieces, Candy seemed lost, licking her fingertip and picking up the crumbs and popping them into her mouth. She looked up and seemed almost surprised that Pam and the county attorney were still there. She licked off her fingertip and wiped it on a paper napkin.

"Raul got a call one night. He didn't say who was on the phone, but he acted like it was someone who scared him a little. The only person he was ever afraid of was Igor. They'd met in prison, and I think Igor was like...Raul's protection. Is that the right word?"

"There's a prison hierarchy and groups of prisoners look out for each other," Bakken explained. "I suppose he and Igor were buddies who watched each other's backs."

"Anyway, after the call, Raul looked...pleased. I asked him why and he told me he was about to come into some money. He got mad when I asked how, so I let it go. A couple days later, he got another call. After he hung up, he told me I was part of his new job. I got nervous and asked what I was supposed to do. He smiled, in a way that gave me a chill, then he said, 'all you have to do is drop me off and pick me up.'"

"Where did you drop him off?" Bakken asked.

"On a dirt road in the middle of nowhere. He got an orange coat out of the backseat and told me to pick him up at the same spot after dark. I had no idea where I was, so I just sat there with the car idling."

"What happened when he came back?" Pam asked.

"He was all puffed up and excited. After he threw the jacket in the back seat, he told me to move over, and we drove to the house in Askov. Raul took the jacket inside and told Igor he was going to get another teardrop tattoo. Igor smiled and handed him an envelope."

"Did Raul ever say, 'I killed Roger Bartlett?"

"He didn't have to. We all knew that another teardrop tattoo meant he'd killed someone. Igor laughed and said it would be all over the news. The next day I heard about the hunter being shot by Beroun and I knew Raul was the one who pulled the trigger."

"Did you ever hear why Bartlett was killed, or who'd paid for the hit?"

"Igor made a comment about Joe not having to sneak in Caroline's back door for a nooner anymore."

The county attorney had been asking the questions, but Pam put up her finger and leaned on the table. "Was Joe Callahan having an affair with Caroline Bartlett?"

"I don't know who any of those people are. I only knew Igor and I heard a few of the other parolee's names, but that was it."

A knock on the door interrupted the interview. The coffee was steaming as promised, and Candy was so mesmerized by her café au lait that she missed the county attorney's nod to Pam that took them into the hallway.

"She can't link anyone but Raul and Igor to Bartlett's murder."

"But she opened the door a crack. Joe has to be Callahan, Bartlett's partner. And Caroline is Bartlett's wife."

The county attorney bent his head down, deep in thought. "Go pick up Caroline Bartlett. Put her in the other interview room."

"Am I arresting her?"

Bakken shook his head. "Tell her we've got information about her husband's murder. If that's not enough to motivate her to come willingly, tell her she's being held as a material witness."

"What's your plan?" Pam asked.

"Unless she's a stone-cold killer, and I doubt that she is, she'll melt when she hears Ms. Keane talking about Igor and Raul's discussion of her arrangement with

Callahan. If that doesn't do it, I'll hint that Raul is ready to bargain and name names."

* * *

Caroline Bartlett couldn't put her coat on fast enough when Pam told her they had a lead in her husband's murder case. "Who did it?"

"I'm not at liberty to say. The county attorney wants to explain the case to you."

"Have you arrested someone?"

"Yes, we have someone in custody."

Caroline Bartlett's first response appeared to be fear. She quickly composed herself and fired another question. "Has he admitted to the murder?"

"I didn't say it was a man," Pam replied.

"Um…well…I assumed it was a man."

"Why?" Pam asked.

"You never hear about women shooting people."

"We've had a few female murderers over the years, Mrs. Bartlett."

"But they've never shot someone out in the woods…"

"I don't recall the circumstances."

"Is it one of the employees?"

"I thought you trusted them."

Caroline shook her head. "They're all convicts. I mean, don't most of them commit another crime and go back to prison?"

"Most murderers know the victim and only kill once."

"Ah, the spouse or boyfriend. That's the theme in so many police shows."

"Love, money, and drugs are the most common motives we see."

"Well, I didn't do it, so the motive wasn't love. Roger wasn't into drugs, so that leaves money. Was someone stealing from the tire company?"

"Not that I know about," Pam replied. "I think we'd best leave this discussion for the county attorney. He may have collected more information while I was gone."

Caroline sat quietly in Pam's car the rest of the drive to the courthouse. They walked into the sheriff's department entrance and Pam led her to an empty interview room. Bartlett froze when she saw the tiny room with the spartan table and chairs. "Why are we meeting here?"

"This is where the county attorney told me to deliver you. Take a seat and I'll let him know you're here."

"But this is where you bring criminals!"

Smiling, Pam nodded. "Yes, it is."

After knocking on the next door, Bakken popped into the hallway. "Caroline Bartlett is in the next room."

"Keep Ms. Keane calm while I talk to Caroline Bartlett."

Pam waited until the attorney closed the second interview room's door. She'd half expected Caroline Bartlett to come screaming out, but the woman was quietly sitting at the table, tapping her toe. With her hand on the doorknob, Pam was ready to enter the room with Candy when she heard Caroline Bartlett shriek.

"She said what?"

Candy looked comfortable, leaning back with the giant cup of coffee in her hand. "Gawd, who shrieked?"

"A woman in another room just found out she was going to be implicated in a murder."

Candy processed the information. "Caroline who was having the nooners with Joe."

Pam raised her eyebrows but didn't answer. "How are you doing on coffee?"

"Could we make another trip to the restrooms?"

"Certainly."

As Pam and Candy stepped into the hallway, the muffled sounds of a woman crying came from the second interview room. The county attorney stepped into the hallway as Pam and Candy returned.

The county attorney held the door for Candy, then took Pam aside. When he was sure no one could hear them, he leaned close. "Arrest Joe Callahan and book him into jail. I'll have my office draw up a murder warrant."

"But he was out of town when Bartlett was murdered," Pam said, knowing Caroline had thrown him under the bus and ruined his alibi.

"Let's say his alibi doesn't mean much when he paid someone to kill his partner."

* * *

Callahan's driveway was filled with SUVs and an orange and white rental truck. A man wearing a black jacket with a yellow US Marshal logo carried a banker's box out of the open front door and into the rental truck as Pam parked behind Callahan's white Land Rover. Joe Callahan's wife, Katie, was leaning against the back fender with her arms crossed. The Land Rover's interior had been stripped with the seats and interior panels laid on the driveway and grass.

Pam walked to Katie, noticing federal agents walking past the second-story windows. "Search warrant?"

Katie glared at Pam. "Assholes."

"Where's Joe?"

"They arrested him last night. One of the marshals said they were taking him to Minneapolis."

"They didn't bother you?"

"What do I know? I'm just the wife." Katie paused. "I suppose you're here to pile on. They haven't dumped the plants out of the pots yet. You could jump on that."

"Is anything hidden in the pots?"

Shaking her head, Katie watched more boxes and a computer go into the rental truck. "The jokes on them. Joe is too smart to have anything here or at the tire company."

"Where did he stash the stuff?"

Katie looked at Pam, noticing her shoulder patch. "You're a local cop."

"Yup."

"How do you feel about feds?"

"There are some good ones. Others are assholes."

"Why are you here?"

"My boss sent me to arrest Joe."

"Tell him you were too late."

"I guess so." Watching another load being carried to the truck, Pam asked, "Since your truck has been trashed, do you need a ride?"

"I'll call an Uber."

Laughing, Pam shook her head. "Uber hasn't got much of a toehold in Pine County. I suppose a local farmer might give you a ride in his pickup if you hitchhiked."

"What's in it for you?"

"What do you mean?" Pam asked.

"If you give me a ride. What do you get out of it?"

"The feeling that I helped someone."

Katie pushed herself off the SUV and turned toward Pam. "I suppose someone's rolled on Joe by now."

"Rolled on him?"

"Bartlett's murder."

Pam shrugged. "All we've got is the cons from the tire company and they don't rat out other cons."

Katie surveyed the mess around her. "Bastards even took my cellphone and wallet."

Pam nodded toward her car. "Get in. Where do you want to go?"

Wedging herself between the console computer and the door, Katie looked around. "Looks like this is built for speed, not for comfort."

After backing out of the driveway, Pam drove away from the house. "Yeah, considering how many hours I spend behind the wheel, the police special cars aren't user friendly."

"Am I in trouble?" Katie asked, staring straight ahead.

"I don't know. Are you?"

"Joe and I can't testify against each other, and I think he's the only…"

Pam glanced at her passenger. "He's the only one who knows what you're guilty of?"

"Will I have anything left after this is over?"

"I suppose it depends. If the feds convict him of RICO crimes, they seize everything purchased with the cash."

"What's RICO?"

"It's a federal law intended to catch people involved in organized crime. They've expanded it to include people who've been operating any criminal network."

"Like smuggling and money laundering?"

"I think so, but I'm just a cop. You need to ask that question of a lawyer."

Katie turned her head toward Pam. "Pull over."

"We're in the middle of nowhere. I'll drop you in town."

"Pull over. I want to talk."

After easing the car to the shoulder, Pam turned to Katie. "Talk."

"I can't testify against Joe, but I know where the skeletons are hidden."

"Okay. What do you want me to do?"

"Take me to someone who can make Joe's life miserable, and maybe arrange so I have a few crumbs to start my life over."

"What skeletons?"

"I know where the money is. I know who Joe uses for laundering money, and how he gets the money to them. There are bodies nobody knows about."

"But you can't testify."

"I'll hand you the keys to the door. It's up to you to open it and prosecute the people involved."

Pam smiled and pulled onto the road. "I've got a pen and paper in the console."

"Can we go somewhere I can get a drink?"

"Sure."

Tobies parking lot was filled with a mix of SUVs and cars, mostly buying baked goods.

Katie hesitated, then nodded. "No one will notice that we're here?"

Pam chuckled. "Not on a weeknight."

Pam led Katie to a corner near the kitchen where the waitresses were wrapping silverware in paper napkins. Pam pushed the napkins aside and pulled out the chairs in the corner, facing the room. An irritated waitress named Trish rushed over, about to yell at them for taking over the table. She saw Pam's uniform, then recognized her. Trish's frown quickly faded as she gathered the silverware and napkins. "We haven't seen you in a while, Pam."

Katie fidgeted with a display placard showing the appetizers. "I'd like chicken wings and Coke."

"Anything for you, Pam?"

With her stomach rumbles reminding her she hadn't eaten since breakfast, Pam nodded. "Sure, a burger basket and Diet Coke for me."

Pam set a yellow legal pad on the table and pulled a pen from her pocket. "Tell me about the skeletons."

Still fidgeting with the placard, Katie didn't look up. "Here's the deal. Everyone thought I was Joe's airheaded trophy wife, so I was as invisible as the Degas painting on the wall." Katie looked up, then pointed at the legal pad. "Write that down. Those assholes probably won't even notice that there's a two-million-dollar painting on the wall when they pack up all Joe's shit."

Pam noted *Degas painting.* "Got it."

"Anyway, they talked like I was an invisible fixture who delivered drinks and prepared appetizers. It suited Joe and I never pointed out that I have an accounting degree from St. Thomas University and an MBA from Wharton. After the visitor's went to bed, Joe had me make notes about the discussions."

"Is that what the feds are collecting?"

Katie laughed as the waitress delivered their drinks and rushed off. "They'll never find those notes.

"They're tearing the house apart," Pam replied. "I'm sure they'll find every nook and cranny and drill the locks on a safe if there is one."

"They'll get the gold maple leaves and Krugerrands out of the floor safe, but they won't find the things they really want."

"What do they really want to find?"

Katie looked around. "Joe's Las Vegas connections."

Pam poised the pen over the notepad. "Joe was connected to the mob?"

Before Katie could answer, Trish was back with their food.

Katie drained her Coke and held up her glass.

After hovering over the basket, Katie picked up a chicken wing and chewed the meat off of it. "So, all these guys would come and go, delivering information, money, contacts, and laughing about some poor schmuck they'd buried in the desert. Joe laughed, I delivered drinks, and later I'd write it all down. It was Joe's insurance policy."

"Where is Joe's insurance policy?"

Katie wiped the grease off her fingers. "Let's leave that for the end. It'll be my one bargaining chip, so I'm not left a penniless divorcee."

"You plan to divorce Joe?"

"I'm not going to hang around for decades, pining over my poor incarcerated husband, and visiting him in Joliet or Leavenworth. I plan to get on with my life."

Pam dipped a too-hot fry in ketchup and waited for it to cool while marveling at

Katie's brains. She knew what she wanted and how to work the system to get it. "But the mob guys won't be happy with you."

Katie shook her head, bouncing her short dark hair as she chewed on another chicken wing. "First of all, the shit is going to hit the fan. Everyone will assume Joe rolled on them to get a deal and witness protection. Secondly, in a week, I'll be blonde. In a month, I'll have boobs, a butt implant, and a different nose. No one knows my maiden name, and I'll be far from Minnesota and Las Vegas."

Pam wiped her fingers and picked up the pen. "You were going to give me information."

"Write *RBC Toronto*, then I'll give you a number."

Pam made the notes. "Okay, what's that?"

"It's one of Joe's investment accounts."

"You had the number memorized?"

Katie tapped her temple. "I remember numbers like bubble-headed bimbos remember the phone numbers of hairdressers and fashion designers."

"Ah, the accounting degree."

"Credit Suisse, Zurich." Katie rattled off another number. Pam filled a page with the names of banks and account numbers."

"Why did Joe have all these accounts?"

Katie finished her Coke and held the glass up so the waitress would bring another. "Some were for outgoing payments. Others were primarily for passing wire transfers to other accounts to muddle the financial trail. They're intended to make it hard, if not impossible, for the forensic accountants to trace."

"Why did Joe have all this?"

"I set it up for him, so we'd have money even if the feds, RCMP, EU tax people, or mob came looking."

"But the mob guys wouldn't ask him politely for these numbers."

Katie shook her head. "Joe could barely remember his phone number, much less these account numbers. His buddies know that I'm just an airhead Joe kept around as a trophy wife."

Pam flipped over the page. "Where are the skeletons?"

"Let's break them out by city. Start with Las Vegas, then write Toronto, Madrid, Mexico City, Lima, Buenos Aires, and London."

As Pam wrote, she asked, "Why are you here, in Pine County?"

Katie smiled. "Because it's nowhere. We're off the grid. We get cable TV and the internet, but he conducts his business elsewhere."

"Why was he involved in the tire company?"

"It was a front and something to keep Joe from getting bored. He liked hanging around with the cons." Katie paused. "And he was screwing Caroline."

"You knew he was having an affair?"

Rolling her eyes, Katie took a sip of her Coke. "He wasn't having an affair. He was screwing Caroline. She was recreation, that's all."

"And you didn't care?"

"I suggested it."

Pam set down the pen. "I'm confused."

"Have you seen Joe? He's fifty, overweight, with hair plugs, and a gold chain. Would you want that sweating hulk humping you?" Katie shuddered. "Besides, he was sampling the show girl line up in Las Vegas, call girls in Toronto, and Mexican bimbos who had who knows what. I didn't want to even think about what STIs he was spreading around."

Pam studied her pen and thought, *My life is so sheltered.* "Joe had Bartlett killed so he had unfettered access to Caroline?"

Katie snorted. "Bartlett was asking too many questions about the cash flowing through the tire company and Joe's constant travel. Having Caroline was just a fringe benefit."

"We have Bartlett's killer in custody. Is he going to roll on Joe?"

"That Mexican gang banger doesn't know shit. He only knows Igor."

"So, Igor handled the contract arrangements for Bartlett's murder for Joe."

"Joe owned Igor."

"I thought Igor was the meanest sonofabitch in the prison. Did Joe know Igor's human trafficking contacts?"

Taking the last chicken wing, Katie shook her head. "You're only scratching the surface. Igor is wanted for Bosnian war crimes. One call to Interpol, and Aleksandr Lianin would be on a plane to The Hague to face charges as a hit team leader during the Bosnian war."

Pam wrote, "Igor/Bosnian war criminal," on the pad and underlined it.

After three hours in Tobies back corner, Pam had a dozen pages of names, places, bank accounts, bank deposit boxes, boats, airplanes, artwork, and houses. "That's it?"

Katie poured down the last of her Coke and stood. "If that's not enough to put Joe away forever, you're the most inept cop who ever wore a badge."

Pam stood. "We're good. Let me introduce you to our county attorney. I think he can help you figure out how to put Joe away and maybe even leave you with a crumb or two."

Pam dialed Tom Bakken's phone number while Katie was in the ladies' room. "Tom, we need to talk right now."

Bakken sounded like he'd been asleep. "I'll meet you in the office at seven tomorrow morning."

Pam covered the phone while Trish cleared the table and left their bill. "I've spent the evening with Joe Callahan's wife. I've got pages of assets, contacts, and details of crimes from all over the world. You need to talk to Katie now. She might recant everything she's told me tomorrow."

"Okay, um, my office in forty-five minutes."

Katie walked out of the rest room and searched the room for Pam. "Put on a pot of coffee. I'll be at your house in ten minutes."

"Wait! You can't bring a suspect..."

"Make that seven minutes, Tom. I'll turn on my flashers and siren."

"This had better be good."

"Tom, it's solid gold."

Chapter 20

Floyd was in a back corner booth of Crazy Mary's Café when Pam and C.J. walked in. He got up and hugged them both before signalling the waitress for coffee.

Floyd looked at Pam whose light complexion highlighted the dark rings under her bloodshot eyes. "Luke kept you up last night?"

"We'll get into that later."

Accepting that, Floyd looked at C.J., who looked equally tired. "According to the newspaper, an unnamed Pine County Sergeant was involved in a shooting last night. I assume that was you."

"Yeah," C.J. said as the waitress poured coffee for them.

The waitress opened her order pad. "Are you ready to order?"

Pam put up her hand. "Coffee's good."

C.J. took a deep breath. "I want a farmer's breakfast, medium rare steak, crispy bacon, eggs over easy, whole-wheat toast, and crunchy hash browns."

With the waitress gone, Floyd smiled. "Do shootings make you hungry?"

Shaking her head, C.J. said, "Life's too short to waste time dieting."

Floyd held up his coffee cup in a toast. "Amen to that."

"What happened last night?" Pam asked. "You've been in shooting review meetings since I got to the office at 8:00."

"I…" C.J. let out a breath. "I'm not ready to talk about it. What happened to Bartlett's partner, Callahan? The sheriff said you spent the morning locked in the county attorney's office."

Pam smiled. "Callahan's wife threw him under the bus. She named names, gave up account numbers, and laid out all his shady operations in both the US, Canada, and beyond. Raul's girlfriend is singing too. The county attorney is convening a grand jury to consider first degree murder charges against both Raul and Callahan—if he can pry Callahan loose from the US Attorney."

Floyd leaned back and pointed at the television. "The sheriff looks like he just won another election." He waved at the waitress. "Turn up the sound on the TV."

The sheriff was just completing his remarks to the reporters from the courthouse steps. "…and luckily, my sergeant was uninjured during the incident."

Floyd looked at C.J. "Did you walk into another life-threatening situation without backup?"

"Igor was killing people. I had to intervene."

"It sounds like you were too late anyway."

C.J. looked down. "By the time I realized what was going on, most of the parolees had already been shot."

"Why did he snap?" Floyd asked. "He'd been living with those guys."

C.J. shrugged. "Kurt Olson said Igor was a psychopath. He was controlling himself, but Raul's take down and the feds busting in on the smuggling were more than he could handle. I suspect he planned to jump in his car to make a run for it if I hadn't shown up."

Pam's phone rang and she pulled it out. She listened for a moment, then handed it to C.J. "It's the sheriff for you."

"We're watching your news conference from Crazy Mary's."

"Why aren't you answering your phone?"

"My phone got smashed last night and I haven't replaced it yet."

"You ran out the door after the shooting review board before we could talk."

"Yeah, I was talked out and you rushed off to meet with the reporters."

"We need to talk about what 'waiting for backup' means when you get back to the office."

C.J got up and walked outside. "Do I still have a job?"

"Are you kidding? How could I fire a hero? You have a job, but we need to talk about ground rules and following orders."

"John, I'm always going to do what I think is right."

The sheriff sighed. "I know. But try to humor me when I give you an order. At least pretend that you're going to comply."

Pam and Floyd were deep in conversation when C.J. returned to the table. Floyd reached out and pulled C.J.'s chair out. "Do you still have a job?" he asked with a smile.

"Yes, but I've been thoroughly lashed about following orders." C.J. looked at Pam. "So, the Medicare brace fraud is the only case left open."

Floyd cleared his throat. "Actually, the Kanabec County Attorney has that."

"When did that happen?" C.J. asked.

"While you two were running all over the county, trying to catch a murderer and smuggler, a woman showed up at my house with a great deal on a new knee brace. We had a long talk and she...confided in me that she and her husband were running the brace scam out of their house in Grasston. I called the Kanabec County Sheriff's Department, and they sent a car to transport her to the jail in Mora. Since it involves Medicare, it'll probably end up on the U.S. Attorney's desk at some point. For now, they've been charged with fraud and haven't made bail yet."

Swirling her coffee, then swallowing the last of it, C.J. smiled. "You just can't stop being a cop, can you?"

"It was fun, but I don't need to go back full-time. Besides, Mary's got an offer on the flower shop. We may be traveling. I think Hawaii might be very nice in January."

Chapter 21

The dispatcher paged C.J. as she finished her arrest report. Annoyed at being delayed from leaving the office, she didn't look at the caller ID before picking up the flashing line. "Yeah."

"Your cell rolled over to voicemail immediately the last few times I've called. Are you blocking my number?" Eddie asked.

"No, my cell was crushed in the mess at Askov. What's up?"

"Do you have supper plans?"

"I thought I'd grab takeout on my way home to walk the dog."

"Are you open to a change of plans?"

"If supper can wait until after I walk Bailey. She's been cooped up in the apartment all day and needs to pee and burn off a little energy."

"I'm still in Duluth. It'll be at least an hour until I get near you. What's your dining preference?"

Laughing, C.J. replied, "Somewhere outside Pine County. The options here are limited."

Computer keys clicked in the background. "Yelp says the best place to eat in... Never mind, the best place in that town had a three-star rating."

"And that's the best?"

"Hang on, I'm trying a wider search. There's a steakhouse on Highway 210, just east of the Carlton exit. It has four-stars and it'll split the difference in our drives."

"Sounds lovely. I'll take Bailey out, take a quick shower, change, and meet you there in an hour."

C.J. pushed the speed limit on her drive home, assuming no trooper was going to pull over a sheriff's department car going eight miles-an-hour over the limit. She waved at her downstairs landlord before racing up the steps to her upstairs apartment. Bailey was sitting in her bed, staring at the door when C.J. unlocked it.

"Are you going to lie there sulking, or are we going for a walk?"

Bailey got up slowly, yawned, farted, then sauntered to the door. Her tail wagging gained speed when C.J. pulled the leash off the peg next to the door. Although short-legged, Bailey was a muscular fireplug and C.J. had to bound down the steps two at a time to keep from being pulled into a face plant. The walk down the street gained urgency as they neared the first power pole. Bailey sniffed it intently before squatting to leave her own scent with that of the myriad other canine visitors. That done, Bailey yanked on the leash and dragged C.J. to the next pole, repeating the process.

"Here's the deal," C.J. explained as Bailey finished her second potty stop. "I've been invited out for supper and you're not coming along. We're going back to the apartment and you're going to wait quietly for me until I come home from supper."

Bailey turned her head to listen, her head pushing up rolls of skin as she stared at her master. Ignoring the plan to return to the apartment, Bailey tugged at the leash, intent on inspecting yet another power pole.

C.J. braced herself and resisted Bailey's insistent tugging. "No. We're going back." Giving in after a short tug, Bailey followed a step behind as they walked the block back to the apartment. "Quit sulking. I've got a life too."

At the back door, Bailey sat down, refusing to budge. C.J. looked at her watch and realized her time to shower and change was down to almost nothing.

The back door opened and Bruce, C.J.'s downstairs neighbor stepped out. He immediately read the situation as Bailey's tail started to wag. "Looks like Bailey's not ready to go back upstairs."

"Bailey's being a shit, and I'm meeting a friend for supper in fifteen minutes."

Bruce squatted down and Bailey rushed to him, wiping slobber on his knee. "We can dog-sit while you go out. It's probably better to have Bailey downstairs watching television with us than to listen to her howling in protest."

Rolling her eyes, C.J. said, "She doesn't…"

Bruce smiled. "Not usually, but sometimes she's very unhappy with you."

Handing over the leash, C.J. turned Bailey over to her neighbor and raced up the stairs. Her hair was still damp when she got in her car.

Eddie was sitting in a booth reading a menu when C.J. walked into the restaurant. He stood and smiled as she approached. "Welcome to the most highly rated restaurant at the Carlton freeway exit."

Sliding into the booth, C.J. picked up a menu. "I've heard the casino is good."

Eddie sat across from her. "Okay. Welcome to the most highly rated restaurant on the east side of the Carlton exit."

The waitress walked over after taking an order from a nearby table. "Can I get you two anything to drink?"

"Diet Coke for me," C.J. replied.

Eddie nodded toward the back. "They have a bar if you'd like something stronger."

"Not tonight. I'm still wound up and alcohol might…"

Smiling at the waitress, Eddie said, "Just the Diet Cokes tonight."

The waitress left and C.J. looked up from her menu, sensing Eddie's stare. "What's up?"

"You look keyed up."

"I haven't recovered from the adrenaline rush yet."

"Alcohol used to seem like a way to avoid nightmares, but it never worked."

C.J. searched his face, realizing he'd been in Vietnam and still fought his own battles with PTSD. "It took a while for me to realize the solutions to my problems weren't in a beer bottle."

"You caught onto that faster than me." He hesitated, "and you have the work demons and the death of your husband."

C.J. set the menu aside as the waitress delivered their sodas. "The special is a twelve-ounce ribeye with your choice of potato and the salad bar."

Closing her eyes, C.J. considered her dinner options. "I've been living on fast food for five days and I ate a massive, greasy breakfast. I think I'll go with the salad bar and a baked potato."

The waitress turned to Eddie. "I'll have the steak special, medium-rare."

Writing their order in her pad, the waitress said, "Help yourselves to the salad bar."

"You know, you could've ordered the steak special for almost the same price and brought the meat home to Bailey."

"Bailey is not getting a rib-eye steak!"

Eddie slid out of the booth. "Let's get our salads."

Back in the booth Eddie said, "I listened to the evening news just before I left. They replayed the morning news conference. The sheriff was kind with his praise of your role in the case."

"Can we talk about something else? How was your day?"

Eddie set his fork down and wiped his mouth. "Your day was so bad you'd rather hear about the post-mortem exams we did today?"

C.J. was sipping her soda and snorted, grabbing her napkin to wipe the Diet Coke from her face. Eddie laughed at her and made C.J. laugh until she was close to tears.

"Oh, geez, I sometimes forget where you work."

Eddie looked around at the dozen other diners who were staring at them and smiling. He leaned across the table. "I think that's literally gallows humor."

Tipping her head back, C.J. drew a deep breath and let it out. "No, that was breaking the tension of a long few days. Thank you."

"Thank you, Charlene. You've rescued me from a bowl of soup eaten in front of the television."

"I prefer C.J."

Eddie shook his head. "You've chosen that moniker for your job in a man's world. I'd prefer to call you Charlene when we're away from all that macho bull."

"Only my mother calls me Charlene. And it's usually Charlene Joy, what have you done now?"

"Charlene is a pretty name. It's as pretty as you are."

"You're the only colleague who calls me Charlene." She paused, "well, except for the sheriff. I think he calls me Charlene because he knows it annoys me."

"We should do something fun this weekend."

"Please tell me there's something more interesting in Duluth than the Hinckley craft fair I went to last weekend."

"Bentleyville."

"You mean the Christmas light display that's set up in Duluth's Canal Park?"

"Yes. It opens this weekend. We'll walk through Bentleyville, look at all the lights, then go over to Grandma's for coffee."

"And then?"

"Then you kiss me on the cheek and drive home."

"No expectations?"

Eddie set down his utensils and wiped his mouth. "Listen, my job doesn't lend itself to making friends. The only people I deal with are the Medical Examiner, dead bodies, and grieving families. I really don't

363

want to mess up my one friendship by throwing sex into the mix."

"You're sure?"

"I'm absolutely certain."

C.J. finished her dinner and set the plates aside. Eddie refused her attempt to split the bill and paid. They stopped outside the restaurant door and Eddie put out his hand. "Let me walk you to your car."

C.J. took his hand as they walked. "This is going to test our friendship, but…"

"But, what?"

"I'm a mess right now, and I need to talk through what's happened to help me process it." C.J. glanced at her watch. "I need to rescue Bailey from the neighbors and take her for a walk. Will you drive over to my place and walk with Bailey and me?"

"Of course."

"It seems so much to expect…"

Eddie shook his head. "Let's go. If the walk isn't enough, you can make popcorn, we'll sit on the couch, and talk while we watch a movie."

"You'll do that?"

"I was your nursemaid after you were shot. I'm happy to be there for you now."

"But…"

"Isn't that what you'd do with your female friends?"

"It's been years since I've had a girlfriend who's willing to listen to my cop experiences. They want to talk about reality

364

television series and their children. They all get freaked out when I start talking about shootings, drug dealers, dead bodies, and PTSD."

Eddie laughed. "This is a two-way street. I'm going to tell you about the autopsy I had this afternoon."

C.J. smiled and looped her arm around Eddie's elbow. "Perfect. Let's go pick up Bailey."

* * *

Pam had just put Luke down for the night when her cell phone rang. Before she could even say hello, the sheriff's voice boomed over the speaker. "Where the hell is Charlene? Her cell rolls over to voicemail and she's not returning messages left on either her cell or her home number."

"I haven't seen C.J. since I left the courthouse. Her cell got broken in the confrontation in Askov, but I don't know why she's not answering messages on her home phone."

"Holy Mary, mother of God…"

"You're praying?"

The sheriff sighed. "Father Mike had a blasphemy discussion with me last week after I missed an easy bowling spare and let loose with a few choice words." He paused. "Do you think she's out with the morgue tech?"

"I really don't know what her plans were. She might be walking the dog. Is there something I can help with?"

"My phone is about to melt after all the calls I've had this evening. Your presence has been requested at the Minneapolis Canadian consulate tomorrow morning at ten. Apparently, you and Charlene are meeting with a representative of the Crown Court."

"I don't understand. Is there a problem?"

Chuckling, the sheriff composed his thoughts. "Your meeting between Callahan's wife and Tom Bakken prompted him to call the US Attorney to discuss whose case against Callahan took precedence. Apparently, no one was willing to disturb the US Attorney at 2 AM over a custody question. That pissed off Tom, who called his friend in Canada. That call precipitated an exchange of secure emails with the information you collected from Katie Callahan. Seizing assets and crimes in Canada, the Crown Court drafted an extradition request to the State Department, in Washington. Somehow, they were able to roust the US Attorney, asking what the hell was going on with the international criminal they had in custody. Of course, his underlings had been handling the case and he didn't have a clue what they were talking about."

"I opened Pandora's box."

"Oh, you opened a lot more than Pandora's box. There are calls flying back and forth between Ottawa, Washington, Toronto, and Minneapolis. They take a break once in a while to bitch at me for not having Katie Callahan in custody. Where is she?"

"After we got through talking to Tom, he agreed she wasn't a suspect in any Pine County crimes and couldn't testify against her husband. She called a friend from Bakken's home phone and a woman picked her up forty-five minutes later."

"You have no knowledge of her plans?"

"None."

"That's what I told the Assistant US Attorney. He was fuming. The FBI had her passport, but he said she had access to enough money to buy a small airline that could fly her anywhere in the world."

"I'd say that's probably true. She told me within a month she'd have had enough plastic surgery so that even her mother wouldn't recognize her."

"Call whomever you need to call to find Charlene and make plans to be at the consulate at ten. If you don't reach her in the next half hour, call me back and I'll have someone dispatched to her house and I'll notify the state patrol that she needs to be notified of an urgent matter." He paused.

"Call me whether you find her or not. I need to know what's going on."

After searching her contacts, Pam found Eddie Paulson's cell number. "Is C.J. with you?"

"Pam? Um, yeah. We're walking Bailey."

"Could you hand her your phone?"

"Sure."

"This is C.J."

"Go back to your apartment and listen to the messages on your recorder."

"I thought I'd leave them until morning."

"The sheriff is frantically trying to reach you."

"Why? Are there riots in Pine City or something?"

"I don't want to repeat the story. Just listen to your messages, then call the sheriff." Pam paused. "By the way, get out your clean uniform. I'll pick you up at 7:30."

C.J. handed the phone back to Eddie, looking perplexed.

"What did Pam want?"

"Apparently the sheriff wants to talk to me ASAP. We need to go back to the apartment."

* * *

C.J. and Pam parked in the Hennepin County hospital ramp and walked two blocks down 7th Street among the late morning commuters. Shaking her head, C.J. said, "I understand road rage. If I had to commute into Minneapolis every day, I might kill someone."

"Yeah, I get a little stressed out during the Pine County rush hour, you know, if I see more than five cars on the way to Pine City."

The guard at the consulate entrance picked up the phone as soon as he saw their uniforms enter the atrium. "Here are your visitor badges. Someone will be down shortly to escort you upstairs. You can wait near the elevators."

"I wonder what kind of dog and pony show this is going to be?" C.J asked.

"You know as much as I do, and maybe more. You've had conversations with the Canadians during the Callahan investigation."

The elevator doors opened and a young man in a gray suit stepped out. "I'm Barry Comstock, the *charge d'affaires*." His smile was warm and his handshake hearty. "Thank you for making this trip on such short notice." He ushered them into the elevator and touched the button for the top floor.

"We're a bit confused about why we were asked here," C.J. said.

"I'm afraid I'm not aware of the nature of your visit," Comstock said. "I have reserved the conference room and arranged for coffee and tea."

Comstock led them down a hallway lined with photos of Canadian cities and mountain landscapes. He opened a door to a room with floor-to-ceiling windows overlooking downtown Minneapolis. The center of the room was filled by a polished cherry conference table surrounded by chairs. A group of men and women, all wearing suits, were gathered around a small nook at the end of the room. They looked up and smiled when C.J. and Pam entered.

"May I take your coats?" Comstock asked.

A tall man wearing a blue three-piece suit and red tie approached them. His salt and pepper hair was carefully combed and his smile exuded warmth. "Deputy Ryan and Sergeant Jensen, I'm Ian McMurtrie." He shook Pam's hand. "We've been reviewing the information you supplied to Tom Bakken. You certainly hit the mother lode."

Pam smiled and nodded to C.J. "My partner was key to breaking this case. All I did was act as the scribe."

McMutrie turned to C.J. "Sergeant, it's nice to connect your face to the voice on the phone. I hear you had quite a harrowing experience when the smugglers were arrested."

"I'm sure your Canadian officers have the same hours of boredom and moments of excitement."

"Very few of them are ever in circumstances that require them to discharge their firearm."

"I prefer that situation myself," C.J. said, feeling red creeping up her neck.

McMurtrie led them to the coffee and introduced them to the other dignitaries in the group. A woman in a gray skirt and ivory blouse shook their hands. The gold badge on her waist was a circle of maple leaves around a blue border with a buffalo head in the center. At the top was a crown. "I'm Vivian LaCroix," the woman said, her voice having a slight French accent. "I'm the token law enforcement representative."

McMurtrie checked his watch, then cleared his throat. "I apologize, but the US Attorney will be in the office shortly and I'd like to express our deep gratitude to you two for your arrest of Joseph Callahan. The information you've provided will allow the Crown Court to prosecute him and recover millions of dollars in criminal profits." He gestured to a photographer who moved to the front of the group as LaCroix picked up two velvet boxes from a small table.

LaCroix drew a breath, then smiled. "I'm sure that you appreciate the sensitive nature of the information you've recovered, so we're unable to have a public ceremony." She nodded to the photographer who raised his camera. "Sergeant Jensen, on behalf of the Canadian Crown Court and the RCMP, I'm proud to make you an honorary member of the Royal Canadian Mounted Police." La Croix opened the box containing a badge similar to the one on her waist and held it out to C.J. while the camera flashed.

The ceremony and photos were repeated for Pam.

McMurtrie shook each of their hands for another set of pictures. "I'm sure you understand that this badge is symbolic and confers no Canadian arrest authority." The Canadian chuckled. "However, there is a card under the velvet with your names, granting you unrestricted crossing of the Canadian border with your firearms."

Smiling, C.J. said, "I don't suppose it'll get us back into the US as easily."

McMurtrie grinned. "I'm sorry, but that's beyond my authority."

The Canadians quickly shook Pam and C.J.'s hands, then exited the room, leaving them with LaCroix. "Please, pour yourselves a warm cup of coffee and sit down."

Gathered at the end of the long table, LaCroix set out coasters with red Maple Leaf logos. "Speaking as one cop to another, you two pulled off one hell of a coup. We've been trying to crack open

Callahan's operations for years and have only scraped the surface. What you two accomplished was extraordinary."

"Thank you," they said in unison.

LaCroix stood, ending the discussion. "By the way, I've never presented honorary badges to anyone before. They were brought in by courier this morning. You obviously can't wear them, but I was told there are two Maine FBI agents who proudly display them in their offices."

LaCroix escorted them to the elevators and shook their hands. As the elevator descended, Pam opened the box and looked at the badge. "Wow. What are you going to do with your badge?"

"I suppose I'll show it to my mom and dad, then hang it in the living room. How about you?"

"Travis has a wooden box with his military insignias. Maybe we'll store it with them. It'll be something we can show Luke someday."

C.J. paused at the consulate exit, watching the people passing. "On second thought, I don't think I want an obvious reminder of Igor and the events leading to his death."

Pam held the door open for C.J. "Talk it over with Eddie. He'll have the right answer." When C.J. didn't respond, Pam asked, "What's wrong?"

"This week has got me so messed up. I want to scream, cry, punch the wall, and hug my dog."

"Yup. I'm going to spoon into Travis' back and hold him tight, thankful for what I've got."

A tear leaked from C.J.'s eye and she wiped it away, hoping Pam hadn't noticed.

"You miss your husband."

"Every day."

Pam stopped and grabbed C.J.'s elbow with her eyes sparkling. "I think we should pin on our RCMP badges, march into Sepanen's office, and tell him he's buying us dinner."

C.J. smiled. "He'd laugh us out of the building."

"So what? Let's do it!"

C.J. pushed Pam toward the parking ramp. "You know we'll chicken out before we get to Pine City."

"Maybe, but doesn't it sound like fun?"

"It does."

The End

2021 Bestselling Author
Dean L. Hovey

Dean Hovey is the award-winning and best-selling author of three mystery series. He uses his scientific background, travel, and life experience to create life-like characters, gripping storylines, and memorable locations. One reviewer said Dean creates characters he'd like to invite over for a beer and discussion.

Dean and his wife split their year between Pine County, Minnesota and Arizona.

BWL Publishing

bwlpublishing.ca

www.ingramcontent.com/pod-product-compliance
Lightning Source LLC
Chambersburg PA
CBHW070205120726
47909CB00001B/259